"Begging. This is me begging."

"I knew you would push the limits of our agreement, Matt Armstrong." One side of Brooke's mouth curled up. "And I knew you would be very hard to say no to, so count me in."

Sweet relief settled over Matt.

He normally kept future plans few and far between. But with Brooke, it was easy to imagine finding some other reason to keep her close by when the festival was over.

"You are as dangerous as everyone warned me, but for a completely different reason," Brooke said.

"Yeah?" Matt asked.

She nodded. "I was advised to prepare myself to be snared by your handsome face."

"I'm not handsome?"

The dramatic way she rolled her eyes startled a deep laugh from him.

"Your heart is more trouble than your face. It's good. It makes other people want to do good, too."

"Now I know you're flirting with me. And I'm helpless in the face of compliments."

Dear Reader,

Thank you so much for visiting Prospect, Colorado! I have enjoyed meeting all of the Hearsts and Armstrongs, but there is a special place in my heart for the youngest in each family (why, yes, I am also the youngest and I understand what a mixed blessing it can be!).

When beautiful, polished Brooke Hearst meets charming, handsome Matt Armstrong in *The Cowboy's Compromise*, there's definitely a spark. They're both struggling, out of their depths and aware that their families are watching. Brooke and her dog, Coco, are passing through Prospect on their way to a new beginning *somewhere* when surprise puppies lead to an agreement: Matt will be her on-call veterinarian in exchange for her help with all the details of the town's big festival, Western Days. Everyone's in town. Failure is not an option for any Armstrong.

When I drove into Prospect with Sarah Hearst that first time, I had no idea how much I was going to love this place or the people in it. Celebrating Western Days with them all has been an adventure. I hope you've enjoyed the journey as much as I have.

To find out more about my books and what's coming next, visit me at cherylharperbooks.com.

Cheryl

THE COWBOY'S COMPROMISE

CHERYL HARPER

HEARTWARMING

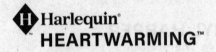

Harlequin®
HEARTWARMING™

Recycling programs for this product may not exist in your area.

ISBN-13: 978-1-335-05139-4

The Cowboy's Compromise

Copyright © 2025 by Cheryl Harper

Harlequin Enterprises ULC
22 Adelaide St. West, 41st Floor
Toronto, Ontario M5H 4E3, Canada
www.Harlequin.com

Printed in Lithuania

MIX
Paper | Supporting responsible forestry
FSC® C021394

Cheryl Harper discovered her love for books and words as a little girl, thanks to a mother who made countless library trips and an introduction to Laura Ingalls Wilder's Little House books. Whether the stories she reads are set in the prairie, the American West, Regency England or earth a hundred years in the future, Cheryl enjoys strong characters who make her laugh. Now Cheryl spends her days searching for the right words while she stares out the window and her dog, Jack, snoozes beside her. And she considers herself very lucky to do so.

For more information about Cheryl's books, visit her online at cherylharperbooks.com or follow her on X @cherylharperbks.

Books by Cheryl Harper

Harlequin Heartwarming

The Fortunes of Prospect

Courting the Cowgirl
The Right Cowboy
The Cowboy's Second Chance
Her Cowboy's Promise
The Cowboy Next Door

Veterans' Road

Winning the Veteran's Heart
Second Chance Love
Her Holiday Reunion
The Doctor and the Matchmaker
The Dalmatian Dilemma

Visit the Author Profile page
at Harlequin.com for more titles.

CHAPTER ONE

SPRINGTIME IN NEW YORK had been Brooke Hearst's favorite season ever since she'd moved to the city after college. Life in southern California had meant plenty of sunshine, but the Big Apple offered the whole range of weather choices from season to season, and sometimes day by day. In March, the dreary gray sludge of winter melted away, and the sidewalk buzzed with people determined to enjoy the warmth. Joggers, parents with strollers, busy professionals making important phone calls and seniors soaking up the sun created an always-changing landscape that she had never grown tired of. Last March, she had lined the five steps up to the front door of the brownstone she and her husband had renovated with large black planters of fuchsia petunias, because bright pops of color were her favorite ways to decorate.

As her great-aunt Sadie Hearst used to say, "When in doubt, add pink." Sadie's NYC home had been a stylish jumble of things she loved;

no rhyme or reason, no central design theory or color palette drove Sadie's decisions. She'd built her Colorado Cookie Queen empire in exactly the same way: doing only what she loved.

This year, the brownstone's steps were as bare as her ring finger.

So were most of the walls inside.

Sadie, too, was gone, and the hole she'd left in Brooke's life was unmistakable.

The money Sadie had left her great-nieces and -nephews had recently been disbursed by Sadie's lawyers, so buying out her ex-husband's half of their townhome should be simple.

But stalling the sale of the townhome until she'd received her inheritance had taken every creative idea she could dream up. It had also burned through the last of Paul's affection and goodwill. He was determined to sell the place— to anyone but Brooke.

Losing her great-aunt, her marriage, her purpose as a politician's wife *and* her dream home in the space of a year? Not even a beautiful spring day could combat this grief.

Brooke pressed her forehead against the glass and considered getting dressed to go out for a walk. It would lift her mood, but only by delaying the inevitable.

With this full day off from her part-time job as a barista at Brew Time, she needed to make some difficult decisions. Her life had been on pause for so long, thanks to her husband's change of heart about 'til-death-do-us-part and their back-and-forth divorce mediation.

Facing the end of the dream she'd built during her first visit to the city with her great-aunt was painful. Making New York home had been her single focus. She'd studied art history in college with the vague plan of working in a museum or gallery. The Guggenheim had captivated her from the first time she spotted the building, and Brooke had always enjoyed paging through the books in her mother's art studio while she painted. After her mother died, those books had been a connection to her. Art history had felt right, and at eighteen, she hadn't been too concerned about finding a job.

Working part-time in her father's small art store had been easy enough, after all. He'd called her his *assistant manager* because she frequently took his assignments and built efficient processes for herself and his other part-time employees to follow. Messy, week-long annual inventories became streamlined quarterly events completed in an afternoon. When she'd found a cheap, easy payroll system to eliminate his paper filing system, he'd teared up. Asking an artist to provide tax records had led to more than one bookkeeper having to "cut back on their client list"—starting with his shop.

He was an amazing artist, a great teacher, a good father—but an indifferent business owner.

Brooke had never worried about finding or keeping a job, because taking all of that—someone else's start—and building it up had been so simple. Figuring out what to call that as a career? Not as easy.

Meeting Paul at the University of Southern California had replaced vague *someday* notions with a concrete plan.

A successful, ambitious husband who fully intended to be governor someday and a gorgeous brownstone on the Upper West Side of Manhattan, not too far away from her great-aunt Sadie's comfortable apartment, were signs of her dream coming true. Soon, volunteering to help local candidates campaign while building strong connections for her husband's future filled her days and left plenty of time to be the partner Paul needed to grow his law career. Dinners with clients. Chairing charity events. Hosting election-night watch parties. Every event had been planned carefully, and Brooke had learned to swim in political waters. Crowds had never been her thing, but they were easy enough to navigate once she learned how.

Everything had been going according to their plans.

Then Paul had started pulling away, spending less time at home and, eventually, he confirmed her suspicion—someone else was about to replace her in the picture-perfect political couple.

Ending the marriage had been difficult, but it was nothing like letting go of this place.

It was the true death of her dream.

Over the last few months, presenting a calm, steady demeanor when she talked to her busy, thriving sisters had become nearly impossible, but it was important to keep up the appearance of control.

For Brooke, it had always been important to pretend that everything was fine.

Even after her ex-husband appeared in about-town gossip with the daughter of "old family friends."

And especially after she'd wheedled her way into working part-time at the coffee shop around the corner—like it offered a six-figure salary instead of minimum wage plus generous tips and all the coffee she could drink. Her résumé was bare of "real" jobs for the length of her marriage. And there weren't many art stores offering good pay and benefits in her neighborhood.

They would have been able to find better qualified candidates anyway.

And even after coming to terms with the fact that their "friends" had all been his, she had to act as if everything was going to be okay.

She was on her own in New York.

Pure stubbornness meant that Brooke always looked her best and smiled to sell the lie that she was thrilled with her newfound freedom. Everything was still perfect.

On the outside.

Inside, Brooke had sold every piece of extra furniture, art, and even her beloved convertible to keep making the mortgage payments until Sadie's estate was settled. It had taken some time to sell Sadie's LA and New York real estate and distribute it to Sadie's heirs, including her seventeen great-nieces and-nephews.

Ironically, now that she had the money at hand, the time for negotiation had run out.

Her phone rang but she didn't pick it up.

All three of the people who might be calling her had moved to Sadie's hometown—Prospect, Colorado—an Old West silver boomtown in the Rocky Mountains.

That distance was all that kept her father and sisters from realizing how bad things had gotten for Brooke.

Because Paul had pulled his dirtiest trick yet. He'd taken the only piece of leverage that remained: the puppy he'd given her on their last anniversary.

Four weeks ago, Paul had left a scribbled note to suggest she return the signed real estate agent's contract when she was ready to pick up Coco and bring her home. Coco was fine, of course, but she should be curled up in a tiny ball in Brooke's lap right now.

After pleading with Paul over the phone and then calling him every name she could dig up from the darkest recesses of her brain, Brooke had tried talking to their divorce mediator. Since Coco had never come up, there was no decision regarding her care.

Coco had been a gift! Brooke had lost track of the number of times she'd tried desperately to explain that when someone gave a gift, they no longer held any ownership. It was logical.

But she needed something stronger than logic to get Coco back.

The police had said a version of the same thing.

"So…he wins." Brooke hated the way her voice echoed in the emptying space. "I'll deliver the papers and pick up my dog. Get this place listed and then I'll…find another place to live. New York is filled with them. This will be easy, especially now that I have money to spend."

No. It could be simple, even if it wasn't easy.

Brooke wiped under her eyes and sniffed

loudly as she dragged over her laptop. Maybe looking at real estate listings would spark some energy. Her face and hair would need some intense work before she could face Paul to give him everything he wanted, along with the signed real estate agent's agreement, and be bulletproof.

She opened her laptop and picked up the card she'd kept inside. Sadie's lawyer had mailed it with the thumb drive containing a video from Sadie. The card made her smile. The photo of an ornery goat said "I'm about to butt in" underneath it. The joke was so Sadie.

She'd already downloaded Sadie's video and centered it on her desktop.

She'd avoided watching so far. It seemed so final.

But today, to put off searching for a new place to live, Brooke hit Play.

Sadie Hearst's beautiful face immediately filled the screen. Her improbably dark hair was perfect and she was wearing the bright red lipstick she always favored, but she was propped up in a hospital bed.

Brooke wondered how long Sadie had been sick before anyone in her family had known.

"Brooke, girl, I sure have missed seeing you around my kitchen since you moved to the Big Apple, but we all knew you were destined for New York City. I'll never forget the first cab ride we took down through Times Square. How old were you that spring break? Nine? Ten? At that time, it wasn't much to get excited about, but you pressed your nose against the glass like it was a fairy tale. I hope, by now, you've learned that New York City is much more beautiful and exciting *outside* of Times Square." Sadie winked, her eyes sparkling as they always had. "That's where the Hearst comes out particularly strong in you. This faith in the way things could be. Now me and your oldest sister, Sarah, we got a stronger streak of understanding how things are—good, bad and ugly—while Jordan is convinced things can always get worse somehow. I love that all three of you girls were also blessed with that faith. That even if things are hard now, someday they will be better. The Hearsts always hope for the future, but you, Brooke, go beyond that. You know it's all going to work out as you dream. I love that about you."

Brooke wanted that to be true.

Sadie cleared her throat and accepted the glass that someone handed her. "Thank you, Howie. Couldn't get through this without you." When she raised her eyebrows at the camera, Brooke shook her head in amusement. As she recalled, Sadie's lawyer Howard Marshal was as far away from a *Howie* as anyone she'd met, but Sadie didn't let things like dignity deter her.

"Sure is hard to hold on to that faith in this old world, Brooke. Life isn't easy, is it? What do I always say? Today we plant the seeds and hope we get to see the flowers. You and your sisters are my favorite seeds ever, my girl. Water, sunshine and a safe place to grow. You've had all that, and you are all ready to bloom." Sadie cleared her throat. "I figure you three have already discussed my daddy's old fishing lodge and what to do with it. I bet Jordan has strong feelings, most likely the opposite of yours, and Sarah will try to find the middle ground. Same as it ever was. It works for the three of you, so I can't complain about it, but I wanted to take this chance to tell you something important, something no one ever told me. Learning it while I'm running out of time is a real problem."

Sadie made the *come closer* motion to the camera. "Don't lose sight of what you have while you're fighting to make that dream come true."

Sadie paused and Brooke clenched her hand over her heart. The ache there triggered more tears.

How did Sadie always have the right words?

She'd been gone for months now, but this message was landing at exactly the right place at the right time.

Sarah, Jordan and Brooke had decided to take the Majestic Prospect Lodge and reopen it, and that decision had created an avalanche of other projects in Prospect. Her sisters were rebuilding the whole town at this point.

While she listened to their excitement from her slowly emptying brownstone.

What would Sadie have to say about that decision?

Was she losing sight of what she had, her family, because she was clinging to New York?

"Don't stop dreaming, my girl. Don't know where I'd be if I hadn't chased the wild inspiration to start a cooking show from Prospect, or that I ought to write a cookbook, or that I should answer phone calls from network executives." Sadie tipped her nose up to demonstrate what she thought of their important airs. "Our dreams can take us places. Your sisters need that part of you. And you deserve to make all your dreams come true." Sadie smiled. "Just don't lose something wonderful because you are hanging on too tightly to a daydream that doesn't suit you anymore. A thing I know for certain—dreams can change. One minute, you're strolling among the blooming roses in the prettiest garden you can imagine, and the next, there's a robot telling you that your car is being repossessed." Sadie's lips curled. "I blame the alarm clock for that part."

Sadie's smile faded. "I was getting too serious. Had to slip a joke in there so you would know I'm still me in this hospital bed. I love you, Brooke. You remind me so much of me when I had my whole life ahead of me. Big things can happen for us dreamers, but please remember that if the dream doesn't end how you expect it, it can always be more than you ever hoped for. Take this lodge and the money and build something wonderful, my girl. Know that I'm as proud of you as a mama cow is of her newborn calf." Sadie winked. "I'm amusing myself by imagining the way your lips would twist at that comparison, but you better never doubt my love. I'm always gonna be nearby to remind you of that. All right, Howie. Nailed it in the first take, as usual."

The video stopped and Brooke rested her head against the couch as tears rolled down her cheeks. The grief was overwhelming.

Inhaling slowly and exhaling through her mouth eventually pressed some of the emotion back, but before she was ready to return to the real world, her doorbell rang.

Had thinking of Paul earlier conjured him up somehow?

While she tried to determine whether she was ready to confront her ex, Brooke pulled up the doorbell camera app.

When she saw two women instead of one man, she bent to get closer to the screen.

"Sarah?" Brooke exclaimed before she registered that Jordan was standing next to her sister. She dropped the laptop on the cushion next to her and hurried to the door, tugging down her silk T-shirt and smoothing the hairs that had escaped her messy bun.

Weird chuckles broke through her tears as she yanked the door open. "Sarah! Jordan! What are you doing here?"

Sarah pointed at Jordan. "Take the other arm. She's walking but she might as well be drunk for all the tripping and stumbling. Whatever Dr. Singh gave her to make it through the flight from Denver is wearing off, but not fast enough."

Brooke immediately helped guide Jordan onto the couch and then turned to throw her arms around her oldest sister. Sarah looked around at the empty room but didn't hesitate to squeeze her tightly. "Oh, Brooke, why didn't you tell us sooner? We would have been here." She pulled a tissue from somewhere and pressed it against Brooke's cheeks.

The words wouldn't come, so Brooke shook her head and clung tighter as the tears fell.

Sarah did as she'd always done, waited patiently while she ran her hands up and down Brooke's back. Losing their mother had changed them all. Sarah had done her best to mother them, even when she'd still been so young herself. When the right words wouldn't come, she'd always resorted to hugs like this.

Even if there was no other comfort in the world, Sarah would be there with open arms.

And Brooke had missed them terribly.

Eventually, Jordan sat up. "When did we get here?" She brushed her dark hair out of her eyes. "And where is *here*?"

Sarah sighed before she urged Brooke down next to Jordan. "This is Brooke's house, Jordie. You walked all the way through the airport, claimed your bags, got into a cab and followed me halfway down the block until I realized I'd passed Brooke's address. You don't remember any of it?"

Jordan covered a jaw-cracking yawn with one hand. "Of course I remember that, but Brooke's house had expensive furniture, artwork on the walls. Remember the tour that she gave us over the phone? The daffodils Dad painted were in the bedroom. There was a piece hanging right there." She pointed at the mantel over the fireplace. "I can't remember the artist's name, but it was a woman playing a flute." She turned to Brooke. "I didn't hallucinate that while I was drugged to keep my entirely logical fear of plunging to my death in an airplane under control, did I?"

Brooke shook her head and yanked her middle sister into her arms. Ignoring Jordan's inelegant grunt was easy enough as she squeezed tightly. "You didn't, but holding on to this place while I waited for Sadie's estate… It hasn't been easy. You two were putting everything, all your time and money, into the lodge to get it open. So I sold some things to make the mortgage payments here. All I had to do was hold on long enough for my part of the inheritance to come and I did." Even if the struggle would be for nothing, Brooke wanted to convince Sarah and Jordan that everything was going to be fine. "I can't believe you risked plunging to your death for me, Jordie."

Jordan patted her back. "I did. And as soon as I wash my face and grab a cup of coffee, you can point me in Paul's direction. I just want to talk…at first." The grim determination in her tone suggested Brooke's ex wouldn't like what came after talking.

Brooke snorted and realized that the tears were slowing. "As much as I'd love to hear what you'd say to him, I can't allow one of my favorite sisters to be arrested for assault or battery."

"We could make bail, but I appreciate your concern," Jordan said as she brushed tears off Brooke's cheeks.

Sarah crossed her arms over her chest as she paced in front of the fireplace. She was studying the dining room and the kitchen as she walked.

There wasn't much left to hold her interest so she soon slammed to a stop. "Instead of demanding we sell the lodge or harassing the lawyers for a loan or something while we waited for Sadie's estate to settle, you've been selling off your pieces of art and *your life*." She pressed her fingers against her lips for a moment. "The urge to lecture you is so strong right now, but we literally just walked in the door and I spent the entire flight here telling myself that I was going to be supportive and loving and not bossy." Her clenched fists suggested she was fighting a losing battle.

Jordan elbowed Brooke before saying, "How long do you think you can keep that in, Sarah? Should we start a timer?"

When Sarah narrowed her eyes at Jordan, all three of them laughed. Then Brooke tugged her oldest sister's hand and Sarah plopped down on the couch next to her. "I don't know how you knew how desperately I needed you both here, but I'm thankful. I'm…" Brooke bit her lip as she fought her instincts and went with the truth. "I'm struggling right now."

Jordan squeezed her hand. "From you, those words are the equivalent of a cry for help. That's all we want to do. Help. We're here for you as long as you need us."

Brooke frowned. "What about the lodge? It's

fully booked for Western Days in a few weeks. All I've heard from you for months is how many things still have to be done to be ready for this big festival weekend where the revitalized town and the modern Majestic Prospect Lodge make their debuts."

Jordan tried a confident smile but it was more of a grimace. "Dad and Mia can handle it. If they can't…" She waved her hand as if the answer was clear before saying, "Well, we'll get them help. Wes and Clay are keeping an eye on everything while we're here. The whole town is ready to pitch in wherever they're needed."

Brooke knew their father had plugged in immediately to help with whatever Sarah and Jordan needed. All three of them were happy to have him returning to his old self, involved and excited after sleepwalking for entirely too long after their mother's death. Mia Romero was the travel writer who'd moved to Prospect to work on a book about Sadie's life. She was staying at the lodge and working there part-time to help out while she researched. That didn't seem to be enough personnel to run a lodge, but everyone in Prospect had a job to do to get the festival off the ground.

"And then there's the new Sadie Hearst museum, with its grand opening scheduled for the same weekend," Brooke said as she turned to

Sarah. "How do either of you have time to come save me?"

"If the museum's not ready, we'll open later." Sarah rolled her eyes. "As if anything in this world is more important than you, Brooke."

Brooke desperately wanted something airy to say back, to convince them that this was a low point but she'd be on top again any minute, but…nothing came.

The loud growl of Jordan's stomach interrupted the heartfelt moment between the sisters. "Sorry," Jordan said sheepishly. "I need roughly two thousand calories and a nap and then I'll be ready to do whatever you need, Brooke. Are we packing up the rest of your stuff? Going apartment hunting? Plotting some mayhem of the getting-even variety that your ex will never expect?" Jordan cracked her knuckles. "All three? Please say all three."

"Calories are easy. Let's start there." Brooke stood up to grab her phone. "Chinese okay? There's a place around the corner that has the best kung pao chicken I've ever had in my life." When her sisters nodded, Jordan still a groggy half-second slow in every reaction, Brooke ordered enough food for six.

The timing of their arrival was perfect, but was it an actual sign of a new direction or a coincidence? Sadie had never trusted in coincidence, so Brooke had her doubts, too.

Her oldest sister had picked up Brooke's laptop and noticed Sadie's face, frozen on the screen. "While we wait for the food, want to tell us your plans? You have plenty of money now, so is it going to be New York real estate or…?"

The open-ended question was where Brooke had gotten hung up every single time she'd tried to decide where to go next.

But then, she'd been alone.

The arrival of her sisters… Sadie's reminder of the lodge and Prospect and changing dreams…

What if she needed some breathing room to make the right choice?

The mountains of Colorado should give her enough space to dream big.

And there was almost nothing else there to keep her busy, no shopping or museums or shows, so she would have plenty of time to think. It was time to let go of the brownstone.

"What if, instead of general mayhem, we have a very specific but chaotic plan?" Brooke asked as she stared at the real estate agent's contract. "There's not much here to pack, but it could be a good time for me to leave the city for a bit." Especially if she found a magnificent way to steal her dog back in a manner that thumbed her nose at her ex-husband. Jordan would be especially helpful in that regard.

"Do either of you need help getting ready for Western Days? In exchange for unpaid labor," she said with a grimace as she realized this would be another job that wasn't "real" enough for her résumé in the end, "I'm camping on the couch and eating your food for three weeks or so."

That should be enough time to make plans, right?

The way they both immediately nodded frantically surprised a snicker from Brooke.

"Yes. I can think of three different things right now that you can do at the lodge without breaking a sweat," Jordan said before wrinkling her nose. "The no-sweat thing is definitely not a promise, though."

She'd been feeling left out of the work in Prospect, but maybe there was still some room for her.

"One problem—Jordan needs to get the first pill out of her system before we add a second. Carrying her through the Denver airport is beyond me." Sarah patted Jordan's shoulder.

"What if we rent a large SUV, load up the few things I want to keep, and drive back to Denver?" Brooke was making up the plan as she went, but getting Coco out of Paul's apartment and onto a plane seemed much harder than driving a getaway car. "It will take longer, but think of all the places we can explore in the middle."

Sarah bit her lip. "After I finish imagining all the arguments the two of you will have, I'll get right on that."

"I know it will take extra time to drive instead of fly, but..." Brooke walked over to Jordan and held out her hand. "I need your help plotting a dog heist and a generally spiteful goodbye. In exchange, we will skip putting you in a flying tin can, and I promise to let you choose the radio station and all the pit stops we make."

The slow smile that blossomed on Jordan's face reminded Brooke of her great-aunt Sadie. They'd all gotten pieces of her personality, but Jordan had inherited more than her share of the mischief. "Spiteful, you say? That's my favorite kind of goodbye. You have yourself a deal. I definitely want to visit the ball of twine in Kansas and you know I'm a sucker for gas station souvenirs. In exchange, you can set the temperature and I will spot you three wrong turns where I swallow every single one of my snarky comments."

Brooke shook Jordan's hand and they both turned to Sarah.

"This is going to end in tears. It always does when the two of you are forced into confined spaces," Sarah said slowly, "but I can't turn my back on the promise of free labor for Western Days. Everyone in town is already working on the festival, thanks to Prue Armstrong's persuasive volunteerism and her son Matt's charming manner, so finding extra hands for the lodge or the museum will be difficult. If you both will agree to hold off on telling stories about the injustices done to you by having to share a single bathroom growing up until at least the Colorado state line, I'm in." Sarah pulled them into a hug.

"Food. Sleep. Rent an SUV. Load it. Go steal a dog. Cross-country road trip." Jordan nodded. "My plan was to move you and then make Paul regret all his life choices, but this is honestly turning out to be so much more fun than I expected."

Brooke giggled along with her sisters, relieved they'd somehow known she needed them and arrived right on time. All the questions that she had were still there, but this one step was going to take her to the next fork in the road. After a few weeks in Prospect, she'd have to make some hard choices, but for now, she was happy to be moving forward with her sisters.

CHAPTER TWO

ON SUNDAY AFTERNOON, Matt Armstrong took off his hat and set it on top of the Western Days binder as he watched the crowd milling around the second floor of Prospect's Mercantile. The building was part of the historic section of town, but it had been renovated a few times in its hundred-plus years to serve as the unofficial gathering place for important town occasions. His mother and father had split the bottom floor in half after their divorce, building a hallway with doors for each of their businesses down the middle, but the second floor was a large, open space with room for plenty of chairs.

That space was filled this afternoon.

Most of Prospect had assembled for this Western Days status update, and, as the one supposedly in charge of the festival this year, his nerves were threatening to riot. The April weather was a tad warmer than normal already, so the windows were propped open to let the breeze in.

None of that air made it to his spot at the front of the room.

Today, every Western Days volunteer in the room would be shifting from planning to doing, and everything had gotten serious. For some reason, he had no trouble standing on a stage or hosting the Halloween costume parade in front of all of his neighbors, but being the man responsible for the biggest tourism weekend the town had all year long had him perched on the edge of an anxiety...occasion. He couldn't label it an attack. Not yet.

Matt Armstrong didn't panic. He was easygoing and good in emergency situations, for the most part.

But add the fact that this Western Days weekend was the centennial celebration, so it was the biggest weekend in a hundred years or so *and* relaunching his mother's dream of making it the biggest and best festival in Colorado, it was a miracle he had any hair left on his head.

Since they were taking their spots and locking eyes on him, it was definitely showtime.

The front rows were all Armstrongs as long as he included the Hearst sisters, and he did. His brothers Wes and Clay would be marrying Sarah and Jordan as soon as they could clear this festival weekend and talk the two women around. They took up one row with an empty spot between Sarah and Jordan for the third Hearst sister, who was absent for now. Dr. Keena Murphy, his brother Travis and the two foster sons Travis was raising filled out the row behind them. On the other side of the aisle, his brother Grant had taken up the perfect spot to heckle him, unless Mia kept him under control. Being the youngest of the five adopted Armstrong sons meant Matt could always count on at least one of his brothers to give him a hard time. Rose Bell, Patrick Hearst and his parents filled out the row.

It should have been reassuring to have all of his family up front.

It really wasn't.

"Took you long enough, Brooke. I wanted to introduce you to Lucky and Dante," Jordan said to her sister as the third Hearst sister plopped down next to her. "It's a bathroom. How long can it take?"

Matt had met Brooke as soon as she arrived in town, but she'd managed to keep her distance from their messy family togetherness so far. He couldn't decide if she was shy, aloof, superior, exhausted or some combination of the four, but she was the least like Sadie Hearst of any of the Hearsts he'd met so far.

Sadie's warmth had been immediate. For Sadie, "never met a stranger" didn't go far enough.

Brooke hadn't gotten that easy personality, apparently.

"What is your problem? I wanted to see the quilts, Jordan. I'm not even sure why I'm in this meeting," Brooke answered before darting a glance his direction to see if he was listening to their conversation.

He was.

"It's an all-hands-on-deck meeting. Everyone *staying* in the lodge is *working* on the lodge. This means you." Jordan poked her leg. "You said you'd help with the flower beds and I'm holding you to that. Since the lodge is opening during Western Days, we have to be here."

"I said I'd help with the beds because you wouldn't give me a pillow until I promised," Brooke hissed back as she rubbed the spot on her leg. "What do I know about gardening? I lived in the city, remember? Big city. Lots of traffic. Few flower beds."

Matt bent his head down to hide his twitching lips as Sarah leaned forward. "We'll get gardeners to help. You keep the project on track. We've had this conversation." Her big-sister tone was *I'll turn this car around right now.* She'd had a lot of practice squashing her sisters' arguments.

Brooke crossed her arms over her chest before she spotted that Jordan had done the same thing.

Then she relaxed her arms and smiled at Sarah. "You're right."

When Wes took Sarah's hand in his, it was impossible to miss the way Sarah immediately relaxed.

Matt knew the pang he felt as he watched was jealousy plus something else, but he couldn't figure out why it happened. Being single was his choice. His brothers were happy coupled up, but he was fine on his own. That was simple.

And he was stalling here. The only way to get through the meeting was to get it started.

"Okay, let's take care of business so we can get to the food, the reason you all showed up this afternoon." Matt smiled as the conversation around the room quieted.

Then his mother stepped up beside him and Matt tried not to let his concern show on his face.

"What'sa matter, baby? You're pale." His mother patted his arms. "It's a good turnout."

She was right about the size of the crowd, but he knew how her "help" was going to go. He was the youngest, and he often played that up, but his mother and her public displays of affection for her "baby" would be so much sweeter if there was no crowd watching.

"Yep, every single neighbor that you've *encour-*

aged," he said with heavy emphasis on the last word, "has reported for duty."

Her encouragement was almost impossible to wiggle out of.

Matt tugged at the collar of his plaid button-down shirt as he realized that if he had been close enough to listen to the Hearst sisters' conversation, they were definitely able to hear everything his mother said now.

Dread tangled with embarrassment to make a knot in his stomach.

"Better get started. If the food gets cold, the crowd will grow restless." His mother tapped his cheek. "My handsome boy. I'm so proud of you."

Matt glanced at Brooke Hearst before he realized what he was doing. Her eyebrows rose at his mother's sugary tone, and he could feel the heat of embarrassment on his cheeks.

After his mother sat, Matt cleared his throat again and scanned the crowd. Lindsay Thompson and Dani Garcia were standing at the back and they both gave him friendly waves. Since he'd dated them both at different times, it was a good thing everyone knew he was happy to be single as well.

"A little over three weeks until the big weekend, so it's time to finalize all the volunteer crews for the different areas of Western Days. Each crew is critical to the success of the weekend, and I don't have the words to express how much I appreciate every person who has shown up to help." His voice wavered and he rolled his eyes. "I guess pretending that I'm not nervous is impossible, so I'll add that, too."

Polite chuckles lifted from the audience here and there.

He firmly told himself not to check on Brooke's reaction to that because it wasn't important.

Matt pointed at the front row. "Grant, let's talk about progress on the Cowboy Games, our new event, first." He'd taken a page from his mother's book and *encouraged* his brother to take on these games, and he was proud of the way that had all worked out in his favor. Grant was still grumbling about it now and then, but this new event was going to be exciting.

"Thanks to Sam here," Grant said as he waved to where the retired postal worker was sitting, "who offered up his land and barn to host the event, and the advice of everyone I've dragged into sponsoring Prospect's growing rodeo club, as well as the most beautiful woman in the world…" He paused to wink at Mia. She blushed and gave him her own scowl before Grant held up his hands in surrender and continued, "We've got the outline for five events for our first Cowboy Games. Coed pairs will compete and be scored based on time to finish or overall performance.

Our celebrity judge, rodeo star Miss Annie Mercado, will arrive in town on Friday, where she will stay at the Majestic Prospect Lodge, and all events will be run on Saturday. We have a team signup website, thanks to Mia, and a nice cash prize for the winner provided by our sponsor, the Cookie Queen Corporation."

Grant was prepared to sit down, but Matt prodded, "And the events are?"

Grant's side-eye was murderous as he answered, "The timed events will be a riding relay, mucking out stalls, a three-legged hay bale race, laundry washing and hanging on a line, and then we'll have a cooking challenge where one contestant from each team, randomly chosen by a coin flip, has to prepare a steak and a good cup of coffee on an open fire. We expect the last one to separate the winning team from the rest. If you'd like to sign up, we still have a few spots. There's a link on the Western Days website." Grant shot him a look as if to say *Satisfied?* before he slid down in his seat.

Mia squeezed Grant's leg. Was that a silent *good job*? Matt ignored the fleeting notion about how nice that must feel. It would be good to have his own Mia helping to run this meeting beside him right about now.

"All right, on to food," Matt said. He flipped through the intimidating spreadsheet for the festival food plans. "Lucky has the vendors all set and ready to pull into town, starting the Wednesday before the festival opens. Some of them will be located at the Garage, but we'll be closing down the main street on Thursday morning. Reg McCall will work with the street crews to set the detour signs before the stage goes in. Some food vendors will be located near the Homestead Market on the other end of town as well. Lucky, is there anything you need to add here?"

From the back row, Lucky stood and said, "My volunteers will mostly be runners, helping to keep all the vendors in business, but we'll also remove trash and make sure the town is presented beautifully. Dante will have a side-by-side with a trailer. We can communicate on the two-way radios that each committee head will have to make pickups as needed. Everyone on my list has done this before, so we're set, but if anyone has any questions or would like to make suggestions, come talk to me."

Short. Sweet. Matt loved everything about Lucky's style. She and her husband were real pros.

"Let's move on to the crafts portion of the weekend. Prue?" Matt offered his mother the floor, and she swept up to stand next to him. She was wearing a big…scarf-y thing with ends that fluttered with each broad movement she made.

"Isn't Matt Armstrong the best?" his mother said as she motioned clapping and waited for the rest of the crowd to follow. Grant crossed his arms over his chest. The rest of her sons skipped the applause as well. "He was reluctant to take the position, but I am pleased with how he's stepped up."

This time, he couldn't stop himself from checking on Brooke Hearst's reaction to his mother.

When their eyes met this time, she wrinkled her nose.

In a second, his blush was back.

And she'd confused him again. That was not an aloof expression on her face.

"He has also started showing up to meetings on time since he was volunteered for this," Wes murmured and everyone around him chuckled. "This has been a learning experience for all of us, hasn't it, Matt?"

He bit back a retort about his busy vet practice and the emergency calls all over the region that he often had to make last minute. Matt looked to his mother. He motioned to her to continue her report.

"As you can see, we've started hanging the quilts for the competition." She waved a hand behind them where four quilts were displayed and roped off to keep anyone from getting too close. "This week, we'll finish every one of the indoor displays here and around town. The outdoor displays will be distributed to their spots the first day of the festival, and I've designated people to be responsible for hanging those and bringing them in if there's any bad weather. But there won't be any rain." She said it firmly as if Mother Nature knew better than to mess with Western Days weekend. "Once the street is blocked off, we'll set up partitions for craft vendors at either end, well out of the way of the parade route. Judging and announcements on the baking contest and the quilt show will take place on Reg's stage across from Bell House as usual on Saturday afternoon. The winner for the raffle quilt, our big fundraiser, will also be drawn at that time, so better buy your tickets first thing."

When she perched proudly in her seat, Matt said, "Okay, that leaves progress on the museum, lodge and restaurant." Matt scanned the crowd. "Any restaurant issues we need to troubleshoot at this point, chef?"

Rafa stood. "No, Jordan and I have worked out a simple but impressive menu for the weekend. Mia will post it to the lodge's website next week. Faye has been assisting with provisioning the kitchen, and Brian Caruso has promised to be on hand for the restaurant's hard launch at the festival."

Matt nodded. He had no doubt the Majestic's new restaurant would be ready. Everyone involved was a professional. "Sarah, Jordan, which one of you wants to go first?"

Brooke stretched back out of the way as her sisters had an intense staring match over her lap to fight it out, but Sarah finally stood.

"We're clearing up a punch list of minor repairs this week in the museum and we're waiting on the delivery of a sign for the window to advertise the test kitchen and studio that will be going in after Western Days…not before. After." She pointed at Jordan, who nodded firmly.

Jordan was losing sleep over everything that still had to be done on the lodge, so Matt knew she was not interested in any other project before Western Days.

Jordan stood. "And the lodge is…almost there. The siding has been restored, thanks to the efforts of Clay Armstrong and his team, and the facade is nearly perfect. We're early for a big landscaping push, but I'd love to have some volunteers out to the lodge the weekend before the festival to work on Sadie's flower beds, cleaning up the restaurant's deck, the dock, whatever we can get done. We're having plants delivered, so we'll be cleaning out the beds and putting in flowers to add some color. The rooms are ready, and we have some part-time help training with

Mia next week on housekeeping and the reservation system." Jordan twisted to survey the room. "What am I forgetting?"

Clay ran his hand over her back. "Not a thing. You're going to be ready for this."

Jordan inhaled slowly before exhaling. "I hope so. We want Sadie to be proud of what we've accomplished." She moved to sit down but popped back up. "The marina! I don't know that it will be gassed up and ready for boats by Western Days because we're still working those logistics out, but the convenience store will be open on Saturday to show visitors what we'll have to offer. We'll have a sign-up sheet for volunteers because we don't want anyone to miss the excitement in town. Faye is going to whip up some of Sadie's famous Cowboy Cookies to hand out to each visitor. It's where we all started this Cookie Queen journey, so it's important."

Then she folded down next to Brooke, sweating as if she'd run a marathon.

Matt shook his head, impressed with how Jordan was tracking all the moving pieces. "What you've accomplished around here is impressive. Thank you both for everything you're doing to make this weekend the best we've ever seen in Prospect." He glanced over at the enormous black Western Days binder on the table next to the wall before saying, "Unless anyone has anything else we need to discuss…"

Matt had almost decided he could relax but his father raised his hand and every one of the muscles in Matt's neck tightened. "Yeah, Dad?"

Walt pulled his earlobe. "Maybe I missed it, but I ain't heard any updates on the parade or the talent show yet."

Matt froze. It was impossible to get enough air in his chest suddenly. Why couldn't he remember who was responsible for those items?

The high school principal, Brad McHenry, stood slowly. "Yep, all the high school clubs are standing by to work on floats, but we haven't gotten any information on the sponsors yet. Normally, by this point, Dr. Singh would have sent me a list of the businesses who want to hire a club to build a float for them, then he delivers the collected sponsorship and materials fees." He knotted his hands together as if he knew the news was going to be bad. "Every one of those clubs depends on the sponsorship funds to pay for events during the school year. Working on the floats is also an excellent after-school activity that everyone enjoys, Matt. I hope we aren't going to lose that."

Keena said, "Dr. Singh is away working on a medical mission." Then she added, "If setting up the float sponsorships was something I was supposed to pick up, like running the clinic while he's gone, I didn't get the memo."

Concerned murmurs popped up here and there throughout the room as Matt tried to kick his frozen brain into gear. Should he have talked to Keena about the parade sponsorships? He was sure it was one of the tabs in the giant binder.

Serving as the only large animal vet for three counties, running his practice in town, assisting with animal rescue as needed, working out at the ranch and generally living his life hadn't left him much time for Western Days, but he'd managed to stay on top of things…until now.

"Oh, those kids do amazing work. That parade has been a part of Western Days for all one hundred years. We haven't forgotten that." Prue immediately stood and pointed at the binder. She'd painstakingly built the all-important binder when she'd handed over the reins of the festival to him this year. "Matt's been planning, haven't you?"

At this point, he had no choice but to go with the lifeline she tossed. "I've got a list of sponsors and as soon as I have the sponsorship fee checks in hand, I'll bring everything over to the high school so you can get the clubs working."

The principal nodded. "Soon?"

"Yep, this week." Matt had no idea how he would make that happen, but the festival was in three weeks so he didn't have much of a choice.

Those kids were already going to be pushed to the limit to get the floats done on time.

Satisfied, the principal sat back down.

"And the talent show?" Reg McCall asked from his spot next to the potluck table. "I've been practicing a number from *Annie Get Your Gun* to kick off the show, but I definitely want to do a country number, too. As last year's winner, I get to perform at the beginning and end. Remember?" His voice was anxious but firm. Reg lived to perform and everyone knew it.

"Reg has perfected 'There's No Business Like Show Business.' The crowd will love it," Keena murmured. "And if he doesn't take first place again this year with whatever Garth Brooks song he goes with, the whole medical clinic will be in trouble." As the clinic's office manager, Reg's happiness impacted everyone there, patients and staff alike.

"I'll put up another page on the website for anyone interested in performing at the talent show. It'll go up tonight, somehow, and the deadline to sign up will be Friday at…midnight," Mia said slowly, obviously aware that someone had to keep Matt from drowning. "Matt can work out auditions this weekend…?"

"Of course, that's the next thing on my list. I've been the emcee for years, so I know the usual suspects, but if we have more acts than we have time for, we'll do auditions on Saturday. I'll hammer out the order for the show at rehearsal… the Thursday before the festival opens." Matt scribbled notes down on a scrap piece of paper before pasting on his best charming expression. It usually got him out of trouble, but this might take something bigger. Food was his last resort to keep the mob in front of him happy.

Besides that, if there was any other Western Days activity that he'd forgotten, he didn't want to hear about it at this point.

"All right. Time for food! I'll send out emails with all the crew assignments this week, along with the phone number of the captain in charge of each volunteer team. You know where to find me if anything else comes up." Matt closed the binder with a thump, which had become his way of adjourning meetings. The chatter started immediately as the crowd turned to mill around the long line of tables holding all the potluck offerings. He ignored the clatter as people moved chairs and tables around to create seating for the meal and took a moment to inhale slowly.

He knew, even without having eyes in the back of his head, that his family was about to descend.

"Why do I get the feeling you weren't telling the whole truth about how prepared you are to finish up strong for Western Days?" Wes said as he stopped next to Matt.

"Yeah, you were definitely tap dancing up there." Clay crossed his arms over his chest.

Grant clapped him on the shoulder. "Mama's baby boy better check the trusty binder."

"I don't guess any of you would like to help?" Matt asked as he turned in the circle his brothers had formed.

Travis sighed. "Sure we would, but you're going to have to explain to Mom *why* you need help."

"So not happening." Matt nodded. "That's what you're telling me."

They were grinning when Sarah and Jordan joined them. Wes wrapped his arms around Sarah to give her a sweet kiss. Clay braced himself for impact as Jordan tossed herself into his arms. That left Brooke hanging back, so Walt and Prue ushered her into the family group as they also joined.

"Matt, you could use some help, couldn't you?" his mother asked as she raised her eyebrows to explain to him that he better say yes. Matt wondered if Brooke understood that his mother had started *encouraging* her participation in Western Days. It started with a firm but not painful hold on Brooke's hand that made it impossible to fade back into the safe crowd.

Matt could use help, and the idea of working with Brooke was somehow much more appealing than working with any of his brothers. "Of course, there's still so much to do." Matt met Brooke's stare as he turned up the wattage on his best smile. It never failed to catch a woman's attention. From there, he usually introduced himself, asked for a phone number or, in this case, negotiated some urgently needed help with Western Days. Then he would accept Brooke's reluctant offer to help and charm her into forgetting it hadn't been her own idea in the first place.

But Brooke nodded politely before tugging her hand free. "It sounds like you have some things to discuss. I believe I'll head over to the potluck table to see what we have for dinner."

Matt pasted a pleasant expression over his shock as he and his family watched Brooke navigate the potluck table. She appeared unaffected by the ripple of disbelief she'd left in her wake.

She'd extracted herself from one of his mother's plans and seemed perfectly at ease with her decision as she hugged her father and stood on her tiptoes to study something that Rose Bell had pointed out on the potluck table.

If she was as immune to his mother's high-pressure sales tactics as she seemed, Matt was impressed.

Even if she was pretending, she was really good at it.

He hadn't expected her to free herself so easily. From his mother, or himself. Was that why he admired it so much?

When was the last time a beautiful woman had knocked him off balance that way? He'd devoted a lot of time and effort to becoming an expert in two areas: veterinary medicine and charming women. Both came naturally to him and he enjoyed every minute.

But Brooke Hearst had demonstrated she wasn't susceptible to his particular brand of charm. His winning smile had missed completely.

And his entire family had been witness.

Now everyone turned to gauge his reaction.

"That is not the way it usually goes, is it?" Grant drawled.

"I don't believe I've ever seen a woman turn away from the bottomless pools of his deep brown eyes that easily," Clay added.

"I still have to poke Keena now and then to get her brain back in gear when she runs into Matt unexpectedly." Travis caught Keena's hand before her elbow connected with his side.

Matt knew he deserved every bit of their ribbing. Prue and Walt had become foster parents when they'd taken in Wes, then decided to adopt him. They'd continued fostering, and over the next couple of years, had taken in Matt's other brothers: Clay, Travis and Grant. As the youngest and the last of the boys to arrive at the ranch, he was frequently the target of his brothers' teasing, and he accepted it as his role in the family. Each of them had one. Wes, the "oldest" because he was the first foster kid at the Rocking A, was the leader, the good one. Clay, the successful architect and builder, was the smart one. Travis, the hero, had retired from the army and immediately opened up the ranch to the next generation of foster kids who needed Prue, Walt and the Rocking A. And Grant had been the bad boy superstar of rodeo before he'd returned to Prospect and assumed his role as Number One Fun Uncle.

Matt was the baby. They'd all gotten used to thinking of him as the one who got out of the hard work because he was the youngest, despite the fact that he'd gone to school and managed a thriving vet practice. But family was everything to Matt, and he understood his place in his.

Wes could have taken this job getting the town ready for Western Days without a hitch, sailing into a successful event without breaking a sweat.

But he'd been smart enough to show up to the first planning meeting on time.

Matt had depended on being the youngest and

his mother's "favorite" to help him slide out of a serious workload for the festival…and been caught in the trap, complete with massive black binder filled with lists of things still to do, things that have been done, people to call and details that he absolutely must not forget.

Except, yeah, he'd *actually* forgotten a couple of big things.

Which is why it was unfortunate Brooke had freed herself from the group without hesitation.

Women loved him. They always had.

And he loved them right back—but never for too long.

Running into one who was…completely unaffected was new.

His mother hummed. "Gotta say, I had this neat little plan in my head where we nabbed all three Hearst sisters for Prospect. How could Matt lose when Brooke finally showed up, husbandfree and as pretty as a picture?" Sarah and Jordan hadn't shared much about Brooke's life in New York, but everyone knew she and her husband had divorced. He hadn't heard any details on why she was here in Prospect instead of enjoying life as an heiress in the city, but he wasn't shocked his mother had been making long-term plans involving the two of them.

She was the queen of strategy.

And she'd been dropping broad hints that it was time for Matt to settle down like his brothers.

Sarah and Jordan Hearst had become the sisters he never had, so it made sense for Wes and Clay to make it all official.

Matt had only expected the pressure on him to increase once Grant toppled into love with Mia.

If he'd considered it, he might even have expected Prue Armstrong to set her hopes on the youngest Hearst sister.

"But…" His mother grimaced. "Maybe we'll all have to keep looking." She patted his shoulder to console him, as if he'd been the one whose romantic aspirations had been foiled.

Matt turned his back on Brooke. Not that she noticed. She was making conversation with Reg McCall near the meatballs, and he immediately regretted that he knew that.

"I'm too young to get married, Mama," Matt said with a teasing wink as he did every time she brought up his love life. "Focus on getting these boys hitched first."

Travis cleared his throat as if he had an announcement to make while Keena waved her hand dramatically. "While we're on the subject of weddings…"

His mother added up the clues first. "You got engaged!" Everyone in the room turned to find out what the excitement was about, so Keena spoke to the room. "Actually, we got hitched. In Las Vegas!"

Matt would have laughed at the dead silence that fell as everyone waited for Prue's reaction, but he was so happy to escape the spotlight that he kept his mouth shut.

Travis's youngest foster son piped up. "We were the best men, and then we walked forever and ever but I saw the coolest fountains! There were lights tall as a building shining on the water when it shot up with music, like the fountains were dancing." Micah raised both thumbs. "Highly recommend."

Matt squeezed his shoulder, amused at how the kid never hesitated to leap in with his opinion. It was nice to be the youngest sometimes.

The rest of Matt's brothers were waiting along with the crowd on Prue Armstrong's reaction.

"And whose suggestion was eloping?" his mother asked sweetly. "We all know how much this town loves a wedding, don't we? The first of my boys to get married and I missed it?"

Keena raised her hand immediately. "Prue, it was my idea. We didn't want to wait until Western Days was over, or until Dr. Singh returned from his medical mission trip so the clinic would be staffed long enough for a wedding and honeymoon. Plus it was just…time. We're a family, and this was the last step." Keena wrapped her arm through Travis's before slinging one arm over Damon, their teenage foster son, and tugging him into her side.

Was she planning to deflect his mother's disappointment with cute kids?

That might work.

Matt watched his mother struggle. She loved nothing more than planning events and she'd been dreaming of her sons' weddings.

But Dr. Keena Murphy had never been one to wait around for anything, and she'd quickly learned how to work with Prue Armstrong.

His mother appreciated boldness. Keena had identified Prue's strategic strengths early on and had used them to her advantage when it was time to convince Travis they belonged together. Keena was smart.

And every single one of the women his brothers had brought into the family had become Prue Armstrong's favorite people in the world.

"Well, I guess we'll have to throw a big ol' party out at the ranch…when time permits," his mother said politely.

Keena immediately took his mother's hand. "And you know I don't have the party-planning ability to pull something like that off, so I'm counting on your help to make it special."

Matt hid his smile as they waited for Prue's reaction.

His mother tapped her chin. "How long do you think it will take to build a dance floor? We're going to need some kind of covering, too. Midsummer? Early fall?"

Travis met Matt's stare and silently exhaled because he'd known this announcement was going to be touch-and-go. Most of the time, Prue Armstrong was the easy favorite to win in any race, but Keena had introduced a wild card.

"Guess we're one step closer to our own new *I do*, Prue," his father said as he waggled his eyebrows.

She sniffed. "Since you haven't asked and I haven't said yes, I'm not sure how you figure that." Then she stretched up to press a kiss to his lips. "But you might be right, cowboy. Better get Keena here to help you plan a big splashy proposal."

Everyone in town except Prue and Walt had been certain their divorce was a mistake, and the split had taken years to mend, but there was a betting pool going on which Armstrong would be first to marry and who would be last.

Keena and Travis had rocked the odds by eloping.

Prue turned back to take Keena's hand. "Are

you hungry? Let's go get some food and you can tell me all about this adventure."

When his family turned to head for the line at the food table, Matt collapsed against the wall, both arms wrapped tightly around the Western Days binder.

He was happy for Travis and Keena and even for his mother, who would throw the party to end all parties with enough time, but he had so much work to do right now.

His eyes traveled to Brooke again. He needed help and Brooke had time. Somehow, he'd get her to agree and promise to keep the truth of his complete lack of preparation a closely guarded secret.

Tomorrow. When there was no audience watching.

And *after* he made his vet rounds at three different ranches to check on livestock at the crack of dawn, then put in a full day in his veterinary office in town. After all that, he'd jump right on this parade problem. He pressed the heel of one hand to his eye, hoping the pressure would ease the budding headache.

On second thought, he should get a jump on it tonight. He'd make a plate of food and head back to his office-slash-bachelor-pad-slash-Western-Days-planning-headquarters to start a list of float sponsors to call on.

Somehow, he would do that without watching Brooke Hearst reconnect with her sisters.

And the dent Brooke had put in his ego would eventually disappear.

CHAPTER THREE

THE NEXT DAY, Brooke stared up at the leafy canopy that covered her favorite spot next to Key Lake. The lake outside Prospect was one of the town's biggest attractions, or it had been while Sadie's old fishing lodge had been in business. Today, there wasn't much traffic out on the lake, but Jordan was hoping that would change when the Majestic and its marina were open again.

Inside the lodge, Jordan's hard work was evident. When Sarah had arrived in town to inspect their inheritance, closed up for fifteen years or more after Sadie moved to LA, the place had been a wreck. Today, the dusty floors gleamed again, all the cobwebs were gone and Jordan had restored or replaced most of the furnishings inside while keeping the history of the lodge in mind. A new roof and repaired wooden siding outside meant the Majestic appeared timeless.

Sadie would be thrilled at what Jordan had pulled off with the help of Sarah and the Armstrongs next door. All twenty rooms were already booked for the Western Days weekend; the restaurant would be ready in time, too. The amenities were simple: clean, comfortable rooms with beautiful views of the glittering lake out front. The essences of the Majestic remained the same, but the place sparkled with life now. Her middle sister had a history littered with unfinished jobs, but not even bats in the lodge's attic had chased Jordan away from the Majestic.

And Brooke had watched it all happen from New York while her life was unraveling, but she was proud to be a Hearst, even if her contributions to Prospect were negligible at this point.

So far, Brooke's first proper order of business upon arrival at the Majestic—after sleeping for twelve hours—had been to dig out Sadie's old hammock and string it up in the same spot it had hung when she was a little girl. The trees were larger now, but when Brooke thought about the Majestic, this quiet cove tucked away from the lodge's view had always been one of her favorite places. It was near the lodge but not too near, and on slow days like this one, the only sounds came from the trees and the muted lap of the lake's small waves landing on the shore.

She and her mother had spent lazy days here, sometimes together, sometimes separately, but always with a book. Sarah and Sadie had stayed busy, bustling here and there around the lodge with to-do lists to conquer, while Jordan had shadowed their father and jumped at any chance to hop in the boat and head out on the lake.

Brooke and her mom had been perfectly content right here, reading and listening to the breeze.

After her mother died, Brooke and her sisters had grieved in different ways. Their father, distant in his own pain, had packed them up to move from Denver to LA for a change of scenery. Sarah had immediately stepped up to mother her sisters and their father, taking the lead around the house and keeping Brooke and Jordan whole. Only Sadie's arrival in LA had given Sarah any chance at being a normal teenage girl. Jordan had done her best to disappear, hiding away in their mother's art studio until Sarah forced her back into the real world.

And Brooke, as the youngest, tried desperately to pretend everything was the same when absolutely nothing was normal anymore. She had wanted to be like her friends, into silly boys and hair and makeup, so that's what she did.

Her heart was broken, but her life went on. During the day, Brooke helped Sarah and teased Jordan in her small attempts to make their home "normal" again.

But at night, she'd hold tightly to her books when sleep wouldn't come. The right story could get her through until morning.

Being out of step with the rest of the Hearsts—who were all in on Prospect, the Majestic and Western Days—had been bothering her, but falling into this hammock had turned the key in a lock that Brooke had forgotten about. They'd had so many good summer days here.

"Coco, I'm not sure it's warm enough to be here," Brooke murmured as she rubbed the dog's ear between her thumb and finger. Her corgi was unconcerned about the temperature, as her current bed, Brooke's stomach, came with built-in heat. "I guess twenty pounds of dog stretched out on top of me will keep me from getting too cold, huh? Good thing you're so fuzzy."

Coco sighed happily and blinked sleepy eyes, content for the first time since she'd been gathered up from Brooke's ex-husband's apartment and carted across the country in a basket.

"How can that possibly be comfortable?" Jordan asked as she loomed over the hammock.

"You found me." Brooke had expected that the wave of Western Days preparation would wash over her sooner or later, but she'd hoped for more time to soak in the peace of Key Lake before Jordan ran out of patience.

"If you were hiding, you should have picked a different spot," Jordan said as she scratched Coco's neck, "and a different color of camouflage. Sadie's bright orange hammock was never subtle."

"But it was Mom's favorite color," they both said.

"And Sadie loved picking out things that Mom loved," Jordan added.

"Yeah," Brooke said softly, "and now I miss them both."

"Hold on. I'm coming in." Jordan threw her leg up over the side of the hammock and wriggled in next to Brooke and Coco. Brooke held Coco tightly while the hammock swayed wildly. Jordan finally settled down with a happy sigh. "Sorry. If it's any consolation, this place brings those emotions right to the surface, but it also changes them so that they're less bitter and sweeter the longer you stay here." She stared out at the water. "Not sure how that works, but you miss them with a smile on your face."

They were both quiet, swaying gently, when Sarah walked up. "Are you already giving each other the silent treatment? It's been ten minutes. I had to make a phone call."

Brooke sighed. "No, we were communing with nature. We try to fight only when you're around to keep things from getting out of control."

Jordan snorted. "You got here just in time. I was about to dump Brooke out of the hammock and tell her to find something to do around here, but I can't disturb Coco."

Sarah crossed her arms over her chest. Brooke watched her face as their oldest sister carefully crafted a response that would navigate smoothly between her and Jordan. "We didn't bring you here to put you to work—"

"But that was definitely part of the bargain we made…" Jordan waggled her eyebrows.

Brooke sighed. "Fine. Give me a job. A small one. An easy one." She turned to Sarah. "And we might as well test if the old hammock will still hold all three of us. It took me a minute to remember how the tree straps work, but I'm almost certain I got them placed correctly."

"Almost certain, hmm?" A worried frown creased Sarah's forehead but she immediately put her leg up to perch on the side of the hammock and eased in on the other side. The hammock swayed and Coco snorted at all the commotion.

The three of them froze as they waited to see if the ropes were sturdy enough, but after a loud squeak of protest as the straps pulled taut, the only sound was the wind in the trees around them.

"They definitely do not make things the way they used to. This hammock is sturdy." Sarah held up her hand. "Before we give Brooke any assignments, let's talk about the Western Days meeting yesterday afternoon."

Brooke closed her eyes. She'd expected an immediate reaction to the way she'd bluntly extricated herself from the family circle, but Sarah and Jordan had waited until now.

When she had no way to escape the conversation.

And the weight of her sisters' stares as they studied her was uncomfortable.

"What? I was perfectly well-mannered." Brooke was convinced that was true. Blunt didn't mean rude, necessarily. She'd navigated plenty of similar groups before, so she'd perfected her coping mechanisms. Big crowds of strangers used to tie her stomach in knots, but now she knew how to make polite, meaningless conversation with people she'd just met. Then finding something that needed her attention across the room was a surefire way to leave any conversation she had no interest in.

Unless she was wedged into a hammock with a dog weighing her down.

Jordan leaned over Brooke to stare hard at Sarah. That was her *do something* glare.

"Well-mannered." Sarah sighed. "That's technically true, but the…abrupt way you turned down the pressure Prue Armstrong was building up to…"

"Never seen it done before, and I'm pretty sure Prue was stunned to silence." Jordan rolled her head against the hammock. "On the one hand, impressive, but on the other hand, the Armstrongs have been critical to each step we've made here at the lodge and in town. We owe them so many favors. They might as well be family."

The faint tone of judgment in Jordan's voice set Brooke's teeth on edge.

Brooke hadn't asked any Armstrong for help, so why did she owe them her time? She didn't.

She'd had it up to her nose in providing unpaid labor for everyone else's causes and finding herself with nothing to show for it.

Before she fired back, Brooke forced herself to inhale and exhale slowly.

"I spent years being my ex-husband's right-hand woman, only for him to leave me without any hesitation, and I don't want to wear myself out so that another man can take the credit. I'm exhausted. For the first time in a long time, I'm putting myself first." She shrugged to punctuate her statement and show that she didn't care what they thought about it.

Even if she did care.

"Dinners for his law firm partners, committee chair for his causes, campaign volunteer for his party connections. I did it all and I enjoyed it because we were building something together." Brooke glared up at the bright green leaves rustling overhead. "He and his new wife, the one from the family with the political connections, will now enjoy all that goodwill. The divorce made it clear to me that our work was his work, our friends were his friends and my experience... well, I owed that all to my husband, too, apparently. Working in the coffee shop was well within my skill and ability, but I had to talk my way into the job because my résumé of countless volunteer *opportunities* didn't give me any experience running a cash register or steaming milk."

Watching those "connections" she'd made through hard work disappear in a blink had been a lesson she'd needed to learn. The only real thing Paul had ever given her was Coco. She stared down into her dog's eyes, grateful to have her back where she belonged.

An outcome that she owed to her sisters, so she could be patient and listen to their side of the story about the Armstrongs and Western Days.

Sarah reached over to take her hand. "You convinced us that your life in New York was everything you wanted, but you were losing yourself, weren't you?"

"I did want that life. All of it. In my mind, Paul and I were a team. We were building something important, you know?" Brooke squeezed Sarah's hand. "It turned out I *was* building something… for Paul. For me?" She closed her eyes. The memory of the moment she'd realized how wrong she'd been brought tears to her eyes. "Losing myself is the perfect way to put it. It's a good thing Sadie is still taking care of me or I'm not sure where I'd be now."

Jordan moved closer until her face filled Brooke's vision.

Which was entirely too close for Brooke's comfort but she was stuck in the hammock under a small dog who was snoring lightly at this point.

"Listen to me." Jordan narrowed her eyes. "Sadie made us strong. All three of us. You would have figured it out, but you won't ever have to do it alone. We're sticking together." She nodded firmly and Brooke could see her great-aunt Sadie in every single one of Jordan's fierce features at that moment.

"I expected you to dump me on the ground like you used to do when we were kids," Brooke said as she rubbed her burning nose. Tears would be too much emotion for this discussion, but they were bubbling under the surface at all times lately. "I'm not sure I'm strong enough for you to be sweet."

"I won't dump you—I can't upset Coco," Jordan said as she lay back down. "Once you've crawled across the kitchen floor to lure a dog out of an apartment while the housekeeper has her back turned, you bond with that dog. Coco and I will share that experience for the rest of our lives."

Brooke snorted loudly, causing Coco to tilt her head in concern. "I hope Jane doesn't get into too much trouble. She's good at her job, even if she was dog-burgled in broad daylight."

"Paul should never have taken Coco to force you to sign over the brownstone." Sarah patted Coco's back. "We did what we had to do. He has the papers he wanted to list the house. You have the dog. Paul better leave it at that."

"Yeah," Jordan agreed with a hard nod, "your fiancé is a lawyer."

Sarah slung her arm over Coco and Brooke to pat Jordan's shoulder. "Everyone knows you're the biggest weapon we have, Jordie."

"You're the brains of the operation. Taking the leftover bacon from breakfast made getting Coco's attention a snap," Jordan said. Brooke shook her head as she remembered the way she and Sarah had distracted Jane with the signed papers while Jordan had skipped out with Coco. Someday, she might feel guilty about involving the poor housekeeper, but not today.

Coco, completely unruffled by being the prize in a heist, stood to stretch.

"So..." Jordan smiled sweetly. "Are you familiar with the saying *one good turn deserves another*, Brooke?"

Brooke paused in the middle of following Sarah, who had eased out of the hammock gracefully. Brooke handed her sister the dog before standing.

"Uh-huh," Brooke said slowly. "But you don't have a dog that has been kidnapped, so I'm going to have to owe you until that day, right?"

Sarah's lips twitched before she cleared her throat. "What we have is a lodge to finish getting ready for a big weekend, a list of jobs longer than both our arms and a family member who needs some help."

Brooke pointed at her chest in a question.

Sarah shook her head slowly before waving her hand with the diamond Wes had given her when he'd proposed in front of the whole town at the Prospect Picture Show. "The family is much, much larger now."

With a groan, Brooke rolled her head on her shoulders. "I can't remember if it was in Kansas or Nebraska, but remember when Jordan made me shout affirmations out the window? Because I do. 'I am strong.' 'I am confident.' 'I deserve happiness.' 'I stand up for myself.' That's what I did last night. I protected my *boundaries* politely by leaving the conversation before I could be drafted to save the Western Days parade."

Sarah bit her lip. "We don't know for certain that Matt hasn't got it under control." She held up both hands in surrender when Jordan and Brooke both raised their eyebrows.

"I stand by my affirmations," Jordan said slowly and Brooke knew there was a *but* coming.

"But you're the answer to the problem, dropped right into place at the perfect moment. All your experience is desperately needed here, and you aren't just helping Matt or his family. Sarah and I have invested our lives in Prospect. A successful festival is going to return immediate dividends for the lodge and the museum for years."

"Talk to Matt," Sarah said. "Ask some questions. You can still say no if you want. After you hear him out."

Brooke shook her head. "There were women waving at him from the back of the room. I doubt he has any trouble finding help." She'd already heard more than once about the Matt Armstrong Effect, how his handsome face had a trail of charmed women following him wherever he went. That advance notice about his good looks had helped her build up an immunity before he could catch her off guard with his dark eyes and beautiful curls.

"If the women were at the meeting, they already have assignments for the festival. Besides, just because they wouldn't mind a job that got them closer to Matt, it doesn't mean they're right for this important job." Jordan pursed her lips. "He manages to present a confident, happy persona at all times, but I know this is important to him. In fact, he might be like *someone else* I know who wants everyone to think things are under control even when they're fraying at the edges."

Sarah silently whistled as Brooke registered the way Jordan was comparing her to Matt.

And Brooke could tell that her sister wanted to push harder. Jordan rarely pulled a punch when she wanted something. This mattered to both of her sisters.

"How can I say no to the woman who smuggled bacon in her pocket to rescue my dog?" Brooke grunted as Jordan squeezed her tightly and Sarah clapped.

"My beautiful baby sister. I don't know why you're dressed as if you're about to stroll down Fifth Avenue, but I love you so much right now that I won't even give you a hard time. However, it's a one-day-only offer. Tomorrow, you need shorts and sneakers like the rest of us or prepare to be teased mercilessly." Jordan stepped back. "Giving you fair warning is so adult of me. I am really maturing."

"It's a beautiful dress, Brooke." Sarah held out a key ring. "Mia has some files that Matt will need, stuff that's coming in from the website. Take my SUV and drive them into town? He's working in his vet office today. It will be easy to ask some questions, find out if there's any way to help."

Brooke accepted the keys.

"And stop in at Homestead Market to make sure that our plants are on target for delivery by next weekend? Don't tell me you aren't a gardener. All three of us know you got Sadie's style, so take a look at the order I filled out and add what's missing." Jordan waved vaguely at the red sundress Brooke had chosen in an effort to cheer herself up. She'd gone with flats instead of heels to be practical, obviously. "They sell working clothes there. You should get some."

Before Brooke could complain about how this "simple request" was already snowballing into errands and lists, Sarah and Jordan headed for the lodge, their heads together as they discussed whatever high-priority project came next. The way they had gotten so close while they worked on the lodge provoked a jealous pinch.

At certain times, her sisters had their own unspoken communication that left Brooke firmly on the outside.

How much time would she need to spend in Prospect to make it inside their circle?

"I guess it's you and me," Brooke said as she

stared into Coco's eyes. "Come on. Let's go explore Prospect. When the cowboy makes his pitch, I need you to stand firm, Coco. Tell me to say no. Let's work out a signal." She bent down. "If you think I'm about to give in and say yes, you wag your tail, okay? That will be a reminder to me that we are looking out for just the two of us now. A whole lot of *I would have volunteered but I didn't really want to* for the foreseeable future."

Coco didn't snort, but it wouldn't have surprised Brooke if she did. Instead of letting her dread build up, Brooke went inside to get Mia's files and Jordan's plant order and loaded Coco and her basket into Sarah's SUV. At some point, she'd have to go car shopping for herself. In New York, she'd loved her two-seater convertible, but life in Prospect had a totally different vibe. Sarah's SUV fit.

If Brooke decided to stay in Prospect for a bit, she'd need to consider that.

Brooke slumped against the seat as her thought registered. Would she stay in Prospect?

New York was no longer on the list of possible addresses.

LA had been home for bit. So had Denver, and both options would get her closer to her sisters.

So why didn't either feel right?

"That's the fatigue talking," she muttered to

herself as she drove down the Majestic's lane toward the highway. "Get some rest and then figure out where the next chapter of your life takes place." She rolled down the windows so that Coco could stick her nose out to sniff the air. The lane wound from the lodge's parking lot through tall trees and out between pastureland on either side. When Sarah had first come to Prospect to investigate selling the lodge, the three of them had agreed to sell some of Sadie's undeveloped land back to the Armstrongs. They needed the space since all five adopted sons had come home and were now working on the Rocking A next door. There were cows on either side of the road. It was a pretty picture for a spring day.

And it was impossible to deny how much Brooke enjoyed driving on an open road. The weather was warming up. The grass was green as far as the eye could see across the Rocking A pastures, and pops of bright pink-and-white buds on trees were scattered here and there.

As she drove into town, she noted the oldest part of Prospect—carefully maintained historical facades still standing from the 1800s—was as picturesque as it always had been. The facades of the buildings dated back to the town's founding, but new businesses had taken over some of the spots. Winter was finished, so the wooden sidewalk had been cleaned and bright flowerpots were scattered here and there. As a kid, she'd been unimpressed by the shopping possibilities in the small town. She didn't hold out much hope as an adult, either.

Brooke stopped first at Homestead Market, which had taken over the town's old livery stable, to confirm Jordan's plant delivery was still on schedule. When Coco was loaded into her basket, Brooke marched inside the big-box store with it gripped in one hand and her list in the other.

Coco was no service animal, so her presence might have caused a stir, but dogs in baskets got passes more often than not, in Brooke's experience. Unfortunately, Coco was pushing the limits of the adorable handled basket Brooke had chosen when she was a puppy. Her "fluff" was dangling over the sides, but once she was in the shopping cart, the concept of being more than any old dog still applied.

Brooke wasn't sure how many years it had been since she'd been inside the store that carried groceries, home and garden items, and bits of everything in between, but she wanted to come back with more time. New York hadn't offered many shopping experiences like this small-town everything store. City stores were about convenience with order and delivery for everything. Meandering up and down aisles was a novelty.

Her discussion with the manager of the garden section was easy. He pulled up images to show her Jordan's selections; Brooke changed the colors and some of the quantities to make sure the flower beds had enough pop to frame the beautiful lodge correctly.

Jordan was definitely going to complain, though, since Brooke doubled her order, but there was no sense in doing anything halfway.

Sadie had taught them all that. It was so easy to picture the older woman, one hand propped on her hip while she shook a finger and said, "When we start climbin', we're going all the way to the top."

After loading Coco into the car, Brooke drove farther down and parked in front of Bell House, the beautiful Victorian that served as the town's bed-and-breakfast. The Armstrong Veterinary Clinic had taken a spot a few spaces down along the wooden sidewalk, across from the shady green space that surrounded the B and B.

Faded paint on the exterior of the building said that the place had been the stagecoach office in the early days of Prospect's life as a silver rush boomtown.

If she'd missed the small sign that said "Veterinarian, Dr. Matt Armstrong" over the door, the carved wooden statue of a miniature stagecoach driven by a cat wearing a large cowboy hat would have been a solid clue.

"Silly. No cat is driving a stagecoach. Cats are management only," Brooke said to Coco in her basket before she opened the door and stepped inside the office.

The tiny waiting area was empty, but she heard Matt call out, "Be with you in a second."

"No rush," she responded, annoyed at how her heartrate picked up. When Coco's basket hit the floor, the small dog hopped out to explore the lowest shelves in the room.

Brooke turned to study a poster about how to tell if a dog is overweight before she checked Coco's ribs. They were fuller than she remembered, but Paul had probably been feeding her leftovers for the month he'd had her. If Coco didn't fit in her cute little carrier anymore, Brooke would size up to the backpack she'd seen subway riders use. "*Diet* is a four-letter word, Coco. We don't believe in them. There's plenty of room for exercise at the Majestic."

She stretched her arm. If she was intent on carting Coco around, she might need to add weights to her cardio routine. "It might be time to add more steps to your day, though." Possibly at the end of a pretty leash.

Matt cleared his throat as he bent down to introduce himself to Coco. "Excellent philosophy. Skip the diet. The doctor approves."

The way she held her breath when she spun around to find him bent down on one knee, making funny, sweet, goofy faces at her dog as he said "Who's a pretty girl? You are" was annoying, but Matt Armstrong's appeal crashed over Brooke's head like a monster wave.

He was wearing scrubs.

Coco greeted him with a careful touch of her nose to his cheek.

He grinned like she was as precious as Brooke was convinced she was.

And it was almost impossible to get normal respiration back on track. So much for being immune.

"Who is this?" he asked.

Her first answer was so rough that she had to take a second shot. "This is Coco."

Matt ran his hand down Coco's sides and said, "Well, I hope you postpone Coco's weight-loss regimen until the puppies are here. Mamas needs good food and plenty of rest, don't they, Coco?"

The record scratch that sounded in Brooke's head stopped her brain. "Puppies." Brooke's knees gave out and she hit the seat behind her with a thump. "Coco's having puppies?"

She didn't register whatever it was that Matt

said. His lips were moving but nothing made it through the static in her ears.

When Matt stood, she thumped the file folder of paperwork that Mia had sent in the center of his chest and closed her eyes to stop the spinning.

CHAPTER FOUR

THIS WASN'T THE first time Matt had delivered the news to an unsuspecting pet owner that they were about to have a special delivery. But he hadn't anticipated cool Brooke would melt down as she had. Anyone who could keep her wits about her to avoid his mother's plans had to be pretty steady.

Brooke was dressed for some kind of special occasion in a flowing dress that settled around her feet as she bent forward. It was beautiful, the kind of outfit he imagined ladies who lunch chose for their weekly confabs. She was lovely, even if she seemed to fit in as well as a show pony at a cattle drive. His scrubs were clean. So was the floor of the tiny waiting room, but large bags of dog food and canned cat food formed her backdrop instead of city streets.

When Coco looked up at him, a tiny wrinkle of concern on her brow, he decided to try…something. What did people do in cases like this?

Water. A drink of water seemed like a good place to start.

He wrapped his hand around Brooke's elbow. "Hey, let's go get you a drink. Can you walk?"

Her irritated glare was also a different reaction than he'd expected but it eased some of his concern. It was much more in line with the Hearst character.

"It was the smallest little panic. I'll recover." Brooke stood but he noticed a wobble until she caught him watching. Then he held up his hands and motioned to the short hallway. "I have coffee. I have water. Both are back in the kitchen."

She bent down to kiss Coco's head which reassured him.

As a young vet, he'd been shocked and heartbroken at the way some owners treated their animals. Unexpected puppies could provoke some terrible requests, so he was happy to hear her concern for the dog.

Brooke Hearst couldn't be one of those people, not if the Hearst-Armstrong clan was going to thrive.

"Sorry, baby, I didn't mean to worry you," she murmured as she ran a hand down Coco's back.

Brooke's husky tone settled somewhere in his abdomen even as he happily crossed a fatal flaw off his list of worries. Whatever came next for Brooke and Coco, she would do the right thing.

Then she straightened her shoulders, tipped her chin up and sailed down the hallway gracefully, each step certain as her skirt billowed behind her.

Since he was familiar with shows of confidence, he expected she was embarrassed for having the "smallest little" meltdown in front of him.

"Go right at the end of the hallway," Matt murmured as he watched Brooke and Coco both scan his tiny, cramped office and the exam room across from it. Brooke stopped inside the doorway of what he optimistically called his "apartment" at the back of the building. His hound dog, Betty, stretched slowly before rolling out of her comfy dog bed to greet Brooke with a wagging tail and Coco with some delicate sniffs.

Betty towered over Coco, but Matt wasn't too worried about their interaction. His lazy hound had as much aggression as a sun-warmed sloth, and Coco's wildly wagging stub of a tail was evidence she only wanted to make new friends.

"Kitchen, living room, bedroom and Western Days headquarters all efficiently contained in approximately four hundred square feet. You can choose whatever seat you like, as long as it's the superplush futon that seats two and doubles as an almost comfortable bed, or one of my kitchen table chairs." He waved dramatically at the only choices in the room. If he ever had five human visitors, he'd be in trouble.

Brooke's lips were twitching as she pulled out one of the chairs and sat down. He'd spread the Western Days binder out as soon as he'd come in the night before, so there wasn't much room left at the table itself. She perched her elbow on the edge and said, "That coffee smells delicious."

"Yeah? How do you take it?" He pulled two unmatched coffee mugs down.

"Black, please," Brooke said politely as he handed one mug over. "Who is your friend?"

"That's my girl, Betty." Matt rested against his short kitchen counter with his own mug. "She keeps this place in line."

Brooke nodded and sipped her coffee. "I never used to drink coffee, but I worked as a barista in New York. Picked up some bad habits of the expensive-coffee-drink variety." She turned her mug in a circle and smiled at the picture on it. "I would have said absolutely nothing here matched what I expected for Matt Armstrong, but this does." The mug featured a cat, one paw pointing at its reflection in a mirror, and said "Practically Paw-fect."

"Does my reputation precede me?" He huffed out a laugh. "Veterinarians get a lot of nice gifts like that."

Brooke's lips twitched. "Did your mother buy you this?"

Matt winced at the direct hit. It was a good one, since he knew she'd been listening to his mother's pep talk before the meeting started. "She did not, but that doesn't mean she doesn't support the sentiment."

Brooke's chuckle reignited the warmth in his abdomen.

"This is how I know that embarrassment isn't fatal. If it was, I would have died in eleventh grade when she thought I was robbed of being named Homecoming King. It required a meeting with the assistant principal who informed her that only seniors could win to change her mind," Matt said.

"So," Brooke said slowly, "did she write a letter to the editor or something? How embarrassing is a meeting?"

It was a good question. A woman who hadn't grown up in a small town wouldn't get it immediately.

"I'm the youngest of five." Matt motioned that she could fill in the blanks.

"And they were all kings but you?" she guessed.

He grunted. That would have made his life easier.

"No, not a single one of them, but they did address me as *your highness* in public often enough that other people started doing it, too." When Brooke winced, he appreciated her sympathy. "Yeah. Luckily, Grant never could stay out of trouble for long, so the focus on me eased up pretty quickly."

"And did you win your crown the next year?" she asked before taking a sip. He was glad some of the color had returned to her cheeks, even if he knew his were pink from embarrassment.

"I suspect my brothers made certain of it," Matt said. "I don't know how or why they'd rig a high school vote, but the results do not lie." Her chuckle made it easier to relax.

Brooke nodded. "That's a good lesson."

"I'm happy my embarrassment could help you recover from the shock of Coco's delicate condition. You are young to be a grandmother, but Coco is the one having the puppies." Matt crossed his arms over his chest. "I'm guessing you weren't planning to breed mini Cocos, but you know there's a way to avoid developments like this."

Brooke rubbed her hand across her forehead. "I don't know much about dogs, but I do know that. I took Coco for her shots and all of that puppy stuff when I first got her, and the vet told me we'd need to wait until she was at least six months old to be spayed."

By Matt's best guess, Coco was at least eight

months old, maybe older, but he waited to see if there was more to Brooke's explanation.

"My husband got her for me for a very romantic anniversary gift that might also have been part apology, now that I'm looking back, and then he decided to ask for a divorce." Brooke nodded as Matt winced. It made sense that some of the important pieces of Brooke's life, such as Coco's follow-up appointments, had fallen to the side.

"And I guess some scalawag seized his opportunity to sneak under your radar," Matt said as he wondered how hard it could be to keep a city dog like Coco from fraternizing with bad boys.

Brooke snorted. "Funny you should mention that." She fiddled with the pen he'd been using to make notes for parade sponsorships. "The divorce agreement was pretty simple. Paul wanted to be done quickly, so we agreed to divide everything evenly down the middle."

"Split custody of Coco?" Matt asked. He'd heard of pet owners trying that, but he was curious how Coco was going to get back home to spend her time with Dad.

"We never discussed Coco. She was a gift, so she was mine. Right?" Brooke held her hand over her heart. "Doesn't that make sense to you?"

Matt nodded. He could tell it was an important answer.

At his agreement, Brooke settled a little. "And the only other thing I wanted was the brownstone we bought together right after we moved to the city." She shrugged. "With a healthy down payment provided by his parents. But it was near Sadie's apartment, and I spent so much time renovating that place. I knew I could buy out his half with a hefty premium as soon as Sadie's estate was finalized. So I stalled. He insisted. We argued. And it dragged out…"

"Until…" Matt prodded. He wasn't certain how this was related to Coco's condition, but he knew this was his only chance to get this information out of Brooke.

"He took her. Came in while I was working at the coffee shop right around the corner and took her." Brooke nodded wildly as Matt groaned.

"No way," he said, the sympathetic knot in his stomach immediate. What a hard decision her ex had forced on Brooke. "And *that scalawag* didn't keep a good eye on our girl here, did he?"

Brooke's eyebrows shot up before she said, "Apparently not. That's something I was not aware of until the moment you delivered the news. I tried everything to get Coco back. I offered him way too much money to sell his part of the house to me. I called the police. I begged his parents to intercede. I contacted my lawyer to ask about renegotiating the terms of the agreement." She sighed. "All a waste of time and money. I should have immediately signed the brownstone up to be listed for sale, but I couldn't give up my dream so easily."

That made perfect sense to Matt. "So you had to sign over the real estate to get her back. I'm glad you did. You will take better care of her."

"He hasn't called to check on Coco or yell at me for taking her. Obviously, he wasn't even watching her the way he should have while he had her. Now that puppies are in the picture?" Brooke rubbed her forehead again, leaving a red mark, and he wondered if he should step closer to catch her in the event of another tiny panic attack. "I'm twice as glad that Sarah, Jordan and I took Coco back and hit the road for Colorado."

"*Took* is doing a lot in that sentence." Matt inhaled slowly. "Are you confessing to a crime here or…" He wasn't certain what the legal implications would be, but he'd accept the consequences. No way was he returning Coco to New York.

"This isn't Wes's area of expertise," Brooke answered carefully, "but he doesn't think there will be any legal leg to stand on if Paul decides he wants to make trouble."

Matt tried to imagine what Wes's reaction had been to *that* legal query, but the picture wouldn't form in his head. His oldest brother was the stand-up, white-hatted cowboy in the family—honest, loyal and true. If he was party to an illegal action, Matt would eat his boot.

"Did you ask Wes that *before* you liberated Coco?" Matt asked.

Brooke wrinkled her nose and shook her head. "Your brother's life was a lot simpler before Sarah rolled into Prospect."

Matt frowned. "Another word for *simple* is *boring*, right?"

"So now I have no place to live, no car to drive, no job, no plans and puppies on the way." Brooke covered her face with both hands. "Jordan is going to kill me if Coco damages a single thread or floorboard at the Majestic."

"No, she won't," Matt said. He knew the Hearsts almost as well as his own brothers by now.

Brooke sighed. "No, she won't. She crawled across the kitchen floor with bacon in her hand to help me sneak Coco out of Paul's new apartment. She's in deep with this dog now."

That was a picture Matt had no problem imagining. Laughter rolled out of his chest as he met Brooke's stare. Then she laughed, too, brightening up her face. Both Betty and Coco raised their heads off the dog bed they'd curled up inside together. Half of Betty's hindquarters were hanging out of the dog bed but she seemed perfectly content with the setup.

When it was clear there was no food involved, both dogs settled back down.

"Good food. Plenty of rest. A place where she feels comfortable when the puppies come. That's all she'll need." Matt understood Brooke's concerns, but he didn't want to push her into a real panic. He was already determined Coco would have the finest medical care around. "One day there are no puppies. The next there are. When the puppies are weaned, you find good homes for them and we spay Coco. It isn't much more complicated than that."

Brooke bit her lip. "Right, but…complications? Dogs have those, right? She's too young for this, isn't she? I need Coco to be okay. I can't lose her. This is all my fault and I don't want Coco to get hurt."

Matt felt the twist in his heart as he watched her blink tears away.

No matter how often he'd faced that painful moment when he couldn't save an animal he was working on, it still hurt. Betty was a piece of his heart. Matt didn't gamble with those pieces recklessly. Brooke deserved to understand that this was serious, but she wasn't alone here.

"Coco isn't an adult yet, so she is young for puppies. That adds some concern for her health and the puppies both. Just like with humans, Coco may run into complications, need a

C-section. Good medical care is required. Lucky for you and Coco, you are a VIP to the best veterinarian I know. Family." Most of Prospect's population and the smaller communities around counted as family, too. His neighbors all knew they could call on him night or day. Being an Armstrong meant that there were many ways to track him down if he was needed. Still, he pulled out his phone. "Give me your number and I'll text you so you'll be able to reach me anytime."

Brooke hurried to grab her phone and stared hard at it until she got his text. Her shoulders relaxed and he was reminded of why he loved his job. Helping people who cared so much for their animals felt good.

"Rest easy, Brooke." Matt squeezed her shoulder, and the soft, warm skin shifted under his hand as she exhaled in relief. "I'm good at this job, the vet one."

She nodded. "You inspire confidence. I like that." Then she motioned up and down. "The scrubs and running shoes say *highly trusted medical professional*. Yesterday I was getting *cocky cowboy*."

Matt pinched the legs of his scrubs. "I guess both things are true. I like to dress for my audience. This morning, when I was out on calls in dirty barns, I was a cowboy medical professional in jeans and boots with a stethoscope around my neck. But I got some…biological matter on my jeans." He grinned when she wrinkled her nose. "And here in the office, scrubs are right. Plus, running shoes? Really comfortable." He didn't motion up and down at her dress, but he added, "You're still dressed for city life. Will you be able to transition to Prospect's casual dress code?"

"Jordan called it out as well, but it's a sundress, not an evening gown!" Brooke smoothed out the dress.

Matt agreed. "Yeah, it's pretty, too."

Her eyes darted to meet his. "I didn't bring much with me, so I need to do some shopping at Homestead Market. I got rid of all but my favorites in New York when I was scrambling for cash to make the mortgage payments. I'm still adjusting to the fact that Sadie's money has changed everything for me."

Brooke licked her lips nervously.

Maybe she'd realized how much she was sharing. He had the feeling that she hadn't intended to confess so much. At first impression, he had believed her to be above the mess of everyday.

But she wasn't really. Brooke was doing the best she could with what she had, like almost everybody else.

This was one time being wrong made him happy.

"Thank you." She waved her phone before she shoved it in her pocket. "You could have been less…friendly after last night."

Matt was thrilled that she'd brought it up; this was the perfect segue to make his case for her help on Western Days.

"And if you could find it in your heart to keep my little—" she wagged her head from side to side as she chose the right word "—emotional reaction between us, I'd appreciate it. My sisters are pretty concerned about me already, and the last thing I want to do is add anything else to Sarah's and Jordan's list of things to worry about."

Matt cleared his throat, preparing his pitch as he went. "Yeah, Western Days has us all overloaded right now."

He thought she might disagree with that statement, but instead she nodded. "Jordan sent me into town to deliver Mia's file to you."

At the reminder, Matt picked it up to flip through the pages. "These are printouts of the lists Mia emailed me this morning. Menu at the restaurant. Links for the pages she's building." None of it was new information and printouts were unnecessary. Did Brooke understand she was caught up in a plot to get her involved in the work? "I can add them to the binder."

Brooke pursed her lips as she blinked slowly.

"Obviously, there was an underlying motive there."

Relieved that he didn't have to be the one to point it out, Matt said, "Yeah, that's one thing you'll learn about life in Prospect. There is quite frequently some kind of strategy at play. My mother is the queen of strategy, but I have been impressed with how quickly Sarah and Jordan have stepped up to her level. For that matter, Keena and Mia are in the same league, and Faye has been part of the Armstrong coalition for so long that my mother has taught her almost everything she knows. So many plots."

Matt crossed his arms over his chest as he waited to see which way Brooke moved next.

"I got a speech today about how you are all family. And when family needs help, we show up. I agree that is true. My sisters flew across the country before I even admitted I was in trouble. They are asking me to do this." Brooke sighed. "So…how can I help with Western Days?"

Doing his best to contain the wild joy that pumped immediately through his veins, Matt asked, "Do you have any experience with fundraising, organizing groups or spreadsheets in general? Any? Some? A deep-seated wish to explore the power of Excel? Do you love talking on the phone?" He held his hands out. "I can work with any of the above."

Brooke's lips twitched. "Well, I don't love talking on the phone, but I'm pretty good at it. And yes to all the rest. I've been swimming in New York's political ponds, so I have experience." Her lips firmed into a hard line as she added, "Nothing that I can put on a résumé to convince anyone to pay me to do those things, but we both know that doesn't matter here."

Her last sentence was packed with so much emotion. He was curious, but at this point, all he could hear was the trumpets in his head announcing that help had arrived.

Matt closed his eyes as his shoulders slumped with relief. "You are experiencing the odd combination of dread and resolve that comes with being volunteered. I know that so well, but if you understood how ecstatic your offer makes me... Well, you would still regret being talked into this, but I will owe you such a large favor when this over."

"Help me get Coco's puppies here, day or night, with daily checkups, then help me get them adopted..." Brooke waited for him to nod. "And we'll be even."

Matt offered her his hand. That was the easiest negotiation he'd experienced in a long time. He was relieved to have help, of course.

But he was also happy he'd gotten this chance to understand Brooke better.

She wasn't the ice queen that he'd observed before. Maybe she was reserved, but there was nothing but warm, gooey love in her heart for Coco. Something in her past had set up the walls she hoped would protect her from more hurt like she'd experienced in her divorce.

But she was doing her best to keep all that under wraps.

For Matt, that was different. He loved women and they returned the favor, but he'd been careful to keep professional distance from those entanglements in his job. This gig organizing Western Days was more job-like than veterinary medicine. He'd chosen the people he worked with carefully to keep the festival on track. Old girlfriends waved from the back of the room during his meetings, and no new girlfriends wrinkled those relationships.

Luckily, Brooke was smart and experienced but guarded and careful.

He could easily work with someone like that.

CHAPTER FIVE

As Brooke straightened in her chair, she searched for one of her tried-and-true methods to regain her composure and control of the situation. Would any of them work here?

Only Sarah and Jordan had seen her at her lowest. Matt might consider himself family, but he had a long way to go in her eyes before she'd say the same. She regretted letting panic take control even for a second.

And it didn't help that he was so...kind.

Compassionate?

Was that the right word? Maybe not, but it was difficult to imagine Matt judging her for an emotional response. Something about him made it tempting to relax her guard.

She'd told him things since she'd walked into his office that afternoon that she never intended to share with anyone.

Paul would have dropped at least two separate sarcastic remarks about her reaction to Coco's impending motherhood. When they were together, she would have done her best to brush them off even as she secretly worried she deserved them.

In the grand scheme, puppies weren't that big of a deal, right?

But she didn't know anything about dogs and even less than that about birth.

And Coco was still a puppy herself. Paul's neglect and Brooke's stubborn refusal to give up her New York address had caused this. If anything happened to her dog because of that...

The pressure in her chest threatened to overwhelm her again. Matt's gentle humor and support was unfamiliar, but she appreciated it. The amount of her life that was overwhelming her at this point had broken the pretend-everything-is-fine dam.

But it was not beyond repair. Jumping into the business at hand would be the first bricks of the dam she replaced.

He needed help. That was her most reliable skill.

"I'm guessing you already have an idea of where I should begin with organizing the parade," Brooke murmured as she awkwardly brushed her hair behind her ear and patted the large binder on the table. "All the answers are inside here?"

Matt stepped up to the table but she didn't dare meet his gaze. Her cheeks were still warm, but she might be able to pretend to be in complete control if she kept her head down.

Then he squatted down next to her with a theatrical wince when his knee popped so loudly that both dogs were alarmed. Their heads jerked up, Coco's tilted to the side as if she was trying to place the noise.

"I was going to offer to postpone this conversation until tomorrow morning, but you might have to stick around to help me up off the floor," Matt muttered.

Brooke was amused at his disgusted tone. "We're too young to make noises like that, Dr. Armstrong. We're the babies, remember?"

She forgot her own plan to keep her head down, and this time, when their eyes met, the whole world shifted.

Was it because he was so close? She could see warm gold in the depths of his dark eyes.

Or it might be the scrubs. They turned him into someone she could trust, a handsome *helper* instead of a handsome stranger.

Or it might be that now he'd seen her at a weak point and had accepted that version of her without hesitating. Could that be the key to slipping under her defense so easily?

Very few people had seen Brooke near tears. Matt had joined the exclusive club.

He stood to pull out a chair next to her and sat

down with a groan. "I keep telling myself I'll get some rest as soon as Western Days is done, but being the only vet for miles means long days three hundred sixty-five days a year. Started out at dawn this morning." He motioned over his shoulder at the futon. "Sleeping where I work should leave a window for a catnap." He waggled his eyebrows and waited for her reaction.

"A catnap. Got it." Her lips were twitching as she acknowledged his pun because he was proud of his play on words. "How many other ladies have you charmed with that clever wordplay?"

"You're the first one," he said as he squeezed her hand, "but if it works, I'm going to add it into my routine. Is it strong enough material for the Western Days talent show? I'm the emcee every year and coming up with fresh jokes isn't easy."

Brooke sniffed. "I haven't heard the other material, but I'd say you might want to keep working on it."

"Add that to your list of things to assist with, if you don't mind." He offered her a pen in case she might want to jot a note down.

Brooke immediately shook her head. "That is outside the scope of our agreement, Dr. Armstrong. The parade. I will help get the parade organized. The end. Do I need to write up a contract?" If she could find a piece of paper, she might do it. Having a reminder of the boundaries she was setting could come in handy when he inevitably tacked on the next task. Brooke surveyed the table and decided she'd have to write any notes she wanted to make on her hand. The binder seemed too important to take a piece from. "Parade. That's it. Any stand-up routines belong to you alone."

Matt sighed. "I suppose that's fair. There's no way for me to pretend I forgot I needed jokes, is there? Would anyone believe I overlooked something so important?"

The gleam in his eyes convinced her he was poking fun at himself for the shape of the parade and talent show. Brooke swallowed her grin at his morose acceptance of his own failings. At least he was able to take responsibility for them. That was nice.

Whoever had built the magic binder had loved a good tab, so it was easy enough to turn to the Parade section. When she found the handwritten list, she understood a big piece of the problem. "You don't have an email list already built for past sponsors." She glanced up in time to watch Matt shake his head. She scanned quickly. "And some of these don't even have phone numbers."

"Right. My mother has been the mastermind of the entire festival until this point." He tapped his temple. "She put this together to help me, but

I guarantee you she had zero need for this list because it was all in her head."

Brooke whistled. "Before you do this again, you should build a database or a spreadsheet at the least, with names, phone numbers and an email distribution list. Technology can be your friend."

"I wish you had walked in that door a month ago. I've tackled big challenges, but this stuff..." He grimaced. "If I'd been able to think about anything other than these Cowboy Games and everything going on at the ranch and this rescue group that I've been working with..." He rubbed tired eyes with the heels of his hands. "But I didn't, so I need to call, make a list, collect checks and get a list over to the high school ASAP so that I don't have every teenager in Prospect disappointed for the entire school year. I'm sure I'll be working with the new rodeo club, and I like to hire a couple of kids over the summer months to help out around here, plus I have these two nephews who go to the schools. Then there's my mother... And the way all of my brothers will never let me live this down and I..." He inhaled slowly. "No pressure, but if you could keep the truth of this situation between the two of us, I'll owe you forever. Do I know we're perched on the edge of catastrophe?" He nodded wildly. "But if we could pull the festival back from disaster without a lot of details going to my brothers or my mother, that would be so sweet."

Watching him at the meeting had convinced her he was a happy-go-lucky, charming rascal who might be out of his depth but would ultimately land on his feet. Today, listening to him talk, she understood how much more there was to Matt than what he showed on the surface.

No matter how different they were, they had a whole lot in common as well.

"That means Sarah and Jordan, too," Brooke said slowly.

He wrinkled his nose as he nodded. "Yeah, you probably tell them everything, right? If you could hold back some, that would be great."

"So everyone is going to view you as the hero and I..." Brooke sighed as she wondered how much the credit for saving a festival parade mattered in the big scheme. "Never mind." It didn't matter what anyone in Prospect believed anyway. "Coco and I are going to be spending as much time near the finest canine maternity ward Prospect has to offer until the puppies arrive. Like, sitting inside your office if it's possible. Today, I'll start to work on this list, get in touch with as many sponsors as I can..." She pulled the loose sheets of paper from the binder. "When I call, I need to ask..."

She raised her eyebrow at him and reached

across the table to snag the junk mail stacked next to the wall with the salt, pepper and a purple baseball cap with the Colorado Rockies logo on the front. The back of one of the envelopes offered a good place for notes. The pile of scrap pieces of paper and at least one napkin with notes scribbled here and there in what was clearly a doctor's handwriting sent a cold chill down her spine. Was that his way of keeping track of progress on this big festival that the whole town was counting on?

It couldn't be.

Could it?

He nodded. "Okay, a plan. Sponsorship fees are the same as last year." He tapped the page that listed a breakdown of levels: basic sponsorship to be listed on the website and banners around town, parade entry fee for businesses supplying their own float or marching group, and high school float sponsor with a flat fee for materials and construction.

"Does the town not have a council or someone to head up big events like this?" Brooke asked. Who would normally step up if there were no Armstrongs around?

"The town council approves businesses moving into the historical part of town, leases and things like that, but this festival has always been my mother's baby. I'm not sure who she took it over from." Matt shook his head. "And I don't know how to hand it off, either." Matt studied the ceiling. "Right about now, I sure wish I had a partner."

"In your veterinary business?" Brooke asked. "Or with planning the festival?"

There was no way he meant in life, was there?

"Yes. Both. Either would help, but definitely both," Matt said. "When you said this place wasn't how you imagined my office, what did you picture?"

Brooke straightened and stacked the junk mail. "I'm not sure. This place is pretty…"

"Small. Crowded." Matt nodded. "It really is."

"And this room is the smallest piece of it all. To fit the rest of your life outside work," she added. He was asking a lot of this one room.

"Lately, there hasn't been anything but work, so it's fine," Matt said. "Someday, I will have space and state-of-the-art equipment to fill it, along with a partner to handle the small animals while I work with the horses and cattle." Matt held his hands out as if he wanted her to picture it with him. Brooke held her hand over her eyes as if she was staring into a bright future. His chuckle made her feel extremely clever.

"What's holding you back?" she asked as she scanned the page of businesses and made a mental list of at least five things they should do immediately to make this process easier going forward.

Matt immediately held up his hand to tick off points. "Money. Money. Money. And moving up the priority list of Armstrong projects. First it was buying Sadie's land, then the farmhouse renovation, then the lodge's repairs and Western Days." He shrugged as if it all made sense and he was resigned to that, but Brooke wondered if he was as comfortable having his own wishes pushed back and back again as he was trying to seem.

Everything that had happened was good, important work, but so was his.

Brooke decided to let that thought fade away without picking at it.

"Contact the businesses, confirm their levels of sponsorship, tell them we need a check delivered here this week, get an email address for a receipt. If they're hiring a high school club, ask if they have a theme they'd like or a group they want to work with." Matt reached across her arm to point at one of the names on the list. "Like the Garcia Garage. That's Lucky and Dante. Until her sister graduated, they specifically asked that the debate team do their float so that Lucky's sister's club got the sponsorship money, and they would include extra for materials. Two years in a row of having floats split down the middle to present the pros and cons of electric cars or self-driving cars should have convinced them to give another club a shot, but they're loyal. Some of the kids pick their own theme, some don't, but every business on this list has done the parade many times. They'll know the routine. We confirm they're in. We get the check. Next year…" He mimed pushing a button. "Boom. An email distribution to collect all that information for the school, a link to take in the fees and life goes on."

Brooke appreciated his vision. It was the right way to take care of this.

Then he added, "As soon as we get the crisis averted, can you help with that?"

When she turned to face him, his eyes were wide as he blinked innocently. "What? That is still parade-related. Within the scope. Loosely."

The innocent expression had to be his best attempt at puppy-dog eyes. Since he was a vet, he'd learned from the best. Getting him ready for the next year *was* beyond the boundary she'd set, but she couldn't blame him for pushing the limits.

She stared hard at his stack of trash covered in notes.

"Pretty sure you'll be asked to run Western Days again next year?" Brooke asked. In his spot, she'd be worried about being run out of town by either disappointed Armstrongs or angry high schoolers, at this point.

His shoulders slumped. "Unfortunately, this is now my burden to bear. My mother won't be taking it back, that's for sure. I have spent some serious time trying to find a way to bamboozle someone else into hoisting the magic binder high, but I lack my mother's intense negotiation skills." He sighed. "I can't even convince her to stop making everyone clap for me at the meetings. There's no way I can force her to take the festival back."

Brooke didn't want to sympathize with him, especially about the clapping part, but it was impossible not to. "We don't want to hurt them, do we?"

"She loves me. She's proud of me. How can I complain about that? I can't. I just..." Matt braced his elbows on his knees. "When you're a part of the foster system and you find a family like Prue and Walt have built, you understand how lucky you are. I do. So do my brothers, and she'd happily embarrass any one of us the same way because Prue Armstrong loves wholeheartedly. Her friends. Her family. This town."

"Why do I have the feeling that she may not feel such warm affection for me at this point?" Brooke murmured.

He tilted his head to the side. "Gotta say, now

that I've recovered from the shock, the way you calmly, easily extricated yourself from that conversation last night… It was impressive. She may not love your fortitude, but I bet my mother respects it anyway."

"But I still got wrangled into helping," Brooke added. "So it wasn't truly effective."

"Any victory, large or small, against Prue Armstrong is notable." He leaned closer and she had to remember to breathe in and out like a normal person. "You aren't the only Hearst to square off against her. The cold shoulder she gave Sarah on arrival was epic. And Keena? Dr. Murphy? The one who convinced Travis to get married in a quickie ceremony in Las Vegas?" He pretended to tell her a secret. "I'm not sure my mother has ever won a battle against Keena to this day. So my mother can be defeated. It's just not easy."

Brooke wanted to giggle like a silly teenager at a cute boy's joke. Instead, she inched back and cleared her throat. "I like that you understand that you are blessed, but that doesn't mean you can't see some flaws. Loving someone doesn't make them perfect."

Matt's eyes grew serious. "Yeah. That's it, isn't it?" He bit his lip. "And if you add foster care and adoption on top of all the tangle of family… When I was a kid, people who I didn't even recognize decided they knew me well enough to say how lucky I was to have landed with the Armstrongs. That was certainly true—but what about the loss that put me in the system in the first place? I've struggled to accept both being lucky and being dealt a devastating blow. My mother had her problems. But no one can tell me that she didn't love me, too. I lost her. At eleven years old, I lost my mother, and that's something you don't ever recover from."

Her hand seemed to move of its own accord to his arm, offering silent comfort.

He continued, "I had nightmares… They didn't stop for a long time. Weird dreams that I could talk to my mom if only I remembered her phone number. Night after night, it would be a series of ways I'd lose the paper or the phone or whatever piece it was that I needed to connect to her. Then I'd wake up to a new place where I had to find a way to fit in. The days were filled with family, but the nights were about… I don't know. What was missing, I guess. You might heal, but you're never who you were before. And the threat of losing any piece of that new life is…"

Brooke was caught by surprise at the emotion in his voice and the corresponding ache in her chest.

"It might be a little like when everyone tells you how wonderful Sadie was, and she was,"

Matt said as he squeezed the hand that rested on his leg. "But the reason she was so much a part of your life was because you lost your mother."

The way her heart ached in that moment made sense. She understood every single word because she'd experienced the same kind of loss, but she'd never seen it so clearly.

Matt closed his eyes. "And why am I talking about this? You're easy to talk to, Brooke. We have work to do. Sorry to derail the plan."

Hearing him put into words this mad mixture of emotions that followed loss made her realize he understood a part of her she'd never shared with anyone.

Since no one had ever called her easy to talk to, Brooke wondered how they had connected so quickly, but there was so much more to Matt than she'd seen on the surface. If they were going to be family—and the way Sarah and Jordan talked about his brothers, the wedding bells were imminent—well, she wanted to know the real Matt.

He'd seen parts of the real Brooke through the cracks in her shell, so it only seemed fair.

Matt stood. "My office assistant, Mary Beth, is out this week. Her mother lives in Golden and she had back surgery, so I'm hoping for a few slow days in the office. If you like, you and Coco can take over the front desk? Use that phone and computer? What do you say?"

A tickle of alarm crossed her nape.

"I'm just working on the parade. I'm not a receptionist, too." She didn't want to find herself running Matt's office because she didn't set out the ground rules clearly in the beginning. "Coco and I will be frequent visitors for months, I'm sure, while we're waiting for the puppies to arrive, but we aren't part-time employees."

Matt's confused frown slowly cleared. "Oh, yeah, no... Mary Beth? She handles all the billing, ordering supplies and medication, and so much more than making appointments. No one can take her place." When he squeezed her hand again, Brooke wondered if he was trying to break it to her gently that she didn't have the qualifications she'd need to run his reception area.

Since she'd heard that said in a dozen different ways when she'd been scrambling to find an actual job with an actual paycheck, the sentiment no longer shocked her or hurt her feelings.

Make her mad, though? A little.

But then he said, "And Coco's puppies will arrive in Prospect in just a few weeks, somewhere right around Western Days, if my guess is correct. When Mary Beth is back next week, let's do an ultrasound to pin down how far along Coco is and how many puppies we're having."

"Not months." Brooke felt the crushing pressure in the center of her chest again. "Weeks. I have *weeks* until I have puppies… Some unknown *multiple* of puppies to care for."

"Yeah, possibly while the lodge is filled to bursting with lodgers, the restaurant's launch is launching and Western Days is…westerning." He peered into her eyes. "But don't worry. We're a team—you, me and Coco with Betty for moral support. Okay?"

Brooke licked her lips as she considered asking about how he was going to fit in delivering puppies with all that going on, but she didn't want to hear the answer. Her heart was already racing.

Matt waited for her to meet his stare again and inhaled slowly and dramatically until she did the same.

"One thing you'll learn about life in Prospect," Matt said as he rubbed circles in the center of her back that Brooke responded to immediately but wished she didn't, "is that you are never far from a helping hand. If the job's too big for Coco, you can count on me."

Brooke nodded even as she worried about how easily he had convinced her of that.

In New York, she had learned the painful reality that she was all alone as one "friend" after another turned away. More than anything, she wanted to be able to take care of herself.

But she'd start her fully independent era *after* the puppies were here.

Getting Western Days across the finish line would present plenty of opportunity to stick close to the reassuring veterinarian. As long as she could spend time with the safe, compassionate version of Matt Armstrong, she was in almost no danger of losing herself to the charming cowboy.

CHAPTER SIX

JUST AFTER SUNRISE the next morning, Matt pulled the barn door open at Billy Dawson's farm. The creak of the hinges was loud in the morning quiet. He was not surprised to find Billy stretched out on a stack of hay bales, his feet propped up on the stall where Juniper, a pretty blue-roan quarter horse, was quietly resting. As Matt set his bag down, Billy tipped his hat back. "Mornin'."

"How was your night?" Matt asked when Billy swung his feet down to stand and stretch.

"Not too bad." Billy's neck crackled with each twist he made to work out the kinks. "Both of us got a few Z's in here and there." He ran his hand down Juniper's neck. "We were both bushed from the night before."

Matt tipped his own hat back to study Juniper's eyes. When he'd stopped in the day before, everything about her—her coat, her expression, her stance—had been dull. Today, Matt pulled an apple out of his pocket and took his opportunity to check the color of Juniper's gums as she took dainty nibbles. Pink. Healthy. "I'll get the test results back this afternoon, but we made the right choice to start the IV."

Billy nodded. "Yessir, and I thank you for that. If my Katy-piller's horse got sick or…" He gulped. "Or worse, her heart would be broken in pieces. Sure am glad I called you when I did."

His "Katy-piller" was a granddaughter named Katy who Matt vaguely recalled being horse crazy, so it was easy to understand why Billy was treating this horse to extra special care.

"Me, too. Endotoxemia is best to catch early, but we did it." Matt moved into Juniper's stall to study the catheter he'd inserted into her jugular the day before. It looked good, so he hung and connected the fluid he'd brought to help replace what she'd lost to fever, and moved back to rest against the gate.

"Katy's daydreaming of being a barrel-racing champion with Juniper someday." Billy ran his hand down the horse's nose. "If you hadn't lectured me about the symptoms to watch for, this might have a different ending."

Matt sighed. "It would be nice if I could talk instead of lecture, but you'd be surprised how often I have to labor long and hard to get my point across. The horse is usually the reasonable one in the conversation."

Billy ducked his head and had the good sense

to look sheepish when he said, "A little skin infection turning into something like this… Well, I learned my lesson, Doc. I promise."

Matt knew better than to take Billy's words at face value, but that was okay. Ranching was hard work with a never-ending list of jobs and expenses to cover. He'd be a nag and deliver boring lectures if it helped his patients get well.

"Sure do appreciate you making an early call out here," Billy said. "Soon as we're done, I gotta get some fence repairs made. Winter's been rough up on my northeast pasture, and it's time to move some stock back out. Me and the missus will be taking Katy down to the zoo this weekend. The girl does love her animals."

Since Matt had been an animal lover his whole life, he was glad he could save a kindred spirit some worry.

"If you want to head out now, I'll stay here with Juniper until this bag is done. I want to leave the catheter in for another day in case I need to give her another bag of fluids tonight. Once I have the test results, we can discuss whether to add any other treatment." While Matt spoke, he was eyeing Billy's hay bales to determine if he might be able to stretch out if he was left alone for fifteen minutes or so.

Billy held out his hand. "Doc, you're a real hero."

Matt accepted the handshake, glad that he and Billy had mended their fences after Matt and his daughter, Lynn, had broken up. To him, their summertime romance between college semesters had been fun and light, but he had a feeling Lynn's version of the story had been different. For a while afterward, Billy had been known to shoot murderous stink eye across the restaurant at Matt whenever they met up at the Ace High.

Luckily, Lynn marrying her college sweetheart and having a happy little family, including Katy-piller, had smoothed out any rough edges between Lynn and Matt years ago.

Billy didn't seem in any hurry to leave. Instead, he held Matt's hand as he bowed forward to ask in a confidential tone, "How's the talent show coming along? You know Whit wants her shot on the stage, right? Believe she signed up soon as the web page came online."

Whit Dawson, Billy's wife, soloed in the church choir often enough that she had an almost weekly opportunity to stand front and center, but Matt appreciated a man who was looking out for his wife's, his granddaughter's and her horse's interests all at the same time. Billy Dawson was an impressive multitasker and Matt had had no idea.

"I haven't seen the sign-up list yet, but I'm glad to hear it, Billy. You know we want Prospect's finest singers up there." Matt stifled a sigh at the reminder that he had his own never-ending to-do list. How had he missed how much work went into this weekend?

"Think you'll have to cut any of the interested parties?" Billy ran a hand over his mouth as he waited for the answer.

The Western Days schedule for Saturday was packed, so the talent show, the last big event, had always been limited to one hour. A limit on the number of participants made sense.

Unless you were a performer who didn't make the cutoff.

Matt had tried to mentally prepare himself for that. Facing the people who weren't chosen to perform would be uncomfortable, but he'd expected that to be a problem he'd deal with much closer to the show. Billy had caught him flat-footed today.

Luckily, Whit Dawson was almost guaranteed to be included in the show.

"I decided to call in some help with the auditions this year." *Just this very minute*, Matt added mentally. If he was honest with himself, he needed the help.

"Oh, yeah? Will it be that rodeo rider, Annie Mercado? Katy-piller loves her." Billy's worry transitioned quickly to interest.

Annie Mercado was a rising rodeo star. She'd worked with Grant and Mia to break the rodeo cheating scandal that had brought them together in Prospect. She was coming to judge the Cowboy Games, and she might be willing to add the talent show on top of that. He pulled the gas receipt out of his pocket to make himself a note to ask.

Then he realized auditions would take place before Annie got to town, so his cojudge would need to be someone in town already.

The beautiful, youngest Hearst sister immediately popped into his head. Before he asked, though, he'd need to find the right leverage, something he could barter to convince her to expand the scope of their current agreement. Groveling might increase his chances of success.

"We'll have a celebrity judge for the night of the show, but I wanted to get another viewpoint for auditions as well." Matt hoped that sounded reasoned and logical even if he was making it up as he went along. "That way, I can't pick all my favorites, like Whit."

Billy nodded. "That's fair. Yep. That's fair." He sighed. "Whit has her heart set on finishing first this year. Being runner-up behind Reg McCall all these years has lit a fire, if you know what I mean."

With a slap on Billy's back, Matt reassured him. "Last year, Whit did a rendition of 'I Will Always Love You' that would make Dolly beam with pride. She'll get her shot this year." Reg McCall had stage presence, talent and a zest for both show tunes and old country love songs that made him nearly unbeatable, but there was always a chance.

Billy shoved his hands in his pockets. "My ladies, Doc. I'll do whatever I can to make them happy."

"Smart man. I follow the same philosophy myself." Making his mother happy was how he'd ended up inheriting the festival and the blessed binder in the first place. Matt moved closer to check the IV bag as Juniper snuffled his shirt and hat. "We love a beautiful lady, Juniper." He ran a hand down the horse's neck, satisfied that his efforts to rehydrate her were working.

"Wait 'til you find the one that all your own happiness rests on, Doc, and then come talk to me about it." Billy shook his head sadly. "You ain't seen the half of it yet, young man."

Matt raised his eyebrows as he met Billy's stare. Was *young man* accurate in this scenario? Turning forty wasn't next door, but it was in the neighborhood.

Billy held up his hand to wave off any argument. "The one you marry? Who will raise your kids if you have 'em and take care of you in sickness and in health? That woman can get a man in real trouble. I'm just happy Whit set her sights on this talent show and not something much grander."

As Matt removed the IV line and capped the catheter, he imagined all the things Billy might have been asked to accomplish if Whit's goals had been loftier. He'd spent at least the better part of the night in the barn with his grand-daughter's sick horse, so Billy was a man who showed up for the people he loved.

Matt admired that.

He was currently surrounded on all sides by couples who were building those same bonds. His brothers had stepped up over and over for the women they were in love with, and each one of those women had proven that they would change their lives, their whole worlds, to build something together.

And in doing so, they had doubled the tight circle of people Matt loved.

That expansion made him uneasy sometimes, late at night when he couldn't sleep.

His nightmares were rare now, but the memory of the ache of loss was still sharp.

As a child, crying at night had been his only outlet. During the day, Matt had been focused on charming his way into the safe spot he'd landed in after his life shattered. Having siblings had been new to him, but he'd learned to roll with the teasing and the roughhousing that came along with brotherly love, and Prue and Walt had been steady, firm and caring parents from the minute he met them.

But having his whole world turned upside down once had ignited the fear in young Matt that it could happen again, and he'd been determined to have a firm grip on his new life if the worst happened.

As a grown man, he understood that the threat of loss shouldn't mean much to him. He could take care of himself if he had to.

But that ache? If something happened to anyone in this tight circle, that ache would be impossible to avoid. It might drag him under.

"How did you know Whit was the one, Billy? That the trouble she might lead you into was worth it?" Matt asked as he packed up his bag and gave Juniper one last pat. "I'll see you tonight, Juniper."

When he stepped out of the stall, Billy had removed his hat.

As if Matt's question was a real thinker that needed some extra air.

"Truth is, you can't imagine the trouble going into it, Doc. You find someone you don't want to give up and you jump in with both feet. The trouble comes as it will, and by that point, you love her so much that even things you know you can't possibly do... Well, you cogitate on 'em long enough and the *how* gets clearer. Maybe you succeed. Maybe you fail." Billy thumped his shoulder. "But nothing will do except you try. For her. See?"

Matt grinned. "No, but maybe I'll get it when she comes along."

Billy grunted. "Young fella, if you don't, you will regret it."

"I'll check on Juniper tonight. If everything looks good, I'll remove the catheter." Matt raised his hand in goodbye as he slid into his truck. After he backed down the long lane to the Dawson house and hit the highway, he turned up the radio and sang half-heartedly as the sun rose higher over the mountains. Early morning calls were wearing him out. Busy stretches made it crystal clear he needed a partner in the vet clinic. Finding another doctor who wanted to settle in a small town like Prospect would take some patience, though. Reopening the lodge, creating the Sadie Hearst museum and whatever the Hearst sisters dreamed up next might help his case.

Days like today would make the perfect advertisement. Spring was fully in bloom and turning toward summer with green leaves, growing pastures and blue skies.

"Wish I could head out on the lake with a fishing pole, a cooler of cold drinks and not a single worry," he murmured to himself as he drove into Prospect. The weight of the world settled on his shoulders when he realized how hard it would be to take a vacation day from all his responsibilities. After he'd settled Brooke at Mary Beth's desk the day before, he'd had a slow stream of patients trickle into the office with a few more scheduled for this afternoon. "After Western Days is over."

The shops along the main street through town were opening up for the day, but the sidewalks were empty of tourists so far. Every single business was gearing up for the festival, the largest burst of revenue they'd have all year.

If this weekend was successful, Prospect would be able to count on return visitors all summer long.

The dollars they spent while they were in town could be multiplied into more restaurants, more retail, more jobs.

"No pressure," Matt muttered as he removed the key from the ignition. A gentle tap on his window caught his attention.

Brooke was standing next to the truck with one hand raised in a wave.

He rolled the window down. "I don't usually expect my unpaid labor to kick in until afternoon."

"I asked myself where I could get a good cup of coffee in town, and your office immediately came to mind." Brooke held up the basket and Coco blinked in the sunshine. "We're determined to get all the parade floats lined up today."

Matt chuckled as he slid out. "'Lined up.' For a parade. That's a good one."

When she paused, Matt realized that Brooke Hearst wasn't in the pun business, as many of the Armstrongs were. Obviously, she hadn't intended to make a joke. That meant she had natural talent.

He unlocked the door and let Brooke and Coco in. "I didn't start a pot this morning before I headed out, but I'll do that right now. It is critical to how the rest of this day will go."

Betty ran out to meet them all and he bent down to rub her ears. "Hey, good girl. I missed you."

Coco climbed carefully out of her basket on the floor and both dogs went into joyous spins, sniffing and jumping and zooming around the office.

"So much energy," Matt said and waved Brooke to follow him.

"I figured you took your assistant Betty with you wherever you went." Brooke moved over to the neat stack she'd left on his kitchen table the night before. He had no idea where she'd found an actual notebook but he was impressed.

"Normally, yes, but Juniper was in bad shape

yesterday. Dehydrated. Sweating. Listless. I was afraid of what the situation might be and how long I'd need to stay." Matt set up the coffee maker and pulled Brooke's cat mug out of the dish rack. "But some IV fluid, some anti-inflammatory meds and a good night's rest has done wonders." When he imagined the heartbreak Billy and Katy would feel if anything happened to the horse, he was doubly thankful that her symptoms were improving.

"Good job, Dr. Armstrong." Brooke's shy smile stopped him midpour and he had to scramble to prevent a coffee mess. "That's an important superpower you have. I don't know Juniper, but I bet she's your biggest fan."

Matt finished pouring Brooke's cup as he considered that.

From any number of beautiful women, he would call a statement like that flirting.

But Brooke had been singularly unimpressed with him before yesterday so...

"Juniper is a beloved horse belonging to Billy Dawson's granddaughter. He was thankful for my help." Matt offered her the cup. "It's nice to have fans, but in cases like this, I'm just glad to have a little less heartbreak in the world."

Brooke nodded before carefully sipping her hot coffee. "I'm sure you've got plenty of fans anyway."

Her wicked smile as she picked up the binder hooked Matt, so he trailed behind her into the front office even though he had a million other things to be working on.

"Can I count you part of the fan club, Brooke?" He propped one shoulder against the wall as he watched her settle behind Mary Beth's desk. He was almost as good at flirting as he was at treating horses, but he never passed up a chance to practice.

She pursed her lips as she formulated an answer. "Of Dr. Armstrong? You bet. Big fan. Coco wants the best care and I suppose you are the best veterinarian around."

"The faintest of faint praise." Matt clamped one hand over his heart. "I'm the *only* vet around."

But right now, he was happy Brooke's choices were limited.

Her giggle landed with a silent boom in his chest. Brooke Hearst didn't strike him as a frequent giggler.

"The Matt Armstrong fan club?" Brooke raised one shoulder nonchalantly. "It's pretty big, right? I like small gatherings. VIP service. Clubs with restricted membership."

Aloof Brooke was back and it was easy to understand how she'd fooled him. Her face was unaffected, but the wicked gleam in her eye was impossible to miss at this point.

"Afraid of healthy competition. I get that."
Matt sniffed as his cell phone rang and he fought
back a chuckle at the way her jaw dropped.
Brooke wasn't the first woman to tell him he
got too much attention from others for her to be
seriously interested.

But she would be the only one who didn't
change her mind…if she managed to keep her
distance.

When he read the name on the display, he
moved to set his coffee cup down. The Colorado Horse Rescue was a group he volunteered
his vet services for from time to time. "Hey, Alison. How are the horses in Colorado Springs?"

A staticky break covered her first answer, but
Alison tried again. "Sorry, Matt. This wind's terrible up here." He could hear her walking and
then the noise died down. "Barn will give me
some shelter so you can hear me."

"What's up? I didn't expect to talk to you until
the next board meeting." And since it would be
the Wednesday after Western Days, he would
be in a much better place to take on whatever it
was she needed.

But not today.

He didn't have room in his life for one more
thing today.

"I've got an emergency and you're my fourth
call, so I'm hoping you can help," Alison said

in a rush, as if she was determined to get the words out before he said no. "We've got two sick horses over here at the foster barn. Young horses. My best guess is strangles, but I wanted a vet to come in and run tests on the others in this barn and help us figure out how to quarantine them. I had a vet lined up, but he was in an accident yesterday. Broke both legs. He'll be okay, but he's not up to a day in the barn. The second vet's kid is home sick with a stomach virus. The third told me if he didn't pick up his mother-in-law at the airport at noon, his wife would divorce him." Her laughter had a panicked edge to it. "So…is there any way I can get you out here? Please?"

Matt sat down in one of the waiting room chairs with a loud thump. There was only one answer. "You bet. I've got some appointments this afternoon. Give me a minute to reschedule them and I'll hit the road."

"Oh, Matt. I can't… While you're driving, I'll try to find the right words to tell you how much I appreciate this, but if you can think of a way to repay you, tell me when you get here." Alison's relief was loud and clear.

Matt shook his head. "No need for that. I appreciate you helping the horses. I'll be there in an hour or so."

After he hung up, he let his hands dangle between his legs and waited for the energy to stand.

"No time for a catnap today, huh?" Brooke asked. "I'm beginning to understand that you need more than an office manager here. You need help, even if it's someone to say no when people call with requests."

"I would ask you to teach me the trick you used against my mother," Matt said as his lips curled slowly, "but I'm not sure you're as good at saying no as we all believed."

Her groan reminded him that he wanted more help from Brooke, not less.

"Every single animal rescue group I know is stretching every dollar and hour of the day into two to take care of vulnerable animals. I didn't understand how thinly they're spread until I was asked to join the board of this one. I can't say no. Luckily, this is not a big job." Matt picked up the appointment book Mary Beth left standing next to the phone every night. "I'll reschedule these patients, track down Grant, ask if he's up for a ride to help some sick horses, run out to the ranch to pick him up when he says yes, and then drive for almost an hour to treat sick horses and draw blood from the others before I drop the samples off to be tested, drive back out to Billy Dawson's to check on Juniper, and then…" He held up both hands with his fingers crossed. "Dinner?"

Brooke tugged the appointment book out of

his hand. "The only part of that I can possibly do is reschedule your afternoon patients. You'll have to do the rest."

Her tone was sympathetic. Concern had replaced the teasing glint in her eye that he'd enjoyed so much earlier.

But it was also nice to have someone care about his workload.

"But rescheduling my appointments is not included in the scope of the agreement. Remember?" He certainly hadn't forgotten how firm her lips had been when she'd drawn that reasonable boundary, so he made a half-hearted attempt to take the book back. But he didn't fight harder when she held it out of reach.

"If you'd asked me to do this..." Brooke rolled her eyes. "Or worse, *expected* me to take on this task and gone about your important life because *of course* I would help as I always do, we would have a different outcome here. No one can argue that you definitely need help." Her lips twitched. "What kind of person would refuse to assist someone so clearly in over his head?"

He exhaled loudly as relief settled over his shoulders.

"Besides, I'm terrible at saying no to favors," she muttered, "especially if it involves extended unpaid labor that does not earn a paycheck or actual work experience." Then she rolled her shoulders. "Sorry. That's all on me and nothing about you. This is an easy favor to do for a friend."

The strains of anger in her voice when she spoke of past experiences were definitely giving him ex-husband vibes, another clue to Brooke and her past. He didn't know the story with her ex, but no one appreciated being taken advantage of. Making sure that she understood his appreciation would be important. Easy to overlook, but critical to remember.

She'd also called him a friend.

He didn't want to lose that title.

He loved the animals, but it was nice to have another human standing next to him.

Was that because he didn't feel so alone?

"Call Grant. I'll take care of your appointments and Betty and Coco and the parade..." Brooke made a shooing motion. "I might regret this, but if you have a spare key, could you give it to me? In case I need to leave and come back in to get everything done?"

Matt pointed at Mary Beth's desk. "There's one in the top drawer. Take it. Keep it until Western Days is in the rearview mirror."

"I'm still not a receptionist or an office manager or a phone service." Brooke pulled out the drawer and picked up the key. "This doesn't change our agreement. I'm only helping with the parade, and in return you will provide world-class service to my expecting dog, as agreed."

Before he could approach the "Well, there's this other thing…" right there on the tip of his tongue, she added, "And yes, I know that you never asked me to do this. I offered of my own free will, but it's a terrible habit that I have, volunteering. I'm trying to break it and failing, obviously. I just didn't want you to forget in case I ever get better at saying no."

Matt solemnly bowed his head to acknowledge her terms and resolved to revisit the auditions another time. They were both smiling when he moved back to his office to pack his bag. After Grant answered his call and volunteered to help out as expected, Matt was ready to hit the road.

But he decided to make one quick stop.

In his kitchen, he grabbed the coffee pot and hurried back out to top off Brooke's cup. She was on the phone rescheduling his last appointment of the afternoon. Lillian Schultz, Prospect's librarian, had a Pomeranian named Dewey that required extra hands for toenail trimming. Matt was pleased to hear Brooke repeat the new time for a date *after* Mary Beth returned to the office. Brooke hung up as he raced through the waiting room again, headed for the truck.

"I left a message for the first two appointments, but I'll call back to get them back on the calendar." Brooke tapped her pen on the desk. "The other two have been rescheduled for next week."

Relieved, Matt tipped his hat lower and opened the door. "Text me if you need me."

Brooke nodded and as he stepped out on the sidewalk, he had the strangest feeling. It wasn't déjà vu, because how could it be? He and Brooke had never met before her arrival in Prospect.

But there was something so familiar about saying goodbye this way, hoping she would need to reach out to him somehow, and pausing to memorize her face before he went on about his work.

Almost like this instant would be repeated enough to create a sense of déjà vu in the future.

"Dangerous thinking, Armstrong," he muttered to himself. He didn't build fantasies about futures.

That philosophy worked for him, so he wouldn't be changing it now.

Billy's words about finding the woman who made all the troubles better were fresh in his memory, but he had plenty of horses waiting for him. They'd put Billy's advice and Brooke's beautiful face right out of his mind.

CHAPTER SEVEN

BROOKE WASN'T SURE how long she stared out the door at the sidewalk after Matt left, but it would have been embarrassing if anyone had observed it. Coco's indignant sniff brought her back to the real world.

"Oh, was I too slow in answering your summons?" Brooke murmured as she bent down to pick up the dog. "You aren't fooling me. This is about a treat, not my attention or your affection. However, I definitely needed the reminder that we are not staring after any men and we are certainly not interested in what Matt Armstrong is doing, how hard he works or how sweet he can be."

She'd anticipated a full day away from home, so all of Coco's favorites had been loaded into a bag that coordinated with her basket. Brooke's favorite boutique pet store had sold everything in matching sets. The dog nosed at the tote in case Brooke needed more instruction.

"Don't keep the mother-to-be waiting. I understand." She pulled out the plastic bag that held the last of the expensive all-natural peanut butter bones she'd purchased before leaving New York.

"I'm guessing the Homestead Market will have plenty of treat options." Had high-end dog food reached Prospect? When she was a kid, she'd been shocked and dismayed that her favorite cereal was not available at the only store in town. Was Coco about to come to terms with a similar realization?

Homestead Market was the place that introduced Brooke to the breakfast treat that remained her favorite guilty pleasure: sweet goodness that roughed up the roof of her mouth and came in a box with a weird little sailor on the front. What it lacked in nutrition, it definitely made up for with a sugar high.

Being an adult meant she had to buy annoyingly healthy whole grains and lots of bran most of the time, but the Homestead Market had given her a taste for the good stuff.

Coco was a dog. She didn't care much about her cholesterol or fiber intake. The treat she'd been waiting for her whole life might be hiding in Homestead Market's aisles.

"Why do I have the feeling that you'll enjoy regular dog biscuits as much as these fancy ones?" Brooke asked.

One thing her dog didn't care for that morning was lengthy dialogue.

As soon as Brooke held out the bone, Coco snatched it and huffed to get down, ready to be free to roam again. Betty's manners were so much better when she accepted the treat Brooke offered. Matt's dog sat patiently, took her treat gently and moved to the sunny spot in the middle of the floor to enjoy it at a leisurely pace.

"It's time we look for a finishing school for you, Coco. After the puppies, of course," Brooke murmured. Now that she had time and money, hiring a professional trainer to take over where Brooke had failed would be simple enough. She could ask for Matt's expert advice.

Imagining his pleasure if she were to do that made her want to give it a shot.

"Oh, boy," she muttered. "Are we back in high school, Brooke? Dreaming up ways to get the cute boy's attention? No. Don't. Stop." Spending this much time thinking about him was scary.

He was nice. The end.

She could make a list of reasons that it had to be *the end* as long as her arm.

When she got this parade organized, she should do that.

A preemptive measure against…whatever was going on in her head.

Betty pressed her head against Brooke's leg,

a frown wrinkling the smooth expanse between her ears as if she was afraid she was in trouble. Coco? She was completely unbothered, her stubby tail wagging as she finished her treat.

"Not you, baby. You're a good girl. But I need someone to train my bad habits away. Handsome men are too much trouble." Brooke smoothed Betty's worried frown. "You are also spending entirely too much time on one-sided conversations with dogs, Brooke, so you're going to need a trainer yourself, Brooke."

Determined to knock out the entire list of businesses who had sponsored the parade and floats in the past in one day, Brooke picked up the hot cup of coffee that Matt had insisted on topping off before hurrying out. Had her ex-husband ever done anything like that? In the early days, Paul might have refilled her cup while he got his own, but she couldn't find many examples of him going out of his way, putting his own schedule on hold for a second, to do something thoughtful for her. Paul liked big, grand gestures that people could admire. Gifts that made everyone murmur to themselves about how thoughtful he was.

Like a corgi puppy draped in a big red bow presented to her at the anniversary dinner he'd invited his boss and her husband to attend.

Coco was precious now, but at that moment, on the spot, Brooke had been speechless.

And it had been impossible not to identify the theatrical nature of the whole night.

At the end, on any plain day ending in *y*, Brooke had started to wonder how often he remembered he had a wife instead of an efficient assistant who brushed her teeth at the sink next to him in the morning.

Being cared for, especially in the small ways, like taking an extra minute to bring hot coffee…

Why did that seem so special?

"It's coffee, Brooke. Get a grip and remember how you weren't going to slip back into propping up anyone else—not a husband and not a handsome veterinarian." Opening up the binder to the section on the parade was easy, and she'd marked her place on the list with a sticky note. Brooke picked up her phone.

"Peak Automotive, we're going places," a perky guy said as he answered on the first ring. "This is Rick, how can I help you?" The way the phrases rolled one into another suggested Rick had said them in a string like that a thousand times before.

"Rick, my name is Brooke Hearst. I'm calling because Peak Automotive has previously sponsored a float in the Prospect Western Days parade. We have a few spots left. Should we add you as a sponsor again this year?" Brooke tapped her pen on the notebook she'd discovered in Mary Beth's bottom drawer the day before, and wondered if her opener was anything like Rick's. She had practiced it, but she didn't want to sound like she'd repeated it until it was automatic. Talking on the phone wasn't high on Brooke's list of favorite things, but she'd gotten pretty good at making cold calls during the last campaign for city council she'd organized for Paul.

She hoped mentioning *a few spots* suggested Rick better hurry up and say yes.

"Well, now, Brooke, I don't believe we've met, but I had a note somewhere around here..." Brooke could hear the rustle of papers and imagined something like Matt's stack of napkins and envelopes. "My wife ordered me to call Dr. Singh to check on the parade, so I sure am glad to hear from you. I'm in for a sponsorship. I'll bring up this pretty little convertible that came in two weeks ago, and I'll have some of the kids from the baseball teams I sponsor there to hand out candy like usual."

Brooke hurried to make notes under Peak Automotive. "Okay, so you won't need any of the high school clubs to help with a float."

"Naw, but I'm going to send a check large enough to cover one of the clubs and materials for a float. Like usual. The principal can add it to the activities fund for the middle schoolers again this year if he wants to. I get some good business from Prospect, so I like to make an investment. Don't know if BV's Chamber of Commerce will ever get its act together enough to make any of our events as big as Prospect's weekend. They're good at collecting dues, but organizing ain't a strong suit." Rick cleared his throat. "Are you new to town, Brooke? I can't place your name, but I don't get down into Prospect as often as I should."

As Brooke tried to gauge his tone, she checked his address. Peak Automotive was in Bella Vista.

That's what he'd meant by *BV's Chamber of Commerce*. So a chamber of commerce might handle events like Western Days... Did Prospect have a chamber of commerce to take charge?

"I am new around here, Rick, and Dr. Singh is out of town, so the parade planning is running a little later than normal. I'm helping get everything finalized. I appreciate your flexibility, and I'm so glad we can count on Peak Automotive this year. The kids will be excited." She'd tossed that in on her call the day before to Prospect's leading insurance agent when he'd expressed irritation about the delay. "We'll be collecting funds this week. Do you know where Matt Armstrong's veterinary office is?"

"Oh, yeah," Rick immediately said, "Matt takes good care of my tabbies. Jinx and Merlin are pretty shy, but Matt can charm them right out of their carriers and have them vaccinated before they know what's happening. That's pure talent."

As Rick spoke, Brooke had no trouble imagining Matt working magic with his patients. She'd seen Coco's reaction. Cats had to be tough customers to wrangle, since they came loaded with so many sharp weapons. Finding a vet who could do what Rick said had to be special.

"Can I drop a check in the mail? Or if Matt's out this way, he can swing through and pick it up. Beautiful day for a drive, after all." The loud bong of a doorbell interrupted Rick's question. "I'd run it into town, but I'm the only one on the lot right now. Got a guy coming back for his third test drive, and I have that ol' familiar tingle that I'm selling a truck today."

Brooke bit her lip as she evaluated the options. Having Matt pick it up was out of the question, of course, but they were trying to get all the sponsorship fees in and over to the high school as quickly as possible. The key to the clinic was on top of the desk. Maybe she could pick it up for Matt?

Then she remembered she had no wheels.

To get to the car lot.

Where they would sell cars and trucks and other things with wheels.

Brooke tapped her forehead as she said, "Actually, I'll be nearby in the morning. I could stop by and pick it up, if that works better?" Brooke crossed her fingers and hoped she could get one of her sisters to take an hour or two out of Western Days preparation for a spontaneous car shopping expedition.

"Why, sure! I'd love to meet you, Brooke." The cheer in his voice was part friendly welcome and part salesperson seizing any opportunity to meet a potential buyer, but it wouldn't hurt to take a look at his car lot while she picked up the check for the parade sponsorship.

And possibly take the first of her test drives before finding her own set of keys.

After she hung up, Brooke sent a text to her sisters to start the conversation about who could take her to Bella Vista or at least loan her their car for the day.

Jordan immediately responded: Ha. And then No way.

And then her sister added, I've got to get to Fairplay to talk to a toilet paper wholesaler this week. You understand the urgency.

Brooke rolled her eyes, but it was hard to argue.

Coco and Betty had settled back onto Matt's futon and were snoozing happily, so she made a quick trip to the kitchen for more coffee and to stretch her cramped muscles.

A quick check of her phone showed that Sarah's answer was a wobbly I'll try. We're talking with a contractor about the test kitchen going in next door to the museum this afternoon. Fingers crossed he can start first thing in the morning.

Brooke decided there was enough potential in Sarah's answer that she could stop worrying about it. She had reached the end of the sponsor list where Prue had tacked on the hardware store, run by Walt Armstrong, and Handmade, her store. Brooke had a hunch that Prue took care of both of those sponsorships, but there was no phone number listed for either.

And she hadn't reached the level of family where she had Prue's cell number yet.

She was also almost certain that her reception with Prue Armstrong might be…polite. Possibly a little cool.

"Only one way to find out," she muttered to herself before taking a fortifying sip of her coffee. She would stop in at Handmade as she made her rounds of the local businesses to pick up the sponsorship checks for the floats.

"Ladies, you keep an eye on the place," Brooke said as she gave Betty and Coco treats and scratches behind their ears. "Keep the futon safe, you hear?" Both dogs had settled back into their cozy curls in Betty's large-but-not-quite-large-enough bed before she closed the door to Matt's living area.

After she locked the office's front door, Brooke stepped out on the wooden sidewalk and surveyed her choices. Saving the Mercantile, home of the hardware store and Handmade, for last seemed prudent, so she headed in the other direction. It was a pleasure to stroll and stare into the windows along Prospect's historical section. She stopped in to meet the insurance agent she'd spoken to the day before, who was also a notary public.

There was a dentist tucked back off the main street behind the Prospect Picture Show, the old movie theater that showed classic Westerns.

At the bank, she met a couple of tellers, a loan officer and the branch manager, who happened to be one of the ladies she'd seen waving at Matt during the Western Days meeting. It was nice to have the opportunity to meet people in smaller groups. She'd always been much better at making conversation one on one, and everyone had such positive things to say about Sarah, Jordan and their great-aunt Sadie. As the afternoon was winding down, Brooke realized her steps were slowing the nearer she got to the Mercantile.

Almost as if she was reluctant to meet Prue Armstrong again.

That would never do. It was easy enough to picture Sadie in her mind, one of the many times she'd tried to peptalk Brooke out of her own social anxiety and into the comfort of new people and new situations that Sadie enjoyed. Her great-aunt had been bubbly and easy to talk to; Brooke had always admired how easily Sadie converted new acquaintances to real friends.

Pretending to be confident and at ease with the situation was going to be an important first step, so she took a deep breath to slow down her racing heart and planted her hand on the door handle. When she pulled it open, the weird little hallway that the Armstrongs had built to split the Mercantile when they divorced was empty. There was one sad stand of flyers for local attractions and, just beyond, two doors, one that led to the hardware store and the other to Prue's shop.

Long, bare walls stretched out in front of Brooke, but it was easy to imagine it with more interesting decor. Photos of area attractions. A timeline of the town's history. Advertising for upcoming events. Something besides walls that needed a different color of paint at the very least.

Letting the space sit like this, unused, was sad. The Mercantile had been one of the quirkiest draws in town when Brooke was a kid. It had been such a hodgepodge of practical and fun and odd that she and her sisters had loved to poke around inside; it was nothing like any other store in LA or Denver.

This hallway? It could be in any boring office space anywhere. It didn't measure up to the facades out front or the interesting offerings inside either store.

Brooke peeked inside the hardware store, hoping that Walt Armstrong might be available to talk to first. The night of the meeting, his twinkling eyes hadn't dimmed, even when she'd extracted herself from the family conversation. She was sure he would be friendlier than Prue. Working her way up to the real challenge made sense, didn't it?

But she didn't see Walt inside; there was only a young guy who Brooke didn't recognize behind the counter. She turned to Prue's door.

When they'd walked through Handmade on the way to the Western Days meeting upstairs, Brooke had been charmed by the quilt shop. The fabrics and finished models on display had spoken to her. While Brooke had never been the same kind of artist her mother was, she had always loved color.

The bell that chimed as she opened the door eliminated any chance of catching Prue off guard, so Brooke made sure to put on her best smile as she stepped inside. Prue and Walt were seated on either side of a long table with neat stacks of fabric in front of them. Both turned to greet her.

"Well," Prue said brightly, "Brooke Hearst. I did not expect to see you here today. Are you out touring the town?" The words were politely welcoming, but there wasn't much warmth underneath.

Nervous, Brooke licked her lips as she watched Prue and her ex-husband have a complete conversation without saying a word. Walt had clutched Prue's hand when she finished speaking. Giving his ex-wife a warning to be nice? Brooke turned to survey the walls of the store. They were covered in finished projects of all sizes: quilts, embroidery pieces, some of her father's paintings to advertise their upcoming Sip and Paint classes. Everywhere she turned, there was a splash of color, but the quilt hanging beside the door caught her attention.

How had she missed it when she'd hurried through to the Western Days meeting?

"Oh, this is amazing," Brooke said breathlessly, one hand stretched out before she remembered her mother warning her to look and enjoy art but not to touch without permission.

Prue moved closer. "Be sure to buy yourself

some raffle tickets. That's the quilt we'll be raffling off this year, the one me and Rose and some of the other regulars here at the shop put together." She tipped her head to the side. "If we keep on growing this festival, we're going to need to make more than one quilt, I guess. Big plans take big money."

Brooke wondered how much they expected to raise from the raffle.

"Art like this should demand a big price," Brooke said as she managed to return Prue's stare. "I can tell you spent a lot of time making it."

"Are you a quilter? Your sisters didn't tell me that." The interest in Prue's eyes was impossible to miss.

Realizing she was about to take the second strike as far as Prue was concerned, Brooke shook her head slowly. "No, I'm not." But there was something about standing in Prue's shop that made her wonder if… "What do you call this pattern?"

"That's a design Rose and I dreamed up. The basic block is a Colorado Beauty. See? It's a kind of pinwheel made out of a bunch of half-square triangles. Then we arranged blocks made out of different colors to build the mountains." Prue drew a line with her finger in case Brooke needed help getting the full effect. "Rose had a vision, but when it took a spreadsheet to track how many of each color combination we needed to make it come true, I told her I'm designing next year's raffle quilt all by myself."

Prue's tone was exasperated, but something about the set of her shoulders convinced Brooke that she was twice as proud as she seemed. That pride was deserved, of course. The quilt was stunning.

"My mom… She had a million different art interests—needlework, painting, pottery." Brooke smiled as she remembered the way her mother had gotten excited about something new and threw herself into it completely until the next new inspiration came along. "She would have loved your shop."

"Sounds a bit like you, Prue." Walt leaned a shoulder against the door frame.

"After I got rid of a husband and gained all this space?" Prue asked as she twirled slowly. "Had to fill it up, didn't I? Before that, I didn't have enough space to make a pot holder on that kitchen table at the ranch. And five boys commandeered that table at least three times a day. I guess your mother and father figured out the secret to a happy home… Mama needs plenty of space."

She'd been too young to understand how her parents had ironed out their differences, but she did remember her mother stomping out to her studio, spending some time there painting or sewing or reading, and returning to the house with a smile on her face. "Space was a big piece of my mother's happiness. She loved us, but she definitely needed to spread her wings, too."

Prue raised her eyebrow at her ex-husband as if she was saying, "See?"

Sarah and Jordan had explained how Prue and Walt were destined to fail at their divorce. They loved each other too much to stay apart, but Brooke wondered if they were still ironing out the wrinkles that had pushed them apart in the first place.

Like having enough space.

Brooke raised her eyebrows at the way Walt pursed his lips and tipped his hat. "Space, huh? Guess we're still talking about that apartment you insist on keeping. On that note, believe I'll give Roger the rest of the afternoon off and wander back down the hall. He's been making a mess of my store, putting all the gardening tools together and all the bird feeders in one spot. Where is the fun in shopping thataway?"

"We used to love digging around in the aisles of the Mercantile, just to see what we could find," Brooke said. "It was an adventure."

"Exactly! I knew I liked you, Brooke Hearst. I'ma go tell Roger he's infringing on my unique retail experience with his 'efficiency.'" Walt made air quotes above his head before he pressed a kiss to Prue's cheek. "You and me, dinner, beautiful?"

Prue nodded. "You're on, cowboy."

After Walt left, Brooke asked, "Shouldn't all the gardening tools be in the same general area?"

Prue huffed out a laugh. "Only if selling them is your chief interest. Walt likes to take his customers on a rambling journey first. That's not his only unique philosophy, but from across the hallway I find it quirky and adorable. Especially because it no longer messes up the bills I have organized on the desk he wiped clear because he was working on repairing a saddle and needed better light than out in the barn." She sighed. "That might be more information than you wanted. About the only thing that scares me about all this talk of getting married again is that this time, I will lose my temper for good and try to feed him the saddle." She blinked slowly. "Mama is keeping her quilt store for sure."

Prue motioned to the neatly organized desk behind the checkout counter.

"Divorce isn't easy, is it?" Prue asked. "But a woman can learn all kinds of things about herself on the other side of it. How to be happy. What you can live with." Prue sighed as she stared at the door. "What you can't live without. Sad that it takes a heartbreak like that to come to terms with such things, but it would be even worse to never learn them at all."

Brooke ran her finger over the edge of the counter as she considered Prue's words. When her eyes met Prue's, something changed between them.

She realized that, of all the people in her newer, smaller circle, only Prue had been through a divorce.

Brooke's was still a fresh injury, but Prue had the benefit of time and distance.

If there was anyone she could talk to about being lonely and angry and sad and happy and excited and afraid and the entire range of wild emotions being on her own again provoked, it was Matt's mother.

The woman she'd shut down so effectively was her best option for an empathetic listener.

Based on the course of her life lately, that made perfect sense.

"Now then, what can I help you with?" Prue asked, her hands clasped in front of her politely.

"Well," Brooke drawled, off-kilter at how the conversation had started but more confident than she had been walking in, "I've been asked to help out with Western Days and…" She chuckled at the way Prue hooted. "I'm gathering up the sponsorship fees for Matt, so I can get them out to the high school tomorrow. There's this binder?" She raised her eyebrows to make sure Prue was following. "Your shop and Walt's were the last ones on the list. I had a hunch you might be the person to talk to about sponsoring this year."

Prue's smug satisfaction might have been annoying, since being here was clearly admitting defeat, but the situation was too amusing to stifle her grin.

"Let me grab the checks I have already written out and carefully organized where Walt can't get to them and mess up my system," Prue said as she waved Brooke to follow her behind the counter. A long drawer rolled out silently, and Brooke could see clear evidence that Prue was the expert tabber behind the binder. Everything had its place in the drawer; there wasn't a single stray receipt with notes scribbled on the back. "Walt and I always do a float for the Mercantile together and then we ride horses to represent the Rocking A in the parade. I'm excited to have all my boys riding together again. Here's a check for each."

"Did you want a specific club from the high school to work on your float?" Brooke asked as she filed the checks in the accordion folder she'd snagged from Mary Beth's magical bottom drawer of office supplies.

"4-H. We always work with 4-H," Prue answered immediately before she narrowed her eyes. "But we might not be the first ones requesting them this year."

Brooke shook her head slowly. "You're the third to request 4-H."

Prue sniffed. "Well. I suppose that's fine." She raised one shoulder. "All of the kids do good work."

"I'm sure whoever you get will do something amazing." Brooke wondered if this was the first time it had occurred to Prue that she was losing control by climbing out of the Western Days hot seat, but she wasn't about to play favorites.

Not even to make Matt's mother like her better.

Before Brooke could examine why that thought should pop into her head, Prue said, "I'm pleased that Matt succeeded where I failed. Getting you plugged into Western Days was my goal during the meeting." She smiled sweetly and Brooke wondered if she was supposed to offer some kind of explanation about her response on Sunday night. "It's a wonderful way to make friends in Prospect, after all."

"Of course, but I intend this to be a short visit, not my new home." Brooke moved closer to the door, the better to make her escape. Then she stopped, curious about what Prue would say if she knew the reasoning behind her rejection.

"I've spent a lot of time doing things for other people, so when I got here, I was determined to only say yes to the things I *wanted* to do. It was never a personal thing. Ex-husband baggage more than anything. I had done all this work setting up a nice, orderly system for our life and his career, and he just took it and gave it to someone else."

She met Prue's stare and knew the older woman was reading between the lines, picking up Brooke's metaphor comparing their divorces, when she nodded.

"I should have known my baby boy would work his usual magic." Prue waved her hand airily as if her worries about the festival had all been blown away in the breeze, but Brooke was keenly aware that Prue was anything but airy about Western Days, her sons in general and Matt in particular.

"Matt and I worked out an arrangement. I'll help out on a few festival-related things, but I plan to stick close to the best vet in town until my corgi has puppies," Brooke said as she tried to understand why Prue's breezy response rubbed her the wrong way.

When Prue immediately wrapped her hand around Brooke's forearm, the contact stopped them both. "Corgi puppies?" Prue asked. "Is that what you said?"

"Well, we don't exactly know who the father of these puppies is," Brooke said slowly, "but they are at least half corgi, yes. My ex-husband…" She swallowed the rest of the words. Telling and re-telling all the injuries done to her had never been her style, especially not to strangers. "Well, anyway, we'll all be excited to find out what sort of mix we're having."

Prue patted her arm. "Oh, honey, go ahead and tell the truth to shame that ex-husband. I have one, too. I can join in."

Brooke blinked. "You mean…Walt?" He was the only ex of Prue's that she'd ever heard about through Sarah and Jordan, but it was difficult to imagine the twinkly-eyed gentleman inspiring similar anger.

"I love him to bits, but raising five boys in a tiny old farmhouse with a man who was more married to his land, his livestock and his family history than he was to his wife was crushing. As long as the food was good and the kids were happy, he was content. But me…" Prue shook her head. "I was living a life that didn't fit me, and nothing I asked for got through to him. Well, you understand what makes me happy." She motioned around the room with one finger. "Can't be happy with him until I'm happy with me. The divorce got his attention, but only his heart could make him change his life. By heart,

I mean a health scare that shaved years off my life. Walt let Wes and the boys take charge of the Rocking A and learned to enjoy his days entertaining visitors in the hardware store."

Brooke nodded once as she absorbed that. "I can't imagine taking another chance on someone who had hurt me the way Paul did." She sighed. "Honestly, I'm not sure how to take that risk with any man now that I know how it can turn out. I was young the first time, you know?"

"Oh, honey, I do know." Prue patted her arm. "I know about being young and about being afraid. What I had to find out on my own is that divorce changed me, made me stronger. It changed him, too, so we aren't those same people who couldn't make a life. Separating might have been the only way for us to get to where we are, so I can't regret it too much. As far as the fear..." She sighed. "Well, I don't know how you get around it, except to meet the one that it's scarier to walk away from than toward." Then she grinned. "Cowboys—you can't live with 'em, but you can't ever forget 'em, either."

The way the older woman waggled her eyebrows surprised a chuckle out of Brooke.

"What's my baby up to while you're out working? Taking a nap? He used to hole up in any quiet corner he could find to take a nice snooze." Prue shook her head as if she was remembering the antics fondly. "I might have shocked some responsibility into him by naming him the chair of this festival, but he's so good at handing off that responsibility to someone else."

It was no wonder he'd been tired. Matt had told Brooke about his nightmares and crying at night because he wouldn't let himself during the day. He'd wanted to fit in. They had loved charming Matt the most, after all.

The naps had been the result of long, sleepless nights.

But Prue considered them a successful dodge of hard work.

Was that how all of Matt's family viewed him? An adorable scamp who worked only as hard as he was forced to?

While Matt was wearing himself thin to meet their expectations.

It wasn't her place to set Prue straight.

But she wanted to.

So badly.

Instead of spilling all of Matt's confessions, Brooke settled for saying, "He had an emergency call for the horse rescue that he works with. Grant went to help. Matt has been very busy with his practice." She managed to bite back a flow of words about being the only vet around and how much his work meant to anyone who loved their pets as much as Brooke did.

"And everything he's done to make this festival the best ever, of course." Was he in a bind because he couldn't keep juggling all the balls in the air? Yes, but Brooke was convinced anyone would struggle with as much going on.

She was also pretty sure that his mother ought to have some clue about how hard he worked, but she wasn't going to get involved.

"You should definitely ask Matt about his busy day today. Not one nap on the schedule."

She *would not* launch into an irritated list of everything Matt was doing instead of getting enough rest and how his mother should know better. But she couldn't resist saying something to Prue. His family should care to ask.

Brooke held up her folder with the checks. "We'll get these over to the high school. One of the groups will be in touch to discuss the float." And it was probably going to be a 4-H representative because Brooke was reconsidering her plan to flout Prue Armstrong in that moment even if she wasn't sure why. It seemed important to win Prue's admiration.

On that note, she paused in the doorway. "Have you and Walt ever considered doing anything with this empty hallway?"

Prue frowned. "Like what? Tear it down? Even if we remarry, we're going to keep the two shops separate, believe me."

Her firm tone convinced Brooke that no one would be able to change Prue's mind about that, not even the cowboy she couldn't live without.

"No, I meant the walls themselves. You could sell advertising to local area attractions, cover the space with beautiful photographs and listings for Bell House and the Majestic." Brooke bit her lip as she realized she hadn't put enough thought into this notion to be pitching it to anyone, but she was already in the middle of it. "Or you could advertise other events throughout the year, holidays that might draw in crowds. Or add to the experience of visitors by putting up a timeline of the town's history. I assume there are photos of the founding fathers somewhere." She gripped the door as she tried to find another graceful exit. "The Mercantile has always been one of the draws in Prospect. The hallway is valuable space that you could use to do...something."

Prue crossed her arms over her chest as she weighed everything Brooke said.

"Does Prospect have a chamber of commerce?" Brooke asked to satisfy her curiosity.

Prue pursed her lips. "No, we don't. Never needed one."

"Having someone to oversee big weekends like Western Days could be the thing you've been looking for to make it even bigger. Who knows?" Brooke pushed the door open wider, eyes locked on the door at the end and freedom.

"It was good to talk to you, Brooke. Don't be a stranger around here. We'll have you quilting in no time," Prue called out as Brooke left the shop. She was halfway back to Matt's office before her shoulders relaxed.

Then Coco stuck her head through the fence surrounding Bell House and Brooke lost every bit of calm she'd regained. The dog had definitely been inside the office when she'd left. How had she gotten out?

When she saw Matt and the leashes he was holding in his hands, relief made her knees weak.

He was lounging against the fence in the shade of the large, spreading oak in the small greenspace in front of the B and B.

"Did you think she'd figured out how to unlock the door?" he asked. When he slowly shifted, his lips twisted before he smiled at her. Was that a grimace? Maybe he'd been waiting for a while.

Brooke pressed her hand over her racing heart. "I didn't make it that far in my head. I went from fine to panic." A quick scratch under the chin was all Coco could stand still for and she was off snuffling under the azaleas that lined Bell House's front porch.

"Thought they might need a break and I wasn't

sure how long you'd be." Matt gave her Coco's leash when she held out her hand.

"Have you finished up for the day?" Brooke asked as she tried to sneak careful peeks at his face. Something was off, but she couldn't put her finger on why she thought that.

Matt sighed. "No, I dropped Grant off at the Rocking A and had to come back through town to get out to the Dawsons'. Sometimes I need to cuddle Betty before I can keep going, you know?"

At the sound of her name, Matt's pretty brown dog trotted over to give him a long swipe with her pink tongue before returning to her important work.

He grimaced as he wiped it off his cheek. "She knows exactly what I need."

Brooke pursed her lips. "A kiss to keep you going, huh?"

His smile matched the glint in his eye. "A sweet kiss can restore a man's soul, I'd say."

The flutter that settled in Brooke's abdomen caught her off guard. She was not interested in men at all and especially not charming cowboys who never wanted for kisses and who had too many jobs and not enough help to do them all.

But the urge to see what effect she might have on Matt Armstrong's soul was strong in that moment. She brushed her hair behind her ear and forced herself to stand tall.

His low chuckle should have made her angry.

Instead, she decided to treat it like a dare. She bent quickly to press a kiss to his other cheek, the one Betty had missed, before stepping back. "You keep putting one boot in front of the other, Doc. The day's not over yet."

She waved the folder at him. "I have all the sponsorship checks but one. I'll pick it up in the morning before I come in. How's that?"

Tomorrow she'd tour Peak Automotive and leave with one. Talking with Prue… Something about that conversation reminded her that she didn't have to wait any longer. If she wanted a car, she could buy it now. Not in a week or a month or when she knew what she was going to do with the rest of her life. She didn't have to ask anyone's opinion.

If there was a decent ride on the lot, she was going to have her own keys and freedom by this time tomorrow evening.

What was the use of being one of the Colorado Cookie Queen's heiresses if she didn't spend a little cash when she needed to?

Matt tipped his hat back. "Picking up the checks is outside the scope of our agreement, Brooke."

Being reminded of her words made her smile. "Since you didn't technically ask me to do this, it doesn't fall under our original agreement anyway. That's the loophole we used for rescheduling your appointments, right?"

They walked slowly back into his office together, and she was painfully aware of how closely Matt watched her buzz around to gather up all of Coco's toys, treats and paraphernalia. The loud honk of a horn had both humans and dogs turning to the window. Jordan waved from the parking spot in front and motioned Brooke to get in.

"Guess I'll see you tomorrow." Brooke paused in the doorway. "I hope you can get some rest tonight." There was something about him that bothered her, but she couldn't point to anything obvious. Matt just wasn't his usual self.

She hurried out before he could answer.

Whether he'd gone with something flirty and fun or sincere and appreciative, she would have been knocked off balance. He had a knack for keeping her that way.

And as Jordan sped toward the Majestic, Brooke held Coco close and was thankful for a successful day.

If she wished she'd waited to find out how Matt responded, she was going to have to get over that.

CHAPTER EIGHT

MATT WAS EXHAUSTED but satisfied when he parked at the Rocking A that night. The yard in front of the farmhouse was crowded with trucks, so he knew most of his family was already waiting inside. His mother had agreed to push dinner back half an hour so that he could run out to check on Juniper, but he was starving, dirty and already anxious to reach his hard futon and cramped apartment.

Unfortunately, he'd discovered that his reflexes with prickly horses weren't what they used to be.

How much of that was due to fatigue and how much could be blamed on a distracting memory of a pretty smile was something he'd have to come to terms with later.

He rested his head against the seat until he realized he was half a second from falling into a real, deep sleep. The front seat of his truck was marginally less comfortable than the futon, so he forced himself to slide slowly out. Each step up to the porch sent a zing of pain through his hip, courtesy of an irritated mare named Rabbit, of all things. She had objected to his testing and seized his distraction to nail him with a hard hoof to his side. The bruise was going to remind him to be careful where he stepped for a few weeks. Good thing there was a doctor in the family.

Then he remembered he was also a doctor.

Still, having a second opinion from a professional who worked exclusively with humans could come in handy.

Almost everyone was already seated at the large kitchen table when he made it inside. Clay was working in Colorado Springs, and Sarah, Jordan and Mia were absent, but the rest of the Armstrongs were halfway through dinner.

It crossed his mind to pretend he was absolutely fine, but Micah's first move after he launched himself out of the chair at the island that now functioned as the kids' table was to bang hard into Matt's abdomen.

The kid had adopted hugs at high speed as his usual greeting for all family members.

Even that might have been fine, but the arm he threw around Matt's waist landed right in the center of where Rabbit's hoof had also landed and his wince was automatic. He gripped Micah's shoulder and tried to shift the kid over without hurting him or his feelings. "Hey, pardner. What's for dinner?"

Matt met his mother's concerned stare and moved to take his usual seat as Micah listed the menu. "Steak, baked potatoes and asparaguts that I have to eat before I can have any chocolate cake." He motioned over his shoulder at Travis who inhaled patiently and said, "You only have to try it, Micah. One bite of asparagus and your chocolate cake is secure."

"And if you don't like asparagus after you try it, you can bet I will never be serving it at my table ever again," Matt's mother added as she ran her hand down Micah's back. "Matt, I'll make you a plate. Keena…" She motioned imperiously to demonstrate walking around the table to investigate Matt.

"He might want to eat dinner first," Keena mumbled to herself as she stood, "or not have the whole family watching me examine him, but no…" She huffed as she knelt down next to his chair. "What's hurting, Matt?"

"And are we all going to be scandalized if you show my wife here at the table?" Travis asked.

Keena rolled her eyes at him. "At least one of us will be able to withstand the shock."

"Your dinner is getting cold," Matt said as he pulled his shirt up and bent forward. Keena's immediate wince confirmed that she was getting a good look at the issue. He bent his head to check the deep reddish-purple bruise creeping up his side.

"I was afraid she nailed you good," Grant said as he motioned with the roll in his left hand. "The rescue is going to need to do some serious work with Rabbit before she's ready for adoption." He stood to reach for the butter in the center of the table and returned to his dinner as if he'd done his part by offering that tidbit.

"What's the pain like?" Keena murmured as Matt watched his mother smack Grant with a dish towel.

"What's that for?" Grant asked as he ducked.

"That's for not telling me Matt was injured." His mother returned to the stove. "We settled this when you were boys. You don't tattle, but if there's blood or broken bones, you spill immediately."

"There was neither in this case," Matt said as he took the plate she offered him and moved so that Keena could lower the waistband of his jeans. "I'm not bleeding, and I've been all over creation since Rabbit caught me napping this afternoon. If the good doctor has a prescription, I will take it, but otherwise, I'll just let it...work itself out." When Matt realized that Micah was locked in on the conversation instead of his meal, he made a big show out of trying the asparagus and smacking his lips. "A good dinner will definitely help."

"And what else, Keena? Ice? Heat?" His mother handed him a cold glass of tea to drink. "We'll put you up on the couch for a bit so I can take care of you."

Keena squeezed his arm and returned to her seat. "Some ice for swelling. An over-the-counter anti-inflammatory will do unless the pain is too much. If you need something stronger, I can call something into the pharmacy in the morning. Rest. That's about all there is for bruising."

"I can take care of all that from my office apartment, but thank you, Mom." He patted her hand because the last thing he wanted to do was try to sleep while his family tromped through the farmhouse living room.

"You could take my bed, Uncle Matt," Damon said from his spot. "I like the couch." At fifteen, his voice had deepened to where he sounded grown until the odd crack sneaked in to surprise them all.

Matt held his hand up for a long-distance high five. "No way, but I appreciate the offer." He motioned with his fork to his brothers gathered around the table. "You'll notice none of these polecats will offer their bed."

Damon ducked his head. "Micah kicks in his

sleep. Sharing a room with him means you have to learn how to ignore his dance steps all night long. You might not get any rest anyway." His grin at the way Micah swung around to argue reminded Matt of the way he and his brothers had picked on each other when they were young.

And now, for that matter.

Damon wanted Micah to stop worrying about Matt's injury.

Teasing him was a solid way to change the course of the younger boy's thoughts.

Matt had thought he had navigated the whole conversation easily, but his mother was still frowning.

"Mom, it's a bruise. I'll rest better in my own bed." Matt dug into the perfectly grilled steak that tasted like heaven, done with the conversation.

The silence warned him that he was the only one moving on.

"A little birdie told me today that I should ask about your day," his mother said slowly, "but I don't believe she had any idea you had been injured, either." She smiled. "So what else do you need to tell me?"

Matt shrugged, confused by the question. Who was the little birdie gossiping about him to his mother?

"Went out to treat Juniper just after dawn at

Billy Dawson's place. She was feverish and dehydrated when he called me out yesterday. I put in an IV, gave her more fluids this morning and tonight." He took another bite of his steak as he watched her watch him. "When I went into the office, Brooke was there. She wanted to work on the parade sponsorships." He held up a hand because he expected his mother to launch into a lecture about how this was his job, running Western Days, so he should be involved. "Before I could sit down and get started on that, I got an emergency phone call from the horse rescue where Rabbit caught me in the side. They had cases of strangles in the barn, so Alison wanted me to test the other horses and help her figure out a quarantine plan to keep it from spreading. Grant went with me to help. He did not keep me safe, though." He shook his head sadly at Grant. "My big brother let me down."

Matt expected Grant to return a rude gesture in response, but he simply crossed his arms over his chest, patiently waiting for their mother's reaction. "The rest you know. I dropped Grant off and went back to check on Juniper. She's doing well. I'm going to remove the catheter in the morning. And now, here I am, trying to eat my dinner." Running into Brooke and teasing a kiss out of her had been the highlight of the afternoon, but he decided to keep that bit of info to himself.

He pointed at the rolls and Grant, first one and then the other, until his brother handed him one, slathered in enough butter for two.

Just the way he liked it.

"So from sunrise to after full dark, you've been working. Through this injury." His mother pursed her lips. Before he could correct her that the injury had come late in the afternoon, so technically he'd been whole and healthy most of the day, she held up a hand. "And how many days in a row have you been working like that, Matt?"

He frowned. "The horse rescue thing was today, so…one?"

"Sunrise to sunset…how many days?" his mother asked slowly.

"Oh," Matt said as he shifted in his seat and swallowed the wince that accompanied the pain, "between making calls, keeping the office open and Western Days, it's been a long stretch now. Months, maybe?"

Her lips were a tight line. "Without a word about it. The burden of the festival. All of this. You never said a word. Do I have to move you back into this house to make sure you're taking care of yourself?"

"You wanted me to take over Western Days,

remember?" Realizing her tone was displeasure and perhaps some hurt, Matt straightened in his chair and swallowed a groan. "I've got everything under control." Was he lying? Yes, but there didn't seem to be much of an option. He wasn't going to leave the ranch tonight with Prue worried or unhappy if he could help it. His family loved him, even if they didn't understand him or how hard he worked. That was fine. "Brooke has already been a huge help. Next thing I'm going to do is sweet-talk her into helping me get some things set up for next year. If I know you, you're already planning to go even bigger."

When his mother didn't agree, Matt glanced at his brothers for support.

The raised eyebrows around the table convinced him no one else knew what came next, either.

Walt rubbed his hands together as he asked, "Micah, how you comin' along on the asparaguts? Are we having chocolate cake or not?"

Micah waved his empty plate and the whole table clapped.

Before his mother stood, Walt pressed a hand on her shoulder. "It's unanimous. Asparagus is a go and so is the cake. I'll get it." Wes and Travis immediately stood to clear the table, and as Matt watched them work, he realized they'd all learned some better manners since his mother had battled to keep six males fed, clean and out of trouble. If his parents had never divorced, leaving them fending for themselves for a time, would they be where they were?

Her quiet responses while they all devoured dessert were so unlike her that it was difficult to carry on a normal conversation. Eventually Walt took her hand. "What say we go for a stroll and leave this wild bunch with the chores? Want to?"

His mother tangled her fingers through his and nodded.

Before she stood, she bent to press a kiss to Matt's cheek. "Guessing you'll be gone when we get back. By all accounts and purposes, you should already be in bed so you can get started at the crack of dawn tomorrow. Get some rest, Matt."

After they left the farmhouse, Matt rested his elbows on the table and pressed his forehead to his hands. "Why does it feel like *I'm* the one who landed a kick to *Mom's* midsection?" He'd only been doing what his parents wanted from them all. Working hard. Helping neighbors. Stepping up.

Grant gently placed an arm around Matt's shoulders and patted his shoulder hard.

Suspicious at the care and concern, Matt frowned. "Is this bruise fatal, Keena? No way you're being careful not to hurt me now."

Grant placed his hands to his chest. "I have experienced bruises like that more than once. I'm trying to be a more sensitive version of myself." When Wes's mouth dropped open in shock and Travis did a double take, Grant added, "And I appreciate that it might not be easy to keep your head above water when the calm seas you've enjoyed turn turbulent."

Matt nodded. "Yeah, the work has gotten a little...overwhelming lately. Once the festival is over, things should settle down." He hoped. "Might get serious about finding someone to bring in as a partner in the clinic." He'd wanted to wait until he was able to build the office he wanted, but there were larger spaces in town that could work in the meantime.

"Not those seas. I meant being called *Matt* instead of *baby*." Grant held his hands up as Matt scowled.

"That's a change I welcome. Around here, being the spoiled baby is one thing." Matt remembered the sweep of heat to his face from the Western Days meeting. "In the general public? It has gotten..."

"Tired," Wes suggested. "And we aren't helping by piling on, are we?"

Matt wanted to brush off the conversation. This was a silly thing to be holding on to, wasn't it? He hadn't realized how much it bothered him until Western Days and Brooke Hearst collided. Had he even understood how he'd gotten here until he'd explained to her about his fear of losing his place in the Armstrong family when he was a kid?

"I have a lot going on now. My usual ability to roll with the punches is missing." Matt was clear on his place in the pecking order of the Armstrong clan. He was the easygoing one, the sweet and charming one out of this collection of strong, silent types.

As he sat there, he recognized he was doing his best to be strong and silent, too. Maybe that was a problem.

"You sure do. How can we help?" Travis asked as Keena handed Matt an improvised pack of ice cubes in a plastic bag wrapped in a dish towel.

After he pressed the ice to his side with a hiss, Matt grunted. "Now you want to help. What about having to admit my sins to Mom first?"

"We won't make you confess you need our help this time," Travis said.

"Let me take over the parade," Wes said. "Sarah's got the museum under control. Clay's got some more work being done on the Majestic this week that I'll need to run out and check on. Sharita Cooper asked me to do a walk-through of her house to get it ready to rent again, now that Keena's moved in here, so I may need to get some of that set up. Travis can handle the ranch stuff. You can put me to work."

It was so tempting.

Wes was the kind of man who would take the binder, peruse it for two minutes and formulate a plan to finish up everything three days early and under budget.

And he'd do it on top of all the other things he juggled in his life on a normal basis.

His law practice. The ranch. Helping Sarah with the museum and Jordan with the lodge and any number of other people with countless things.

Somehow without losing focus long enough for a mean horse to get in a sucker punch.

"Or," Keena said slowly, "we could let Matt get his jobs done the way he wants them done. Letting the grown man make his own decisions without pulling a string to influence his decisions is a thing you could try." She held up her hands as every man faced her. "I get it. I'm not an *Armstrong* Armstrong, but you need an outside perspective here." She waved a hand at Matt. "He's tired. He needs rest. You made your offer to help. Let Matt figure out what that looks like after a good night's sleep and at least four ibuprofen tonight."

They were silent as they absorbed her words. Eventually, Travis ran his hand up her back to her nape before pressing a kiss to her cheek. "The smartest Armstrong has spoken. Keena's right. We all want to make our own decisions."

Relieved that the pressure was off, Matt smiled at Keena.

She used to freeze in one spot whenever he did that, but tonight, she gave a small shake of her head as if they were all so silly because the answer had been clear.

"You know," Wes said, "if rest is what you need, you could take over Sharita's place. It's close to home without being stuck on the couch. Plenty of freedom still. An actual bed in a totally separate bedroom. Kitchen, too. It's not fancy but there are benefits over sleeping where you work, especially when you work all the time."

It wasn't a bad plan. Having some space to spread out would be nice.

"I was planning to ask Brooke if she's ready for her own place, but not until after Western Days." Wes met his stare.

Almost as if he was evaluating Matt's reaction to that.

"What?" Matt asked, aiming for innocence or ignorance if he couldn't quite manage that.

"You want to tell us how working with the youngest Hearst has been?" Grant propped his chin on his hand as if he was waiting for Matt to spill the hot gossip.

"Honestly, we haven't been together much."

Did he regret that? A little. "But she's easy to talk to, and being able to do the things I need to do without worrying about Western Days falling further behind has been a relief today. Nothing about her suggests that anything other than success is a possibility." He liked that. Everyone could use someone like that in their corner, right?

"Sarah can move mountains. Jordan can knock them down." Keena laughed with them. "It is not surprising at all that Brooke has her own powers. Sadie Hearst must have been amazing."

Since Sadie's move to LA had nearly shut down Prospect and the return of her great-nieces had led to an explosion of regrowth, it was easy to agree.

"And don't forget that she's the little birdie on Mom's shoulder," Grant said.

It was another record-scratch moment. Everyone turned to Grant for an explanation.

"Whatever she said to Mom is what set this whole night rolling down the hill." Grant mimed a sharp dive off a high cliff to bonk hard on the table in front of him.

Wes nodded. "Yeah, she had to be the one to mention that Mom didn't know as much about your life as she thought she did."

Matt recalled Brooke's proud wave of the folder filled with sponsorship checks. Had she walked the whole town to gather them? And braved his mother at the Mercantile after their encounter at the Western Days meeting?

The longer he studied the possibility, the more certain he was that Grant was right.

"Wonder what she said," Matt murmured.

"And why," Grant added.

Keena sighed. "I don't want to be labeled the smartest Armstrong, but I feel it's necessary to help you out when I'm the only one at the table who can." She wrapped her arms around Grant and Travis before smiling at Matt and Wes. "She's standing up for you, Matt."

When Matt checked with Wes, he was relieved that neither one of them managed to catch on.

"For some reason," Keena said slowly, "she thinks someone needs to make your mother understand how hard you work."

Travis pursed his lips. "Shouldn't that be Matt's job?"

Keena turned to him, her lips curled as if he was the most adorable thing she'd ever seen. "Oh, honey. You and your mother… All of you and your mother… You love her so much, and that makes you the sweetest, but you don't want to hurt her, either, so you accept things from her you don't like. You do things you don't want to do. And you hide things if you think you can get away with it." She ran a finger across his eyebrows to smooth the frown there. "Don't make me list all the examples I can name right off the top of my head."

Matt removed the ice pack.

The doctor was right. Of course she was.

"Say it with me..." Keena wrinkled her nose at Travis. "Your mother is strong enough to..."

Together they said, "She is strong enough to handle the truth."

It had the quality of something Keena had said often enough to Travis that it was a mantra they had both memorized. He had a feeling it hadn't been about his mother originally. Keena didn't strike him as someone who wanted less than the whole truth from the people she loved.

"Offer Sharita's place to Brooke." Matt fiddled with his folded napkin. "I mean, if she's planning on staying in Prospect for a while."

The silence that followed his attempt at casually gathering information convinced him he'd failed.

Wes pursed his lips. "Sarah wants her to stay. That means I'm going to do my best to make it appealing."

Matt said, "Hmm," as if that provoked deep thoughts. "We haven't talked much about her plans after Western Days." But he certainly wouldn't mind if Brooke extended her stay.

Having the chance to get to know more about

her when he wasn't running from one job to the next could be nice.

She didn't strike him as a person who fished, but everyone loved days out on the water, didn't they? A day away from work out on the lake was on his mind again.

Keena's snort caught his attention. All of his brothers were watching him.

If Rabbit had been nearby, she might have kicked him on the other side because he had definitely gotten distracted again.

"Is this going to be a love match?" Grant made a temple of his fingers before wiggling them as if he was too excited by the prospect. "A clean sweep of the Hearst sisters."

"I'm too young to get married," Matt immediately said before a sharp twinge in his side provoked a grunt.

"You keep telling yourself that, buddy," Grant said as he patted Matt's shoulder. "Say it again and again. It covers up the tiny, quiet noises of love sneaking right up on you."

Matt grinned, relieved to have something close to normal to end the conversation.

But as he drove back into Prospect to sleep on his hard futon, he couldn't shake the thought of Brooke standing up for him.

He hadn't asked.

Defending him was definitely outside the scope of their agreement.

Not even their loophole covered being his champion to his mother.

What would it mean to have a woman like that around all the time?

CHAPTER NINE

ON WEDNESDAY, Brooke slid out of the top-of-the-line fully loaded silver SUV Rick had shown her after their first test-drive in a sleek, sporty black convertible much like the one she'd had in New York. Giving her car up because she couldn't afford the payments or the secure parking she'd gotten so used to in the city had hurt, but so far neither test-drive had stirred any emotion at all.

Sarah and Jordan had fully converted to country-slash-mountain life in SUVs with hauling capabilities, so Brooke had wondered if she was on the same page.

The appeal was easy to understand, but she hadn't gotten any of the pleasure she'd expected from maneuvering through the twists and turns outside of town.

If she was going to hand over such a big chunk of money, she wanted to feel excited about it.

"That is not the face of a satisfied customer," Rick said as he clapped his hands in front of him, eyes already scanning the lot for another option.

"What if you ordered the convertible in red?" Jordan asked as she hopped out of the front seat to stand next to Brooke. "Red is your color anyway."

Brooke nodded uncertainly as she stared at the convertible. Black was sleek, classic. It sparkled in the sunshine. It was easy to picture her and Coco driving down the street in Prospect. Rick had plans to use it for the parade himself, adding in a jaunty wave and a sign to visit him at Peak Automotive for a test-drive.

But it only had two seats.

And if the top was down, the trunk was full.

She and Coco would barely fit, and they would have no room for their things.

They both needed many things, so room to carry them seemed important.

Since she and Jordan had filled the back of her SUV with bags from the office supply store in a single stop, Brooke had been reminded that her life was completely different now than it had been in New York.

There was a delivery service for every need in the city.

Nothing in Prospect was like that. When she had to buy her own groceries, how would she get them home unless she had some room for hauling?

"Let's talk this out," Rick said, a man who

clearly wanted to make a sale and wasn't ready to give up on this one yet. "Tell me what you liked about each. Maybe there's a third choice."

Brooke pointed to the SUV. "Lots of room for buying and carrying stuff. Who doesn't love that?"

Jordan nodded enthusiastically. "I know you didn't think we could get two entire boxes of copy paper in the back of my SUV along with an entire aisle's worth of notebooks, file folders and pens you had to buy for some reason. We managed it and still have plenty of room to hit the bookstore that made you scream with excitement when we drove into town. Cargo space is important."

It was tempting to argue with Jordan about her description. She *had* emitted a high-pitched noise at the sight of a convenient bookstore, but it hadn't been a scream.

If it had been a scream, it hadn't lasted long.

"Can't argue about the benefits of space," Rick said. "And what else?"

Brooke pointed at the convertible. "I can picture myself driving that one. I had forgotten how much fun it is to drive roads outside the city, accelerating out of curves while the car hugs the shoulder. Plus, my dog is low to the ground. That fits us better, being low to the ground."

Jordan blinked slowly. "You'll have to lift Coco into whatever you buy, Brooke."

It was a valid point, but Rick had asked her what she liked.

He held out his hands to tick off points. "Fun to drive. I'm guessing quick acceleration and turning factor into that. But you need space and a comfortable ride for your dog and any other passengers you might want to include." To his credit, Rick was carefully evaluating the criteria instead of explaining to her what she should be focused on or brushing aside her concerns. This had been Brooke's only concern about the day—dealing with the salesperson—but Rick was doing a great job. She wanted to buy from him.

"And she needs to look expensively beautiful," Jordan said with a wave at the long skirt Brooke had chosen for the day. It was silky and flowed as she walked, but it wasn't fancy by any means. Apparently her sister had no problem ignoring the plain cotton T-shirt she'd paired with it.

So what if the skirt wasn't the denim that Jordan had chosen to wear on their shopping trip; Brooke was completely comfortable.

"Expensively beautiful… That is important to know as well." Rick motioned for them to follow and walked to the front of the lot to a navy blue car. "Luxury. Check. Zero to sixty in about five seconds and takes curves like a dream. All-wheel drive so you can drive it in the city or off-road, and when the weather turns, you'll be ready. There are no limits. Fun to drive. Check. Panoramic sunroof. All the techy gadgets you can dream of, and it's not red, but this deep blue is nice. To me, that's stylish. Check." Rick opened the door. "Let's take this one for a drive."

The tone of his voice was the same one the devil on a woman's shoulder relied on to lure her into making terrible decisions, but it was effective.

"Okay. Let's do it." Brooke nodded.

While Rick raced inside to get the key, Jordan inched closer. "You know that's a station wagon, Brooke." Her tone was scandalized. "A family car," she added.

Had Rick mesmerized her somehow? Because she wasn't in the market for hauling kids around yet.

"It's a *luxury* wagon," Brooke said as she read the sticker affixed to the window, "and it costs more than a college education these days."

"That's saying something," Jordan said as she slid into the back seat. After she leaned her head back to look up, she said, "Whoa. Panoramic sunroof, indeed."

Bright blue sky filled the space as Brooke opened it, pulled out of the car lot and took the *luxury* wagon for a spin through the busy streets of Bella Vista. Outside of town, she hit the gas and felt the familiar thrill when the car responded immediately.

Her hair lifted in the breeze and it was only natural to push the controls on the steering wheel to turn up the music as the wind chased away her worries.

This was how she wanted to feel. Alive. In control. Free.

Before Brooke was too far gone, Jordan tried one more time to insert some logic into her car-buying decision. They were seated in comfortable chairs in front of Rick's desk while he ironed out the financial hoops for Brooke to complete the purchase when Jordan said, "I might be able to see how this fits here in Prospect, but in the city, you could want something different." Her sister raised her eyebrows. "Are you planning to make Prospect a long-term stay?"

It was hard to read whether the idea pleased her sister or not. Jordan and Sarah had ironed out where they belonged in Prospect at this point. They had both fallen in love with Armstrongs, but more importantly, they had found callings. They had work that they were meant to do. There was no doubt about that.

Brooke didn't have either one of those things tying her to this small town, so it didn't make as much sense for her to buy what fit her life here.

If she decided to move to Denver or even back to LA, what kind of car would she choose for herself?

Luxury.

Fun.

Stylish.

None of those things would change, no matter where she was living three or six months from now.

"Apparently, I'm all in for this car, Jordie," Brooke said with a smile. "I appreciate you trying to be all mature and reasonable with me when we know that's not your strong suit."

Jordan slumped in relief. "I had to give it a shot since Sarah's not here, so I was channeling her in my head. But you know me. I say get what you want. If you don't want it next week, there's a solution for that, too."

Brooke threw her arms around Jordan's shoulders. "Thank you for bringing me today."

Jordan patted her shoulder and gave her a worried look when she stepped back. "You threatened to cancel my plant order through Homestead unless I did. Remember?"

Brooke nodded. She had done that. Neither one of them had believed she'd do it, but it was a sister thing. "You were the perfect choice for a car-shopping trip companion. Getting the Majestic ready to open is a big job, and I appreciate you rearranging your plans to help me today."

Her sister's brilliant smile was the best answer.

Of the three of them, Jordan had always been the one in the present. Sarah anticipated the future, planning every step. Even if she would never approach Sarah's skill with planning, Brooke had always been focused on the end goal, a someday thing that she had her hopes set on. Jordan looked carefully at the moment, right where she was, and that directed her decisions. Taking a page out of her book for this part of Brooke's life made perfect sense. Until she knew what the next big dream was, she could try to learn to live for the day.

The thing about having a chunk of money that she'd inherited? It simplified everything.

Feeling alive, in control and free was easy with the right checking account balance.

She didn't have any trouble completing her purchase and waving goodbye to Jordan, who was on her way back to Prospect *without* stopping at the bookstore that Brooke desperately wanted to visit.

Because Brooke had her own keys, her own car and plenty of hauling room of her own.

Flush with the successful shopping day and the freedom of the road back to the Majestic in front of her, Brooke made the snap decision to order a large, loaded pizza before she left town.

It would cool off before she made it back to Prospect, but the only thing better than cold pizza was warm pizza. As long as she had a microwave, she could have everything her heart desired.

After a too short but fun drive, Brooke reached Matt's office.

Her plan was to drop off the final sponsorship check and leave Matt a note. He could handle delivering the money to the principal on his own while she...

Well, it was difficult to imagine what she might fill her time with the next day, but there were so many miles of roads to explore. She didn't have any limits.

For the first time in a long time, she believed that. Anything was possible. For so long, the struggle to hold on to her marriage and her townhome had filled every waking minute. Letting go of those had hurt.

How had one extremely large purchase followed up by pizza voted "best in the county" make her feel this way? Younger. Happier. Optimistic for the first time in a long time.

Caught in the flush of a good mood that had been a long time coming, she decided to share her pizza with Matt if he was interested. If not, that would be fine, too.

Juggling Coco in her basket and the large pizza at the door took a minute, but she let herself in the office and locked the door behind her. "Matt? Are you here?" She paused in the waiting area and set Coco down as she waited for his answer.

When she didn't get one, she moved toward his apartment at the back. "Matt?"

There was still no answer. Maybe he'd walked down to the Ace High for dinner.

The back door that had been closed every time she'd worked in his office was standing open, and she could see through the glass storm door. A little patio area led to the street that ran behind the shops on Prospect's main road. Betty's head popped up in the center so Brooke moved closer to see that Matt was stretched out on a lounger, one arm thrown over his eyes while the other cradled something against his side.

Brooke froze there, stuck in indecision until Coco pressed her nose to the glass over Betty's and both dogs whined. Matt shifted on the lounger and blinked sleep out of his eyes. "Hey, Brooke. What are you doing here?" He held out one hand and motioned her out.

She'd been half a second from strategic retreat, but something about his invitation caught her.

It was almost like he wasn't even awake yet, but the sight of her was so automatically welcome that he wanted her closer. Brooke bit her bottom lip as she opened the door.

This could be dangerous.

Was that why her heart was pounding in a fight-or-flight rhythm? Of course it was.

Listening to her heart was the right thing to do; flight might save her some regrets in the long run.

But at that moment, all she could do was move closer to Matt.

WHEN MATT HAD glanced over to find Brooke framed in the doorway, he thought he was still dreaming. He had been dancing with her in his apartment, spinning her gracefully in a tight circle right there between the futon and his cramped table. Why had the dream seemed so romantic when the setting had been so…not?

Her warm hand squeezing his brought him fully awake.

"'You're Still The One.'" Matt covered the wide yawn that took over before rubbing his eyes.

Brooke bent down to study him. "Are you awake?" Her worried frown reminded him she didn't know what he was talking about.

"I was dreaming. We were two-stepping. You know the old Shania Twain song?" Matt hummed some of it to help her connect the dots and took the box she offered him. The delicious smell brought him fully alert. "Where did you get pizza?"

"I was on a spending spree today in Bella Vista. I went to pick up the sponsorship check at Peak Automotive, and ended up buying Mary Beth some office supplies to replace the ones I took, a few new books for me and a new car... so pizza made sense." Brooke surveyed the outdoor area he'd fenced off, and Matt remembered there was no other chair for her. He patted the end of the lounger.

She perched uncomfortably on the edge before hopping back up. "I'll grab some drinks. What would you like?"

"No, let me..." The sharp ache in his hip reminded him of why he'd fallen asleep in the first place. Ibuprofen had been working its magic.

"What's wrong?" Brooke asked, bending closer so he could smell her perfume.

"I've got a bruise. It's better, but I get a reminder every now and then that I've got to take it easy." He shifted in his seat to stand and she pressed her hand to his shoulder.

"What happened?" she asked. Her no-nonsense tone made him think he better answer. It also reminded him of Keena and Travis and their chant about his mother being strong enough to handle the truth.

Was Brooke?

And why did it feel so important to their relationship to know the answer to that?

"I wasn't paying attention in the barn, and a horse kicked me." Matt held out the ice pack. "So I'm icing the bruise and trying to take it easy."

He didn't like her frown. "It's not that big of a deal. I made a rookie mistake, got distracted. This should remind me not to do that again for a while." He smiled and covered her hand where it rested on his chest.

The way her eyes darted down and back up made him wonder if she'd forgotten she was touching him.

"Do you get hurt often?" She leaned back.

But she didn't remove her hand from his.

Nice.

"In the early days, it wasn't unusual, although it's the cats that will strike fear in a man's heart until he learns their ways." He smiled. "Now, it's pretty rare to sneak up on ol' Dr. Armstrong."

He wasn't sure she was satisfied with his answer, but Brooke said, "Sit. I'll make myself at home and be back in a second." She disappeared inside before he could formulate an argument.

By the time she was back, he was glad she'd

ignored him. Rabbit had packed a punch, the kind where the pain got worse before it got better.

He took the glass of water and patted the end of the lounger. "Sorry. I don't get much company here."

She moved the pizza between them and turned to face him before kicking off her shoes and crossing her legs in front of her, her long, flowy skirt bunched up between them.

"It's a loaded pizza. I hope you can pick off the parts you don't like." Brooke chose a slice and immediately took a bite. The way her eyes drifted shut convinced him it had been too long since she'd had pizza.

"I like it all. I'm easy to please." Matt tasted the pizza. It was good. All pizza was good, right? But he was curious about her reaction. "I can't tell if pizza is your favorite meal or if you were afraid you'd never have it again while you were in Prospect."

Brook nodded while she chewed. After a sip of water, she said, "A little of both? I do love pizza. There's this place in the LA neighborhood I grew up in called Lark's that supplied our dinner multiple times a week. They have the best pizza in the world, but it has been a while. My husband..." She shook her head. "My ex-husband is a vegetarian, so I have missed sausage and pepperoni for a long time. He was not about to pick those off his pizza, you know?"

"Had to order separate pizzas, I guess?" Matt wasn't sure what convinced Brooke to open up with him, but they were in one of those spaces right here and he wanted to know anything and everything.

"Nah, it was easier to be a vegetarian myself. All his events, our meals, grocery shopping... I had to remember his preferences and make sure he had everything he liked, so it was simpler for me to adopt the same diet." She patted her stomach. "For the most part, it was easy enough and healthy, but my stomach is thrilled by sausage at this point."

Her description made Matt wonder if Brooke's ex had needed more than his food choices catered to. He happily made accommodations for the people he loved, but if he was the only one bending to fit into another person's space, he would run out of patience. That's why the expression for compromise was *give-and-take* and not *take-and-take-and-take*.

He hoped Brooke realized that now, but he just said, "It's important to make your stomach happy now and then." He stretched back slowly.

"That is medical advice I will take, Dr. Armstrong." Brooke pointed at his side. "Were you hurting like this last night? While you were out walking Betty and Coco? I knew something was wrong."

Matt grunted. "I am a tough and strong and macho man, Brooke. As such, it is required that I disguise pain in a manly way from all the beautiful women in my vicinity. How else will you be amazed by my rugged appeal?"

He cracked his eyelids open when there was silence at what he thought was a pretty funny answer.

Brooke's nose was wrinkled into amusement.

"That's a relief. I was afraid you were going to take me seriously." Matt winked at her and was thrilled to watch color sweep up her cheeks.

When she sipped her water and immediately coughed as if it had gone down the wrong pipe, Matt decided he should move back to safer topics. "A new car? Congratulations. Give me a ride out to the high school tomorrow so I can experience some luxury. My truck rattles like a BB in a tin can."

Brooke sniffed. "Why would you say *luxury*? How do you know I didn't choose a fuel-efficient compact?"

Matt pursed his lips as he pinched her silky skirt between his finger and thumb. "Let's call it a hunch."

She sighed. "The way I dress. Of course. A clue

that I like expensive things. If either of us forget, Jordan will remind us."

"Hey, I know Sarah and Jordan, too. They like nice things. Who doesn't?" Matt asked.

"Well, you're still going to be surprised by what I picked, but it's got some nice features." Brooke licked her lips. "You could deliver the checks on your own whenever it's most convenient. I don't think that's within the scope of our original agreement. Organize the parade. That's what you said."

Matt narrowed his eyes. "Job's not finished until the registration fees are delivered. Right? Besides, you texted me this morning to have me email the list of sponsors over so the clubs could begin planning. That should have fallen under your responsibilities. This is a nice compromise. Plus, I want to get a new-car-smell fix."

She sighed as Betty came over and jumped on the lounger. "Fine. I do want to drive and drive and drive now that I can. It's a deal." She scratched Betty's ears and waited for the dog to sit.

"You're in her usual spot," Matt said as he shifted over. "Lie down here, Betty."

The look his own dog gave him told him he was wrong, wrong, wrong.

So Brooke stood and they both watched Betty turn around and curl herself into an impossibly small ball with her head on his ankle.

Her happy sigh tickled Brooke. "She's a simple dog. Give her everything she wants and she's content."

Matt was ready to agree when Coco sat next to Brooke and opened her mouth in a silent bark.

"I've been trained pretty well, too." She lifted Coco up onto the lounger. It took Coco three different tries, but she finally settled along Matt's leg with her nose buried under Betty's ear.

"I guess I live here now," Matt said slowly. He shifted to the right as far as he could. "There's room for you right here if you perch carefully."

Brooke crossed her arms over her chest. "I should load my dog up and head home. You can go back to sleep. You definitely need it."

That reminded Matt that he wanted to talk with her about his mother and the discussion they'd had over dinner the night before. He patted the lounger again.

"We need to talk about something serious. Sit." Matt held her stare as he watched her weigh her options.

Finally, she huffed a sigh. "Do you know what the weight limit of this piece of furniture is?" Both of them held their breath as she settled into the spot framed by dogs.

"We could probably get one more dog up here, but that's it," Matt muttered as he wiggled his toes to keep his foot from falling asleep.

Her quiet laughter filled him with so much peace.

That confused him.

Then he realized it made perfect sense. Betty was here. Brooke was here. Even Coco was a warm weight next to him. He had no worries in that moment.

"My mother decided she needed to find out about my workday last night at dinner." Matt turned his head to study her face. She was staring up at the night sky. It was growing dark enough that the stars were peeking out. "Do you know anything about that?"

Brooke immediately shook her head. "I know it's a large group, but I wasn't at dinner with you last night. How would I know anything about your conversation?" Then she very obviously didn't look at him.

So he waited and memorized the lines of her profile—the way the light landed on her cheeks, shadowed the curves of her lips.

Finally, she sighed. "She doesn't understand how hard you work. None of your family does, do they? You talked about working to fit in with this new family as a kid, Matt, and I..." She shrugged. "I understand that, the way you try to make them all think everything is okay with you. I do that. When my mom died, everyone in my family was destroyed. As the youngest,

I guess... I don't know. Watching them reassemble themselves piece by piece made me determined to do the same, but it was so hard. Pretending was the only way I could do it. Sarah was strong. Jordan was tough. In the beginning, I clung to them because my dad faded away. The three of us were all we had until Sadie arrived. I guess we were all pretending to be okay. Eventually, I learned how to do it even better than Sarah and Jordan." She put one hand over her stomach, and her elbow rested against his side and brushed his arm. "It's too hard, Matt. You shouldn't do it anymore. They're your family. They should be the first ones who know when you're in trouble."

This time she turned to face him.

This close, he could see faint freckles across her nose and the way her blue eyes reflected the concern that had prompted her to speak on his behalf to his mother, of all people.

"Are you going to take your own advice?" he asked softly.

The way her eyebrows immediately shot up made him chuckle. "I thought so. It's easy to tell me to bare all to my family, but your situation is totally different, right?"

Brooke sniffed. Her mouth opened and closed. "Therapy is outside the scope of our agreement, too." Her lips crimped in a prim line.

Matt tangled his fingers through hers. "You started it, didn't you? My mother? Remember that?"

Brooke closed her eyes. "I just… Sometimes I have this urge to defend people. I struggle to stand up for myself, but I will battle for others who are being ignored or taken advantage of or…" She sighed. "If anyone is being treated unfairly. It kicked in when your mother started the whole 'baby' thing, like you're spoiled." Then she covered her heart with her hand. "Not that there is anything wrong with being spoiled. I am spoiled. I also work hard, not as hard as you do, but I'm a good person."

"Of course you are," Matt replied as he brushed his free hand over her arm and ignored the twinge in his side.

"I guess if we want them to know us," Brooke said slowly, as if she hated where the sentence was going, "we're going to have to show them. All of it. Even the messy parts."

Matt sighed. "Like a big ugly bruise from a kick that never should have landed."

"Yeah," Brooke agreed, "and ugly, snotty tears when the help you were afraid to ask for shows up to save the day."

"Did either one of them hold it against you?" Matt asked. "Not a single person in my family lectured me for daydreaming when I should have been moving out of Rabbit's way. Almost like they've been caught a time or two themselves and understand how it happens to all of us." He'd never intended to keep his injury or his long days from his family. In his mind, both things were just the way it was, not worth complaining about.

His mother's reaction at dinner suggested she did not feel the same way.

Brooke's dramatic groan had both dogs concerned but only for a moment. "Fine. If you want to be reasonable, I guess our older siblings aren't perfect and can manage to love us even when we don't have everything under control. Gosh."

He was amused by her tone and delighted at the way she tugged his hand closer to rest against her stomach. The shadows drew closer around them.

"New deal—you remind me that my sisters can handle the messy truth about me, and I'll remind you that your family loves you too much to go away." Brooke turned her head to stare at him as she waited for his answer.

"Fair." Matt held on to her hand because there was one more item of business to discuss. "But I have another addition to the scope of our festival agreement—the auditions for the talent show."

She smiled, a confused frown wrinkling her brow. "You need me to organize those, too?"

"Yes…and help me judge." Matt held her hand when she tried to tug it free. "Please? I will beg. Please. I am an injured man."

Brooke groaned again, less theatrically this time. "I don't know anything about music, Matt! You need me to make calls and set up files or whatever, sure, but how can I help with auditions?"

He tipped his head closer. "It's simple. We pick the top twelve and we kindly ask the remaining people to sign up for auditions next year. You had such good suggestions for organizing the parade for next year. Imagine what you can do with the talent show. I know a spreadsheet will be required. You love those, right?"

"I expected you to push the limits of our agreement, Matt Armstrong." One side of Brooke's mouth curled up. "And I knew you would be hard to say no to, so count me in. After we deliver the check to the high school, let's make a plan for the auditions."

The relief that settled over Matt was sweet.

Another man might have wondered how much of it had to do with having another reason to spend time with Brooke, but not Matt.

He was aware that he was acting unlike himself in that moment. He usually kept things light. Future plans were few and far between. Tonight, though, he was relieved to have a built-in excuse to see her.

And it was easy to imagine finding some other reason, something beyond Western Days, to keep her close when the festival was finally over.

"You are as dangerous as everyone warned me, but for a completely different reason," Brooke said softly.

"Yeah?" Matt asked. He wasn't certain he wanted the details.

She nodded. "I was advised to prepare myself to be snared by your handsome face."

He frowned. "I'm not handsome?"

The dramatic way she rolled her eyes startled a deep laugh from him. Both dogs shot him dirty looks before settling back in to numb every muscle in his leg.

"The part of you that's more trouble than your face is your heart. It's good. It makes other people want to be good, too." Brooke poked his chest. "That is a problem with your whole family, you know."

He wrapped his hand around her finger. "Now I know you're flirting with me. Compliments? I'm helpless in the face of compliments."

They smiled at each other as the moment drew out, and Matt studied her eyes as he said, "This moment needs a kiss, doesn't it?"

Her small nod was the agreement he desperately wanted so he pressed his lips to hers.

When she returned the kiss, parting her lips

to draw him closer as her fingers sifted through his hair, Matt felt the effect in every muscle. He was falling but steady and connected to Brooke.

When Brooke ended the kiss, Matt was close enough to watch the worry return to her eyes.

They needed space to figure out where they went next, so he smoothed the skin on her forehead with his thumb.

"If you'll remove these dogs weighing me down, I'll walk you out to your new car." He smiled as she blinked once, twice, breaking the spell. Watching Brooke's face transition back to the composed, confident expression she normally favored bothered him. He liked seeing the real Brooke.

That softness warned him that she was vulnerable here.

Her heart was involved. He had to take care not to break it.

Here, in the quiet of his patio and the peaceful pile of dogs and person on the lounger, it was simple for him to ask for a kiss; that was what he wanted.

But if her heart was involved, he had to reflect on more than this moment.

His relationships were always focused on the present.

With Brooke, he couldn't ignore the future.

CHAPTER TEN

BROOKE WAS STILL trying to figure out how she'd gone from a friendly shared pizza to a kiss as she waited for breakfast the next morning. The kitchen was the most spacious part of Sadie's apartment built on the back of the Majestic. Her great-aunt had always wanted company while she cooked. Sadie would not be impressed by the caliber of meals coming out of it lately, though.

None of her great-nieces had gotten Sadie's love of cooking. Brooke propped her elbows on the island and rested her chin in both hands while Sarah poured coffee into three mugs. Her oldest sister was the only Hearst to have reached a fully alert status so far. A few boxes of cereal, a gallon of milk and a carafe of juice waited on the small island while Brooke and Jordan sat silently at either end. When a mug landed in front of her, the warm and delicious scent hitting her at close range, Brooke's eyes opened fully.

And after the first sip, her brain engaged.

"Ah, there she is," Sarah murmured. "Jordan

needs the full application of caffeine and the daily recommended dose of sugar from her favorite cereal before she switches on."

"Good morning," Brooke said as she poured the healthier whole-grain cereal in her bowl and topped it with milk. Then, after a slight hesitation, she topped it off with a healthy serving of Jordan's preferred sugar bomb. Sarah watched her closely as Brooke tested the first bite of her new concoction. It wasn't terrible.

"Breakfast food innovation. I never thought I'd see it." Sarah took her seat in the middle. "Should I be concerned about Jordan's influence on you?"

Brooke huffed out a laugh. "Definitely, but it's too late to start now." She took another bite. "I'm trying to find what I like. Is it a sporty convertible or an SUV? Nope. Luxury wagon. What about healthy, cholesterol-lowering, low-excitement cereal versus delicious pebbles of pure sugar with little nutritional value?" She took another bite. "This compromise needs some work." It wasn't bad but it also wasn't good.

Sarah nodded as she ate her cereal. "You had a big day yesterday. What is your plan today? How is the parade coming along?"

Brooke chewed slowly as she considered how much detail her sisters needed.

Her first instinct was to keep everything on

a strict need-to-know basis. Hit the high points and toss the conversational hot potato back in Sarah's lap.

"Matt and I are going to deliver the sponsorship checks out to the high school this morning. He wanted to go for a ride in my new car. Something about new car smell." Brooke sipped her coffee as she replayed their conversation. All true.

But there had been so much more. Sarah seemed to understand that because she picked up her own coffee and waited.

Brooke sighed and added, "And now I have to help with the auditions for the talent show."

"You didn't want to be dragged under by another man's delegated tasks," Jordan said as she poured milk onto her cereal. "How did Matt manage to talk you into another job for Western Days?"

Sarah grinned at Brooke. They were both amused at how Jordan literally flipped a switch from zombie to clear, functioning adult from one second to the next. She didn't do anything gradually.

"He asked." Brooke shrugged. "He's got a lot going on right now, so I couldn't say no."

When both of her sisters leaned toward her as if they needed to know a lot more, Brooke sighed again. "Do you want me to say you were right and I was wrong? Is that what's missing here?"

Jordan pursed her lips as if she was considering the suggestion, but Sarah immediately shook her head. "Nope. We need details. That's all."

One of the benefits of living so far away from Sarah and Jordan had been how much easier it had been to wriggle off their hooks when they wanted information. Sitting elbow to elbow like this, refusing to share, seemed so silly. They had already seen her at her lowest, crying in an empty house and liberating her pregnant dog.

"I stopped by his office last night to deliver the last check and finish my assignment." She wasn't going to mention the pizza that never made it to the Majestic, was she? Jordan might never forgive her. "We talked about his day— his very long, hard day. Did you know he'd been kicked by one of the rescue horses the day before? I ran into him that night and he didn't say a word about it."

Sarah rested her elbow on the counter. "And?"

Brooke held her spoon up and watched milk drip back into her bowl. Everything was very casual here. Nothing exciting. "He asked me to help judge the auditions because he might need a second opinion on who made it to the show, so I agreed." The end. That was all the information they needed.

She finished her mixed-up cereal, hyperaware that there was no conversation covering the scrape of her spoon on the bowl or the obnoxious slurp of her coffee that would normally provoke a strong, loud reaction from Jordan so she did it on purpose sometimes.

"You're doing that to distract me from this conversation, aren't you?" Jordan asked. She wagged a finger. "What's the rest of it? What are you hiding, Brooke Nicole Hearst?"

"When Coco's puppies come, I'll need his help. This is an exchange, not a delegation." Brooke watched both of her sisters nod.

"And?" Sarah prodded.

Fighting the sensation of being pinned in place, Brooke blurted out, "I like him." She rolled her eyes as both of her sisters overreacted. Sarah immediately gripped her arm as her mouth dropped open and Jordan pretended to fall off her stool. "Oh, please, you both know he's charming. You warned me about falling for him, remember?"

As long as they'd been in Prospect, Sarah and Jordan had dropped tidbits about Matt's dating history and the Matt Armstrong Effect on women. Seeing him at work, talking to Coco and Betty, leaping into action to help someone who needed him…that was the rest of the Matt picture. None of that had made it into the descriptions beforehand.

"His face is mesmerizing until you build up a tolerance," Jordan agreed, "but warning you not to fall for him doesn't sound like me at all."

"If I'm recalling correctly, all we asked you to do was help him with the parade. Other Western Days assistance is a bonus and we definitely appreciate that, but there was never a hint of romance coming from us." Sarah crossed her legs and leaned back. "In fact, you gave us a brilliant demonstration of your immunity to his appeal at the meeting. His good looks didn't even slow you down."

Brooke wanted to explain to her sisters that he was so much more than handsome, but she didn't want to encourage them. She had already fumbled her answers here, introducing the idea of "falling."

How did she escape this interrogation with the biggest confession still a secret? Surely she'd shared enough to extricate herself from breakfast.

Besides, she wasn't sure how she felt about the kiss at this point. Did she want to repeat it to see what happened next?

Or should she treat it like an odd mistake that had more to do with timing and the satisfaction of a good day than the man she'd been snuggled up to?

And what did Matt think about that kiss? They'd both retreated so quickly the night before that she couldn't make a solid guess on whether his immediate judgment had been satisfaction or regret.

Then she realized there was the potential that Matt might say something to his brothers about her.

Possibly even about kissing her?

Did brothers share details like that the way sisters did?

But if they did and Wes or Clay happened to say something to Sarah or Jordan…

The fallout when her sisters heard it from someone else would be over-the-top.

"He kissed me," Brooke blurted out before covering her mouth with both hands. "I kissed him? There was kissing." Over pizza. But there still wasn't a good reason to add that detail as far as she could see.

The stunned silence in the air would have been amusing if her confession hadn't been the cause.

Sarah cleared her throat, but before she could speak, Brooke slipped off the stool to pace. Movement seemed important at this moment. "But it hasn't even been a full year since my divorce was finalized. I don't live in Prospect. He's a ladies' man with more ex-girlfriends than he knows what to do with. If we tried anything and it didn't work out, you would have to defend me, and his brothers would be on his side and then all this matrimony and happily-ever-after that you both had planned might implode." She stopped her third round of the kitchen island. "If you had let me say no when I wanted to say no, none of us would be here, teetering on the edge of disaster, our only lifelines my willpower and good sense. Do you know how weak my will-power and good sense are?"

As Brooke reversed her pacing direction, she tried to comfort herself that she was getting in touch with her emotions regarding Matt and the kiss.

Even if they were scary and her sisters were going to get the wrong idea.

"Distance. That's the answer. I'll step back, give the—" she waved her hands vaguely as she tried to find a better word than *attraction* "—stuff between us space to evaporate."

"After you take him for a ride in your new car to the high school to finish up the one thing we asked you to help him with. And before you assist with the auditions that you agreed to all on your own," Jordan said before holding up a finger. "And delivering your precious dog's puppies and helping you find them good homes." Then her lips curved in a fake smile. "Sure. The *stuff* between you will have plenty of space to evaporate."

Sarah tilted her head to the side. "I hear you outlining the worst that could happen. The Hearsts and Armstrongs will go Shakespearean and a feud worthy of the Capulets and Montagues will break out." She turned to Jordan. "Romeo. Juliet. Are you following me?"

Brooke giggled at her oldest sister and the way Jordan scowled at her. "And this is where you ask me the Sadie question, right?" She huffed out a breath. "What's the best that could happen?"

Sarah's eyes twinkled as she said, "We already know the best, Brooke." She slung her arm over Jordan's shoulders. "We're living it."

Brooke crossed her arms over her chest as she studied them, the cramped apartment they were sharing, the stacks of things here and there for Western Days, and realized that absolutely none of it fit her definition of a dream life. There was no way Sarah or Jordan could have imagined what would happen when they returned to Prospect.

There was also no way to argue that they both were in the right place at the right time.

Seeing them with the cowboys who'd come into their lives convinced her that Sarah was right.

But Wes and Clay weren't Matt.

And she wasn't either one of her sisters.

There was no guarantee that she and Matt could navigate all the pitfalls and come out on the side of happily-ever-after.

Jordan said, "Remember that you don't have to make a life-or-death decision today. What you *will* have to do is figure out how to be around Matt with all this…stuff between you. Parade. Auditions. Puppies. Life as in-laws forever and ever. The only way to do that is day by day."

Sarah whistled weakly. "That is some Sadie wisdom right there. I'm impressed. I don't get to say this often, but Jordan's right." Jordan's grunt when Sarah squeezed her tightly amused them all. "You better head on into town and figure out what to do today."

Sighing made her feel marginally better and braver.

Brooke nodded. "It is good advice. I'll load up Coco, and we'll get on with this day. Talking with Matt should clear up what the kiss meant. Right? If he thought it was a mistake or, worse, a laugh, my willpower and good sense will grow in strength."

Both of her sisters nodded.

"Before you go," Jordan said slowly, "have you recently become aware of a sweet scent in this general area?" She waved her arms to indicate Sadie's apartment or the whole Majestic.

"Vanilla. Like sugar cookies are in the oven but there is absolutely no one baking?"

The legend of Sadie's "ghost" had started with Sarah's first visit, when the lodge was a dusty wreck. The inexplicable vanilla scent had appeared now and then to different people inside the lodge.

Those people had managed to find the kind of love everyone dreams of.

The official line of the Hearst sisters was that there is no such thing as ghosts.

Hoping that Sadie Hearst had somehow found a way to haunt the three of them in order to matchmake them from the Beyond was illogical.

Their great-aunt had done her best to raise three level-headed, practical women who were too smart to fall for a good story.

But Brooke inhaled deeply.

Because having Sadie nearby when she was confused and lost would have been a blessing.

"I smell coffee. No vanilla." Pasting a smile on was harder than she'd expected.

Brooke reminded herself that was illogical, too. She wasn't dreaming of love.

But the glance her sisters exchanged caused a twinge of pain in Brooke's chest. It didn't feel good to be on the outside, to miss an experience they shared, but what could any of them do about that?

"Okay, good talk, sisters. My head is on straight now and I am ready to tackle this day." Brooke scooped up the breakfast bowls and moved to the sink to wash them before Sarah could drop broad hints that she and Jordan clean up.

Whatever sneaky glances they shared behind her back…

Well, she couldn't see them so they wouldn't bother her.

Sarah called goodbye as she left to go into the museum, and Jordan waved on her way to meet with Rafa about the lodge's restaurant supply order.

After Brooke finished straightening the kitchen, she loaded Coco in her basket and moved toward the door. Before she stepped outside, she inhaled slowly again, but Sadie's ghost was still absent. The disappointment that settled over her shoulders was silly, but that didn't make it any easier to shake.

CHAPTER ELEVEN

MATT HAD EXPECTED there to be some awkwardness between Brooke and him when he climbed into her car, but it had taken an unexpected form. Instead of reserved quiet or painful politeness, Brooke had decided to go for determined cheerfulness and small talk. It was almost unsettling.

But it was also a strong hint as to her own feelings about the kiss and what it did to their relationship.

Apparently, for her, it changed everything, even her personality.

"Thank you for taking a look at Coco to make sure she's progressing well. I was afraid to leave her alone out at the lodge, since Jordan always has a million different tasks going on at once. It's a good thing Coco and Betty are the best of friends. I guess they have to be to share Betty's comfy dog bed the way they do. Coco is a horrible bed hog. Did you see the way Coco turned up her nose at the treat I offered her? Then she begrudgingly accepted it, as if she knew it was the best she could expect. I hope I can find something she likes from Homestead Market's dog food aisle," Brooke said.

Matt considered reminding her that he stocked food and treats and could special order if she couldn't find any other way to satisfy Coco's elevated taste buds, but Brooke tightened her hands on the steering wheel so hard that it squeaked.

"I am thrilled to have such a beautiful day to show off what my new baby can do," she said as she patted the sleek dashboard. "You'll have to let me take it out of town to get up some speed." Her bright smile was beautiful but he noticed her eyes never met his directly. "Unless you're like Sarah and will complain the whole time that I drive too fast."

He shook his head, amused at how she filled in any silent space between them with a solid stream of words. "No, ma'am. My philosophy is that the driver sets the speed and the radio station. Besides, I've been known to exceed the speed limit on a straight stretch now and again." Any time Grant had to ride with him, his brother spent most of the trip gripping the seat, the seat belt or the handle over the window and muttering under his breath about dying. "This car is smooth around curves, for sure."

She offered him her hand for a high five. Was that where they were? High-fiving buddies?

If Brooke had faced him, she'd see an amused smile as he returned her gesture.

This jittery uncertainty in her was so unexpected. It was sweet and human and so adorable that all he wanted to do was kiss her again.

"Prospect School District, home of the Wildcats," Brooke said as she took one of the visitor spots in front of the high school. She picked up the file she'd shoved beside her seat when he had slid in the passenger side before asking, "Are there any teachers here that I can ask for embarrassing stories about Matt Armstrong?"

Then she marched with determination toward the building, careful to keep a step or two ahead of him.

He huffed out a laugh. "That is a question I should have considered before this moment, isn't it?"

Brooke didn't glance in his direction, but her steps slowed as they reached the doors to the building. Matt brushed her hand off the door handle to pull it open for her.

She breezed through the open door ahead of him, the skirt of her dress fluttering behind her. Her preference for pretty dresses wasn't strictly Prospect's style, at least not every day, but he was beginning to enjoy it.

Brooke said, "I'm taking that as a yes, so I'll

keep my eyes and ears open to get the good gossip."

Matt was content to follow behind her as she walked into the front office and told Sheila Bloom that they were here to meet the principal. They had a meeting at ten o'clock.

"Well, of course you do, Brooke." Sheila stood, although her head barely cleared the top of the high counter, and waved Matt forward. He bent over the counter so Sheila could press a kiss to his cheek. Rubbing off the lipstick she deposited took a minute. "Is it okay if I call you Brooke? We didn't get a chance to talk at the Western Days planning meeting, but I'm sure we're going to be good friends." She propped her hands on her hips. "I mean, any friend of Matt's is bound to be good people, you know?"

Was Brooke his friend? Matt waited to see how she answered Sheila's question, amused at the way Sheila bounced up and down. She had been head cheerleader their senior year and still had the energy and brilliant smile decades later.

"Of course you can call me Brooke," Brooke said as she leaned against the counter next to Sheila's nameplate. "All I need is one embarrassing story about my friend Matt here, and it will be like we've known each other for years, Sheila."

The way Sheila's eyes lit up made Matt nervous. They had dated when they were sopho-mores…maybe? He wasn't sure of the timeframe, but he was almost certain she'd been the one to end things and they'd been friends since. How bad could her stories be?

Before Sheila could launch into whatever tid-bit had excited her, Brad McHenry stepped out of his office. "Matt, Brooke, I've got some stu-dents here who are ready to get started on these floats."

Sheila pointed at Brooke. "I owe you a story. Next time we meet, remind me that I want to tell you about how Matt kissed me the first time. Outside the boys' bathroom, of all places!"

Matt managed to swallow his groan but he did not miss the way Brooke's lips twitched as she nodded at Sheila. Then she walked around the high counter to shake hands with Brad.

"I like her," Sheila mouthed at him as she pointed at Brooke. "Don't mess this up," she added with a hiss before squeezing his arm. Was that encouragement? For what, exactly?

Once he entered the principal's office, he found a small collection of students arranged around the table in the corner.

"The kids wanted to make sure they got a chance to say thank-you for including them in this year's parade preparations. This is a big fundraising opportunity that they wouldn't get otherwise," Brad McHenry said, nodding encouragingly at the group. Since Matt's nephew Damon was crammed into the corner and he hadn't heard a word about this gathering in advance, Matt decided this was a spontaneous occasion.

Were any of them prepared to speak?

When Brooke turned to him, eyebrows raised, which he read as a *do something* signal, Matt held up his hand. "We should be the ones thanking you. You all know how much the town depends on Western Days, and the parade has been one of the main attractions ever since the first festival. I apologize that you are getting a late start this year and hope it doesn't cause you too much trouble." He squeezed Brooke's shoulder. "We're so lucky to have had Brooke take charge. She's hustled to gather all the sponsorship checks, along with the materials fees, so all the clubs are in business." He stepped back and waved Brooke forward. She'd done all the important work; it made sense that she should take charge here as well.

She hesitated but eventually smiled. "All we need to do is finalize which clubs will be taking which floats. I have the list of requests here. If it's okay, we'll run down it quickly. If we have multiple requests for a club, you can choose and then we'll make sure everyone has an assignment."

He was impressed with how businesslike the whole process was with Brooke taking the lead.

When it was crystal clear that no one needed his input, he moved back out to the office. Watching Brooke with a goofy grin on his face would get him in trouble sooner or later, so it made sense to find another way to occupy his time. His plan had been to rest his still-sore hip in one of the almost-comfortable chairs out front, but Sheila popped out from behind the filing cabinet she'd been working at.

"Matt," she said excitedly as she squeezed his arm again. He didn't jump but it was close.

"Talk to me about Brooke." She hopped in excited little motions. He guessed she was trying to keep their conversation confidential, but Sheila's whispers were worthy of the stage. There was no way Brooke could miss them if conversation slowed inside the principal's office.

Matt motioned to the hallway and Sheila hurried outside.

"We're working together on Western Days. Brooke has been a huge help. That's all there is to tell." Because he most certainly would not mention the kiss to Sheila before he talked to Brooke.

Sheila frowned as if she was disappointed in him. "But why?"

Matt tipped his hat back as he considered the question. "I was about to mess it up?"

She bent her head down toward her chest as if his obtuseness was completely wearing her out.

"You've got to be swimming in the shallowest dating pool around, buddy." Sheila held up her hand to wave the large diamond that winked in the weak sunlight streaming in through the high windows. "Even the fishies you tossed back have been well and truly caught. And that—" Sheila motioned broadly with her head toward the office "—is a winning catch in there. Please tell me you aren't still in your love-'em-and-leave-'em era. You aren't sixteen anymore."

Before he could figure out how to address anything Sheila had said, Brad and Brooke stepped out into the hallway. "It's a pleasure, Brooke. Next year, we'll get a representative from the high school to take over the administrative details of the parade under my supervision. Having them attend the planning meetings earlier in the year should help us schedule the process better in advance, too. The student council president would be our best bet, but I'll talk to the students involved to see if they have other suggestions. Setting up a class project to build the website to gather the required information from interested sponsors and funds in advance of next year's festival is brilliant."

Matt crossed his arms over his chest as he watched Brooke tip her chin up. She was proud of herself.

She should be. It was a great solution.

Why hadn't she run it by him in the first place? There wasn't much he could do to improve it, but delegating responsibility seemed to be a huge step outside the scope of work she'd agreed to.

Why did that bother him? Since he'd assumed he'd have to run the festival until the next generation stepped up, he owed her for removing one of his responsibilities, didn't he? For some reason, he wasn't feeling much gratitude at this point.

"Matt, do you still want to use the auditorium stage for auditions? I'll have someone there to help with the sound system and lighting on Saturday afternoon." Brad pointed at him as he waited for the affirmative.

When Brooke didn't immediately answer or offer a creative solution to get him out of that as well, Matt nodded. "Yep, that will great."

Brad nodded. "Let me put in a good word for my daughter's dance class before you go. She's been working on her hip-hop moves."

"Excellent," Matt said as he tried to remember how old Brad's daughter might be. He thought she was young, so...

"Yeah, it's something to watch five-year-olds freestyle." Brad pursed his lips. "They have a grip on the *free* part, but they're still learning the *style* of it all, you know? They've been working on a routine called the Electric Cowboy. There are glow sticks and their shoes are neon yellow."

Matt caught Brooke's eye. He was sure they both agreed that this act needed to be included in the talent show, no matter what.

He was happy to have her support, even if he was struggling to accept how far she'd taken it that morning.

"Can't wait to see it," Brooke murmured.

"Give Brooke a tour around the school," Sheila said as she urged him closer. "Relive some of your glory days, and be sure to stop in front of the trophy case, okay?"

Matt waited for Brad to tell them they'd need an escort if they were planning to stay on the school grounds, but Sheila hustled the principal back inside the administration office and closed the door.

"Glory days, huh? Is the trophy case somewhere near the boys' bathroom?" Brooke asked as she blinked innocently at him.

"How did you know?" Matt waved grandly with his left arm. "I'll give you a quick tour and make sure you visit the spot of that romantic first kiss. Then you and Sheila will be able to get into the nitty gritty."

Brooke's lips were twitching as they wandered down the hall.

As they walked, he wondered if he was going to raise his concerns about her taking charge. Things were weird enough between them. Maybe it was better to let that water flow right under the bridge?

Then he remembered their promises to each other to be more real.

"Thanks for letting me answer Brad's question about auditions, but if you want to assume control over those as well, I will gratefully step back," he said and tried to add a teasing smile.

Then he realized pretending to be joking about it was all wrong.

Brooke frowned. "What do you mean?"

Matt rubbed his forehead and regretted opening this conversational door. "Setting up a high school representative. Giving them duties for next year? Unless you've changed your mind recently, you won't be here to see it happen."

Brooke blinked as she walked beside him. "The kids asked about attending next year's planning meetings in the fall." She covered her heart. "I thought that might be too much pressure on you, so we decided on a single representative instead. Since it's clear they're worried about how late they're starting this year, I mentioned your plans to streamline as much as you could, so the principal took that and ran with it... right to the online sign-up and payment system. We brainstormed. If you had stayed in the room, you could have taken the lead."

Her patient smile made it evident that she was reading his irritation loud and clear.

Just as he was picking up on hers.

"I love the ideas, both of them," he said with a sigh.

She nodded. "Your nephew is a smart kid. The online form was his excited suggestion."

"Of course it was. Damon is always planning ahead. I should take a page from his book, I guess." He bumped her shoulder as an awkward apology for being weird and relaxed when she snorted her agreement.

The conflict had been small, but navigating it with Brooke felt big. Neither one of them had walked away to avoid the tension.

What would she have said if he'd gone for full honesty? If he'd confessed that he enjoyed working with her and didn't want to consider next year without her, even if she was doing her best to save him from his own workload with great solutions?

Matt pointed out a few classes as they traveled through the school; some were still being taught by the same teachers who probably wished they'd retired years ago. They peeked through the windows at the cafeteria and he pointed out the gym, a place he'd only visited when required for pep rallies and physical education. When they made it to the trophy case, Matt understood why Sheila made a special note to tell him to bring Brooke here. There was a photo inside of the year Grant had won the State High School Rodeo Association's Best All-Around trophy. Every member of the Prospect Rodeo Club had been gathered around Grant, including Matt.

"Oh, you were so young!" Brooke immediately bent closer to study the picture. "All of you, but especially you."

"And handsome. Don't forget that part. Sheila was extremely impressed by my rugged good looks." Matt leaned closer. "But it looks like I was still growing into my hat, doesn't it?" The tips of his ears had been completely swallowed by the black hat he was wearing in the photo.

"Ah," Brooke said as she turned slowly to observe the hallway. The bathroom was still exactly where it had been. "She was overcome by your cowboy ways right here. Your first kiss happened here in front of this trophy case. Was she your girlfriend?"

Matt pursed his lips. "Do people still remember their high school puppy love at my age?"

She already had this idea about all his "fans." Would a stolen high school kiss be better than a story about a high school girlfriend? He honestly wasn't sure which way to go here.

"So that's a yes, then." Brooke smiled. "And yeah, most people do, but they might not have had the sheer number of faces to keep straight that you do."

She slowly moved farther along the trophy case, scanning as she went. It was tempting to watch her as she cataloged everything.

"Have Sarah and Jordan been telling stories about me? Somehow you've got this impression that I have so many girlfriends, and yet, I've been single since you've known me." Mainly because he was worn out from working dawn to dusk. Sheila was absolutely correct about the shallowness of Prospect's dating pool. His best options for meeting new people had been the board meetings for the rescues he served on in Denver and Colorado Springs, but it had been a couple of months since his attendance had been required.

"Yes, you have been fully single for at least the *whole week* I've been in Prospect," Brooke said dryly, "but I saw the ladies waving at you at the Western Days meeting. Now Sheila. And your face…" She waved a finger. "And overall appeal should mean lots of romance."

"My face and overall appeal…" Matt pursed his lips, uncertain whether she was giving him a true compliment or if he was going to have to take it backhanded if he wanted it. "Does that mean you'd say yes if I asked you to dinner at the Ace High?"

She stopped and faced him. "If I did, the whole town would spontaneously combust, wouldn't it? I expect Sheila already has a plan of who she'll call first if she gets any good information."

Matt inched closer to Brooke as he tried to be logical about where they were. It was definitely not the most romantic location for a second kiss with her.

He hadn't decided how he felt about the first kiss, but her nerves had been clear on the drive here.

"Combust?" Matt tipped his hat back as he considered his response. She understood Prospect well enough that there was no sense in pretending there was any other option. "We will make the nonexistent front-page news for a minute, but it always blows over."

"What about a hometown hero getting involved with a new-in-town, recently divorced heiress? When we break up, will my neighbors run me out of Prospect for breaking the heart of one of the Armstrong brothers?" Brooke asked. "Because we most likely will break up. That's how almost all relationships go, even the ones you want to last forever." Her grimace was cute, even if he understood she was trying to keep things light between them. Nothing about her divorce was light to Brooke. "Will your family hate me for hurting you?"

Matt pursed his lips. "It's interesting that you're the one breaking up with me in your scenario. That doesn't happen all that often." Mainly because he always made it clear going in that there was a time limit to any new relationship. When it got too serious, time was up.

But he understood that he and Brooke had already stepped past that boundary.

"Oh, you're a heartbreaker. You're going to make me sad. So you'll be on the run from Jordan for the rest of your life. That's what you're saying? My advice is to swallow the dinner invitation because there's not far enough to run from my big sister if she's after you." Brooke held her hand out. "Let's save your life now and be friends."

Her grin told him she was teasing, but he knew there was some truth under all of the rest. She had considered what might be between them and the consequences if and when they said goodbye.

"Sheila was a girlfriend. So were the two ladies at the Western Days meeting and a few others you've met but don't know too well yet." Matt took her hand in his and tangled their fingers together. "One thing they have in common? They don't hate me. We don't hate each other. We live in a small, small town and still manage friendly hellos day in and day out."

Matt wasn't sure when he'd decided that it was important to find out what might be between him and Brooke, but presenting an argument in favor of whatever the next step between them might be was coming easily.

As if it was meant to be.

His heart beat as if he was standing on the edge of a long fall, but her smile anchored him in place. He couldn't step back.

"I'm going to have to take your word that we can do this without ending in a bitter war that only comes to a close with Jordan crawling across the floor with bacon in her pocket," Brooke drawled.

Matt brushed hair off her cheek. "We may have to convince her to re-create that, but it doesn't have to get that serious between us. We'll take our time, okay? And I promise to never hunt for ways to hurt you like that. There will be no need to rescue Coco from my clutches if this ends." It was almost impossible to imagine being angry enough to treat anyone the way Brooke's ex had her. Even if it wasn't love, Matt liked Brooke too much for that.

"*If* this ends, huh?" She pursed her lips as if he'd revealed something important to her. Maybe he had.

She pointed with her chin. "There must be something about this bathroom."

"Listen, I firmly believe if it ain't broke, don't fix it." Matt kissed her then, their smiles fading. Brooke settled into his arms, and he could imagine a lifetime of holding her against him like this.

In more private and much more inspiring places than the high school hallway between the bathroom and the trophy case.

When they walked out of the school holding hands, Matt was relieved. The spring in his step irritated his bruised hip, so he settled into Brooke's passenger seat gratefully, but it had been a good day. The parade was back on track. Brooke's determined bright chatter had receded.

And they had figured out the next tiny step between them.

Neither one of them was sure where they were going, but they were going to kiss along the way, and that seemed like a happy compromise to him.

CHAPTER TWELVE

ON SATURDAY NIGHT, Brooke clapped as the last audition for the talent show ended and the performer took a bow. The whole process had taken almost three hours as twenty acts had tromped across the stage to perform. Now she definitely understood the value of limiting the number of performances at the Western Days show. No matter how talented the performers were, it was difficult to maintain the audience's focus for that length of time. Her backside had been sending increasingly alarmed messages to her brain for an hour or so. If she didn't stand up soon, her muscles might revolt.

She and Matt watched Ruby Dodge toss all the various objects she had been juggling into a large plastic bin to clear the stage. Her act had gotten off to a rocky start when she'd dropped two of the four eggs she'd started with. Luckily, they'd been hard-boiled eggs and Ruby had gotten more confident and reliable before she'd reached the glass bottles.

"Dropping the eggs was part of the routine, wasn't it?" Matt asked under his breath as he smiled at Ruby. Before her first trick, Ruby had introduced herself as Matt's physics teacher. She had been retired for years, but it was clear that Ruby was still a character. She was wearing a T-shirt that read "Boom! Here Comes the Science."

"I hope so?" Brooke smiled at him. "I'm guessing corralling kids like you enhanced her reflexes to the point that any missed toss now has to be on purpose."

His humph tickled her. He stood to address the rest of the crowd waiting in the seats of the auditorium behind them. "You're all welcome to wait, if you like, as Brooke and I compare our scores to build the final list of performers. This shouldn't take long. Otherwise, I'll get Mia to post it on the website."

Brooke turned to see if anyone budged from their seats. They didn't.

Her stomach growled, and Brooke hoped the scores were clear and that the performers who didn't make the cut weren't already hangry.

Matt met her stare as he turned back around to sit. "Guess I shouldn't be surprised that absolutely no one was hungry enough to head for dinner instead of waiting, but I'm starving."

"Giving them an option to wait was your first

mistake," she said as she patted his shoulder, "but you were right. This won't take long, thanks to this score sheet that some forward-thinking, clever woman created in a fit of organization and wisdom last night." She'd wavered back and forth on setting up the sheets they'd used to track the performances. After his pointed comments about assuming control of the high school visit, Brooke had wondered if she was stepping on his toes.

From there, she'd fallen down the rabbit hole of wondering if her resentment of the way her ex-husband had taken advantage of her help over and over was her own fault. Had she pushed her way into her role as his unpaid assistant and then blamed him for it?

Now she was glad she'd decided to go ahead and build the score sheets, but the doubt was still there in the back of her mind.

Matt bowed his head in her honor. "Every single word of that was true, of course. I thank you for your skill and expertise while I also pat myself on the back for recognizing your true powers. If anyone is the hero here, it's definitely me."

Brooke laughed as she totaled the last scores on her sheet and tried not to remember times in her past when her husband had managed to offer charming, teasing thanks that also conveyed his honest appreciation.

It wasn't easy to find examples, but they had also been privately issued and usually offered at her suggestion.

Working with Matt had been similar to helping Paul. She did a million different little things that slipped his notice, like the score sheet.

It was still impossible to forget that she was actually enjoying herself.

And Matt was sitting right next to her, doing the work instead of delegating.

That didn't settle the knot in her stomach, but it was a major difference.

Paul had slowly and surely taken all the credit until she'd lost herself, but Matt wasn't Paul.

And Brooke could learn from her past mistakes. These auditions were all up to Matt. She would follow his lead.

"All right. We've previously had between twelve and fifteen acts on the stage." He ran a finger down the list of performers as he ranked his scores from first to last. "Should we compare our winners?"

When he turned to face her, Brooke experienced one of those moments Sarah and Jordan had described to her, where Matt's good looks caught them unawares and they were helpless under his spell.

But he was used to a different reaction from her, so he said, "Hello? Paging Brooke? Are you already deciding what to have for dinner or something?"

Brooke blinked rapidly. "Don't be silly. We don't know what's on the menu at the Ace tonight." She stared hard at her score sheet. "Although I'm hoping for fried chicken. I say that every time I go to the Ace."

Matt tapped her sheet. "Who's your number one?"

"I have a tie. Reg McCall and Whit Dawson. He's got the showmanship, but her rendition of 'Wind Beneath My Wings' brought tears to my eyes," Brooke said immediately. There was no doubt in her mind about either of those performances. Both should definitely end up on the stage.

"Yeah. Those are the easy ones, I guess," he murmured as he squinted at the sheet.

"Did you forget your glasses?" Brooke asked with a smile.

Matt sniffed. "I only need them for reading." He waved the paper. "I wasn't expecting to be reading before you got out of your car, tote in hand, with half an office-supply closet inside."

"And you have so far borrowed a pen, the tape and two highlighters," Brooke replied. She clicked her stapler at him. "You're welcome."

"No spare pair of glasses, huh?" Matt shook his head sadly.

"I'll bring some next time. I didn't know you needed glasses," Brooke continued in a singsong, "and now the rest of Prospect will know unless you pay my exorbitant blackmail."

"No one will believe you," he said before winking at her. "You've got special access. I'll deny, deny, deny."

The way her brain fuzzed at that wink should have been annoying. It would be annoying as soon as she got some distance from its effect.

"Okay, instead of the top, let's move to the bottom. We need to cut at least six acts. Which ones should they be?" Matt asked and bent closer to his paper. "And how do we keep Mrs. Dodge in the mix? I can't cut her. She got me through a vulnerable period in my life." He added, "It was the one right before lunch."

His lips twitched as he waited for her response to his joke.

"Oh, boy," Brooke said, "you're lucky you have time to work on your routine before you have to stand up in front of a crowd." She bumped his shoulder with hers and forced herself to return to the matter at hand.

She'd gotten used to sitting in his office to work on the parade or transferring the list of sponsors to an electronic file that would make the next year so much easier. Matt had brought her coffee. He cuddled Coco as he checked the corgi's expanding middle and calmed Brooke's anxiety over her health. She got to meet a few neighbors who brought their pets in for an office visit on the afternoons he was in.

Their routine was easy. This fun banter between them tickled her soul every single time.

It made sense to be scared of that, didn't it?

Because she was.

Matt set his score sheet next to hers. "All right, we agreed on the bottom four, so that helps." He tapped her note beside the Hip-Hop Highlights. "And this is Brad McHenry's daughter, right? They were terrible but adorable. Every talent show needs that."

"They were part of this three-way tie on my sheet," Brooke said as she bent toward him to read his score, "but you ranked them higher."

"The cute points kicked in." He turned to face her. This close, he was devastating. "I'm a sucker for cute."

The way she gasped was irritating, but Brooke managed to lean slightly away to get her brain reengaged. "Luckily for you, most people are going to respect us going for the adorable choice out of our options. You have your list of cuts." Brooke highlighted the names so he could easily read them and pushed the sheet toward him.

"I don't suppose you want to handle this part?

What if I mangle the names?" Matt pointed at his eyes. "No glasses, remember?"

Brooke pretended to weigh the offer for a half second before firmly shaking her head. "I'm an assistant in this role. You should definitely handle all the official aspects."

He straightened his shoulders. "Okay. It's the right thing to do, but…" He closed his eyes. "I don't wanna."

Before Brooke could wrestle with her own urge to take the task off his shoulders, he squeezed her hand under the table. "Here we go."

Then she had the privilege of watching his face transform. One minute, he was the adorable, sweet man who made her laugh so easily, and when he turned around to face the crowd, he was the charming cowboy again. He thanked everyone, read the list, and made his sincere wish that everyone come back again next year before the performers clattered out of the auditorium.

He answered two questions from lingering contestants about pets, one dog and one rabbit, before he turned back around to take a seat with a heavy, relieved sigh.

"That wasn't so bad," he said before he rubbed his eyes with his hands.

"Because you're good with people. That's why." Brooke gathered up all the materials she'd tossed into her tote at the last minute and realized he was watching her.

"You are, too." He ran a hand over her back that immediately spread goose bumps along her arms. Dangerous.

"In a different way. Mine's efficient. People like to deal with efficiency. Yours is smoother." Brooke couldn't find the right word for his effect, but it was powerful. Magnetic. "Charismatic, maybe."

He grimaced. "That gives me televangelist or politician vibes."

"Well, I have experienced the politician persona up close and personal. You are worlds away from that, I promise." Matt and Paul were both easy in front of crowds, but only one of them had been a politician to the bone. She'd been through the heartache to learn how to tell the difference.

When Matt squeezed her arm, she turned to face him.

"Sorry about that. I wasn't thinking when I tossed that word out." His apology was easy to read in his eyes. That was something else that made Matt unique. Every emotion was there if she knew how to read it.

"It's okay. Sometimes I drag him into conversations he doesn't need to be in. At all. You are nothing alike," Brooke said as she propped her elbow on the armrest between them. "There was a discussion of dinner at one point, wasn't there?" She batted her eyelashes at him. "I could eat."

Matt clapped loudly. "I love it. A woman who knows what she wants. Let's go find out if there's fried chicken at the Ace High tonight."

It was natural to tangle her fingers through his as they stood and walked out of the high school. The student responsible for locking up the auditorium behind them was slouched outside the door. The kid didn't mutter a peep, but there was definitely a smirk on his lips.

As if he'd been waiting for the old folks to put on a show.

"Good thing you didn't kiss me by the trophy case again. We would have had an audience. Your nephews might be stuck in a loop like your Homecoming King loss for days," Brooke said as they paused next to his truck. She'd ridden with him from his office after leaving Coco to cuddle-nap with Betty.

Instead of agreeing, Matt traced his thumb along her jaw before slipping his hand around her neck to urge her closer. His kiss was slow, intense. It bordered on inappropriate for the high school parking lot and audience. When she inched back, she raised her eyebrows in question.

"I've learned a thing or two since I kissed a

girl in front of the boys' bathroom. I'm setting an example for the next generation here." He opened the truck door for her to slide in. "A sprinkle of teasing will be good for Damon and Micah. Builds character."

His slow grin as he closed the door sent that shivery sensation all the way to her abdomen again. She was in so much trouble.

But she was going to enjoy it until the end.

CHAPTER THIRTEEN

ON FRIDAY AFTERNOON, Matt heard Grant greet Brooke and Coco outside the Rocking A's barn. It had been almost a week since their dinner at the Ace High, where they had indeed been center stage even though it had been difficult to find anyone watching them. The weight of the stares had been heavy, but Brooke had been so easy to talk to that he hadn't minded a bit. Their conversation had run the gamut of dating topics: movies, books, her favorite memories of life in New York, his funniest animal stories.

He'd been in the same spot across from a beautiful woman a hundred different times, but he had to admit something about this time and this woman was new.

The fact that he wasn't brainstorming ways to back out of seeing her again while also keeping her as a friend convinced him he was in unknown territory.

During the week, they'd only managed to squeeze in brief visits when she brought Coco in for her daily wellness check. Mary Beth had returned from Golden, well rested, determined to straighten out all the messes he'd made in her absence and overwhelmingly curious about Brooke. Since his office manager was falling head over heels for both Coco and Brooke's style, they hadn't enjoyed much privacy. The preparations for Western Days had hit maximum velocity, so Brooke had been helping with the lodge, the museum and even out at the high school on the Cookie Queen float.

Logically, he knew that they would have managed all the work going into the festival without her, but it was hard to figure out how. He removed his gloves and smacked them on his jeans as he meandered outside the horse paddock to meet her. Betty and Coco were already trotting around, sniffing things in tandem, as Brooke carefully tiptoed through the grass.

"Sandals. In a barnyard. Brave," Matt murmured as she stopped in front of him.

Her wrinkled nose made him chuckle. "I'm finally on my way into Homestead Market to buy practical choices. Jordan threatened to hide every dress I own otherwise." She waved a hand in his general direction. "Are you safe to kiss?"

Matt tilted his head to the side. "Interesting way to formulate that question." He tipped her chin up to press a too-short kiss to her lips.

"I was specifically referring to biological matter on your person," Brooke said as she stepped back. "Barn. Barnyard. It's kind of a theme."

He nodded. "It's a valid concern. Travis asked us to help clean up the barn, so we started there. Then I brought ol' Dusty out for some sunshine and green grass." He stomped his boots to shake off straw and other "matter," then he bent down to get Coco's attention. He ran his hands over her sides and dodged her kisses while he made nonsense conversation that his brothers would no doubt give him grief about. "Healthy mama. We're getting close. Are you fully ready to be a mother of three, Coco?"

As soon as Mary Beth had returned, he'd gotten her help with a quick ultrasound. His best guess was that they were expecting three puppies, but the little rascals were notoriously hard to count.

When Coco trotted away to inspect Betty's discoveries, he stood again, swallowing the groan at the way his hip, knees and other various parts of his body objected. "Plants delivered as expected?"

He picked up a currycomb and clicked until Dusty eased closer. The rescue horse had gotten more trusting lately, especially while Matt was holding out the currycomb. Running it across the horse's back and withers in slow, steady circles calmed Dusty.

It might calm them both.

Brooke sighed as she moved closer to the fence. "They were late, but everything was there. Jordan almost blew a fuse. I asked Mia to lock her into the lodge's office until the truck left."

Matt nodded and convinced Dusty to turn so he could reach the other side.

"One more week and we'll all have survived running our first Western Days. We need her to hold all her fuses for one more week," Matt said as he grinned at Brooke. "Once the landscaping is in, you can all relax for a second."

"Yeah, starting early in the morning and ending whenever, but tomorrow is the last big push on the lodge. Jordan will only be checking in guests after that." Brooke patted her hand softly against the top rail but she didn't meet his stare. "I'm not sure anyone can believe how far she's come in this time."

"You and Sarah have been there every step of the way. All three of you should be proud of what you've accomplished with Sadie's legacy." Matt watched the emotions flit across her face. She wasn't as excited as he expected. On a hunch, he said, "You are an important piece of the lodge's success, Brooke."

She straightened her shoulders. "I am. I get

caught up in this worry…" She shook her head. "Jordan has the lodge. Sarah has the museum. I have…bits and pieces." Her groan of frustration was accompanied by a sharp chopping motion of her hand. Matt wrapped a hand around Dusty's neck but the horse didn't startle. Before he could mention the horse's skittishness as a gentle suggestion against quick movements, she grimaced. "I'm sorry, baby. I got too wild there, didn't I?"

Matt motioned with his head. "Reach into my pocket for a treat."

Brooke raised her eyebrows and he chuckled. Dusty tossed his head but he didn't run away. "For the horse, Brooke."

"Oh," she said as she stepped off the bottom rail of the fence and moved closer. "You have carrots in your back pocket. I have never seen that before."

"Secret veterinarian trick—always have treats in the back pockets. How do you feel about horses?" Matt asked.

Brooke moved back to her spot and held her arm over the fence, carrot extended. When Dusty delicately nibbled on the end, her smile broke through the worry on her face. "I'm somewhere between Sarah, who rides as if she was born in the saddle, and Jordan, who wakes up screaming from nightmares about horses and their teeth." She held the carrot steadily as Dusty made quick work of the carrot and snuffled at her arm as if he could tell she was hiding another somewhere.

"If you're around for a while, we can move you closer to Sarah on the scale," Matt said. "Go ahead and give him the other one. I've got apples in the barn. Dusty needs all the treats he can get. He went hungry for too long before he was rescued."

Brooke watched Dusty enjoy his treat. "I'd like that. The longer I'm here, the easier it is to imagine staying. Wes asked me about renting out the house Keena was in." She glanced at him. "I'm going to do it."

Which pushed them even further into new territory and long-term planning that affected them both.

But the happiness that welled up as she shared the news was impossible to ignore.

Matt clasped her hands and squeezed them. "I'm glad. After Western Days, you'll have plenty of time to figure out what you want to do, your lodge or museum. I'll help."

"In all your spare time, right?" Her face was adorable as she bit her lip. "You've been working around the clock and next week is only going to be busier. This weekend, can you relax for a day or so? We're going to have plenty of help landscaping. Sleep late tomorrow. Eat a big breakfast. Then take a nap. Have a big dinner. Go to bed early." She nodded firmly as he scoffed at her orders. "If there's anything left to do on Sunday, I'll call you first for help. I promise."

Saying no would lead to firmer orders, Matt was sure. She was concerned about him, and he appreciated that, so he said, "I'll think about it."

Her dramatic sigh brought Dusty's head up, but she pressed a kiss to Matt's lips instead of arguing.

He had no intention of following her orders as he waved her and Coco back down the lane toward the highway. There was no way he was going to let her work while he slept.

But he knew he'd stand a better chance of slipping in unnoticed and unchallenged while she was busy. That might avoid a tense conversation and an irritable mood he'd have to charm her out of in front of his mother and all his neighbors.

So, on Saturday morning, he slept late.

After a lifetime of rising before the rooster crowed, that amounted to a few minutes after eight o'clock.

Big breakfasts would never be prepared in his apartment so he settled for cereal and numerous cups of coffee while he cleared up the stack of messages Mary Beth had piled up on his desk upon her return. Apparently, he'd missed a few hundred things that he should have followed up on while she was away. Neither of them was surprised by that fact.

Then he'd pulled on jeans, a T-shirt and his work boots, loaded Betty into the truck, and headed out of town to the Majestic. He was touched when he saw the crowded parking lot in front of the lodge. This might not be the whole town, but the neighbors were all showing up for the Hearsts.

Her annoyed expression was easy to read, though, when he wandered up to the small group gathered around her. While he waited to get her attention, he waved at Dani Garcia and Sheila Bloom. They were both weeding the long beds that bordered the deck outside the restaurant. Then his mother whistled in the time-tested manner of hailing every one of her boys across a long distance and motioned imperiously for him to join her in front of the flats of colorful flowers. He held up one finger and turned to face Brooke.

Her hands were propped on her hips. "I told you not to come today. You have one chance to rest, so what are you doing?"

"You've added denim, but there's still something…" Matt waved his hand vaguely at her attire. She had on jeans, inexpensive tennis shoes and a plain cotton T-shirt knotted at her waist.

"Yeah, she's doing something fancy. I can't put

my finger on it, but these are not regular jeans from the Homestead Market," Jordan said as she motioned up and down at herself as if to show what *regular* would be.

"Go down to the marina and make sure the dock has been cleared," Brooke said and urged her sister down the hill. When Jordan narrowed her eyes, Brooke said, "You're the one who put me in charge here, remember?"

That ended the argument. Jordan trotted away and Brooke's wicked grin made him laugh.

"Whatever my family thinks? I can't rest while all of this is happening. If you're working, I'm working. When you sleep late, I'll sleep late."

Brooke opened her mouth to argue but changed her mind. "Thank you for coming. I appreciate it."

He raised his eyebrows at her reasonable tone.

The gleam in her eyes convinced him she knew how he'd expected her to react. "I was being the old me, I'm afraid, and I'm secretly thrilled you showed up for me." She shrugged. "I'm still a work in progress."

"And you're adorable," Matt said, fighting the urge to kiss her in front of their audience. "Unless you need me somewhere else, my mother has an assignment."

Brooke tucked her hair behind her ear as she shook her head. "Nope. Go."

He was amused at the blush on her cheeks until he turned to see that his mother was locked in on the two of them like a laser beam. Her attention didn't waver, either, as he walked over. "Which flat did you want next?" Her wicked chuckle forced him to face her directly. "Okay, Mom, get it out of your system."

He managed to stand firm when she wrapped her arms around him and squeezed so tightly his back popped. Sleeping on a futon meant a lot of little wear and tear. "If you make a bigger deal out of this, you may scare her away."

Prue cleared her throat as she stepped back. "Good point. My son is so smart. Grab the purple pansies. I've got the pink ones. We're going to fill the pots up by the front doors and you can tell me everything."

Matt nodded at the women who smiled and waved as they headed to the front of the lodge.

Then his mother motioned at the pots and they both sat down. "Take the plants out of the containers like this and then we'll get them in the planters." His mother demonstrated and then dug around in the dirt while she waited for him to follow her instructions. "Is it serious this time, Matteo?"

He grunted as he absorbed the use of his full

name. She only did that when she was prepared to get tough about answers. "It's…" He sighed as he tried to find the way to fill in the blank. "It's early, Mom. But it's not *not* serious."

She frowned. "Not not… So it's at least more serious than usual." She patted his hand. "It's progress. I'll take it."

Matt shook his head. "You aren't worried about me hurting her? Or the other way around?"

He watched her set the plants in the pots and adjust the color placement before filling around them with potting soil. When she was satisfied with the first pot, she said, "I don't want either of you hurt, but there's no way to prevent that if this doesn't go all the way to the end, right?" Her eyes were serious as she faced him. "I know both of you well enough at this point to trust that you'll do whatever you can to avoid that."

He fiddled with his bootlace. "No hard feelings from your first meeting, then?"

Her snort amused him. "Nothing but respect from that first encounter, is more like it. Whenever I tried to picture the kind of women who would be good for my boys, I couldn't. I love you all more than air, so who could be right for you? But I'm telling you, not a single one of you has made a bad decision. Your girl is strong, smart. We talked about ex-husbands, which I know something about. I do like her. The fact that she stood up for you means I could love her like my own." At a sudden thought, she clutched his arm. "Have you discussed horses with her yet? I've come to terms with Jordan's phobia, but the strain of another non-horse person in my family will be difficult on my nerves."

Matt chuckled as he studied her face. Honestly, that was his mother's truest fear. Not a mismatch that would cause heartbreak or what might happen in the future for two people in such different places. She was concerned that Brooke might not like horses.

He patted his mother's shoulder. "I watched her meet Dusty yesterday. Climbed right up on the fence, took a carrot from me and had a nice moment with him in the sunshine. She's not a rider like Sarah, but she won't stretch your faith like Jordan, either."

She chewed her bottom lip before holding up a finger. "Soon as Western Days is over, you need to give her some lessons." Then she immediately shook her head. "Nope, you're busy. The last thing I am going to do is dump another job on you. Grant can do it. He will enjoy that."

It was easy to picture the glee on his annoying brother's face as he got to show Brooke how to ride.

"As long as Brooke hangs around long enough, I'll be sure to get her out for a ride on Lady, okay?" He wanted to be the one to show Brooke the Rocking A. His mother's horse, Lady, had the perfect manners to teach new riders.

"Wes said she's considering renting the Cooper place. She doesn't have a lot of stuff, but Sharita's house is pretty well set up, especially since Keena's been staying there, so it should be comfortable for a bit." His mother leaned forward, eyes locked on his face.

As if she expected some grand reaction.

He was happy that Brooke had mentioned it to him first. For some reason, that seemed important, that she'd shared her plans with him, but he wasn't sure of the impact yet.

"One week. We've got to focus on this festival for one more week." She brushed her hands together. "Then we start planning the rest of your life, right?"

He nodded. "Why don't we get this other planter filled for now?"

"Good idea," she said and pulled it over. They worked together easily, as she gave the orders and he followed them, lifted things, carried them and gathered up the trash.

By midafternoon, most of the crowd had filtered out, leaving the family finishing up small jobs.

When his mother freed him to roam around, he and Betty spent a few minutes staring out at Kcy Lake. For a long time, it had been quiet on this end of the lake. After the marina and lodge shut down, the boat traffic had dried up, but today there were two boats on the far side of their cove. The temptation to take a free day to head out with a pole and some cold drinks called again and he promised himself he'd find the time soon.

On the way back up to the lodge, he spotted an orange hammock strung between two trees.

That reminded him that Brooke's orders for his day had included a nap, so he decided to test it out. When he was inside the hammock, Betty stretched out alongside him. He closed his eyes and listened to the leaves rustle until he fell asleep.

CHAPTER FOURTEEN

Brooke rubbed the tight muscles in her lower back as she watched Sarah and Jordan fuss with the placement of the large planters on either side of the Majestic's front doors. So far, they'd turned both barrel planters so many times that she was almost certain they were in the same position they'd been in when they started.

"Are you aware that those are circular in shape?" she asked. "The concept of the best side is harder to quantify when there are no actual *sides* involved."

"Excuse me? There is definitely a front side and a back side," Jordan said as she motioned at the riot of colorful flowers. "But I have no idea which is which anymore."

"We're done, Jordan. Let's stand back and enjoy it." Sarah towed Jordan away from the front doors by one hand. All three of them rested against the small bridge that joined the Majestic to the parking lot over the small stream that bisected the land on the way down to Key Lake. The days were growing longer, but there in the circle of mountains, the light was slipping toward dusk.

"Really wish Sadie was here," Brooke murmured. "She would have enjoyed every single minute of this day." And the end result would have been perfect. Without Sadie's touch, Brooke had had to rely on the guidance of the volunteers and her own instinct. The beds were colorful, but she wasn't certain they'd gotten anything exactly right.

Even after turning everything in a full circle more than once.

"I can hear the part you aren't saying aloud, Brooke." Sarah draped her arm over Brooke's shoulders. "But only barely because Jordan is also thinking very loudly about how she knows she's forgetting something or made a wrong move somewhere."

Brooke leaned forward to catch Jordan's eye. "I hate it when she does this."

Jordan grumbled, "As if she never had her own doubts about what Sadie would have done in our place."

Sarah tilted her head to the side. "This is not about me. This is about you, and I am one hundred percent sure that the three of us have done something that Sadie wasn't able to."

Brooke grunted when Sarah yanked them closer. "We've brought the Majestic back to life."

She squeezed again. "And we didn't stop there. We're bringing Prospect back to life. If we didn't perfectly capture Sadie's preferred flowers or colors or whatever it is that you're worrying over in your minds, she'd be the first one to tell you there is no one right way." She sighed. "Today we plant the seeds and hope we get to see the flowers. Remember that? She loved to say that when I was trailing behind her like a shadow."

Brooke squeezed her eyes shut as the first tear fell at hearing those words again. "She did say that. In the video she left me. Her advice was about not holding on too hard to the dreams that don't suit me anymore. It's good advice, but shouldn't I already…" What? How did that question end? "I should be so much closer to wherever I'm going by now, you know? Shouldn't I already be a flower at this point?"

Sarah sighed. "The metaphor loses some of its power if you push it too far, but I understand what you mean."

The ache in her chest hurt, but being wrapped up in a hug with Sarah and Jordan added a layer of relief and gratitude. She missed Sadie desperately. They all did, but because of her, they had each other, this place and Prospect. How could Sadie have had any idea how this would work?

The truth was that she couldn't.

But she had planted the seeds and trusted that the flowers would grow.

"Well, now, this is the prettiest sight I've beheld in quite a while," Prue said as she stopped in front of them. "You ladies have moved heaven and earth and you deserve to enjoy this moment, but..." She wrinkled her nose. "Rafa has plated up a neat little picnic for us to break in the revamped deck. Can I interest you in one of the biggest, prettiest, sloppiest Italian subs I've ever seen in my life?" She motioned them up toward the restaurant.

Brooke turned to follow Sarah and Jordan when Prue tsk-tsked. "I believe my youngest is snoozing in your hammock. A brown hound dog's head popped over the edge. I better go and get him. He needs food almost as much as he needs his rest." She inclined her head toward Brooke. "A fact I am doing my best to be aware of now, thanks to a friend."

Brooke wanted to send Prue back and retrieve Matt herself, but she followed Prue's direction and went to find dinner.

But that didn't prevent her from keeping one ear open for Matt's approach, so that when he stepped up on the deck where the Hearsts and Armstrongs were scattered, she patted the cushion she'd snagged.

"Got you this soft seat. Should help with your

hip." She crunched into one of the baby carrots she'd dumped on her plate next to an absolutely enormous sandwich and waited to see if he'd take her up on her offer.

First, Matt placed a box in front of her.

Then he rested his plate on top of it and an icy bottle of water.

Finally, he lowered himself next to her with a lot of theatrical groaning.

"Way to attract everyone's attention," Brooke muttered. They'd been pretty *hey, we're friends* in front of Prospect so far.

Matt immediately took a bite of the sandwich and closed his eyes in bliss. He held up one finger as if he wanted to make a comment in response to her but needed a minute. The way the conversations around them had died down while their audience waited for Matt's next move reminded her of the way all eyes had been drawn to him the minute he'd shown up earlier.

And her uneasy recollection of being cast in her ex-husband's shadow at the events she'd planned for him floated back to the surface.

But so did the reminder that Matt was not Paul.

He eventually wiped his lips with his napkin and said, "I've recently achieved some clarity on our relationship."

Brooke drawled, "Oh, yeah? Clarity is good."

He nodded and motioned between them. "I

don't want to be *you and me* anymore. I want to be *us*." He studied the crowd to make sure everyone was listening. "A couple."

"Us," Brooke repeated as she watched her sisters immediately perk up. The only way to avoid heartbreak for the whole town would be to execute an about-face the same way she had at the Western Days meeting and walk all the way into Prospect. Only there was no potluck table to capture her attention here.

He nodded.

"And I say okay? You chose me and I...agree?" Brooke asked as she tried to read his expression.

"Of course not. I'm going to win you over, though." Matt finished his sandwich.

"As you have successfully won over so many others previously," Brooke drawled in response.

He coughed. "Not really much effort to the winning." He held up his hands when she ducked her chin, preparing to explain firmly that was exactly her point. He was entirely too comfortable with the easy wins. "It was a mutual thing, but I sense some hesitation on your part. I get that, but I'm all in so I'm doing things differently. Here. A gift." He nudged the cardboard box closer to her.

It wasn't wrapped in a brilliant red bow for dramatic effect. This box had been roughed up in shipping, was covered in the stickers and marks required for freight and delivery, and had lost part of one top flap at some point.

Coco and Betty were extremely interested in what was inside, although only Coco was impatient enough to poke it with her nose.

Matt didn't clap his hands to make sure everyone watched, although surrounded as they were by family, they were center stage already.

As far as she knew, the gift was...just because. There had been no special occasion or rocky disagreement, no positive public relations angle here.

"Open the box. I'm dying," Jordan groaned dramatically. She'd never been able to wait patiently on Christmas morning. Her gifts were opened in an explosion of wrapping paper.

Matt rested his hands on his knees as he waited for her to give in.

"Okay, girls, what's inside?" Brooke asked, charmed by the way Matt's eyes shifted between hers and the box.

As if he couldn't wait to see her reaction.

The mangled flaps popped up easily, so she dug around inside to pull out bags of...dog treats? Coco and Betty immediately sat, eyes and ears on alert. That made her audience chuckle.

"You mentioned you were out of Coco's fancy treats." Matt pointed to the bag on top. "So I tracked them down and special ordered them.

None of my regular suppliers carry these. The single source was the one you found in New York. Luckily, nowadays that's no problem. They ship! I ordered both flavors. Just in case you couldn't find a replacement at the Homestead Market that Coco liked as well."

Brooke stared at the bags in her hands as waves of emotion swamped her.

He'd taken the time to research—and special order—her dog's favorite treats.

Just because he knew it would please her.

She pulled out four bags and a note from the shop owner that said, "Brooke, I hope Colorado agrees with you and my favorite customer, Coco! I tossed in a new cookie I'm trying out in the store, a sweet treat. Please let me know what Coco thinks." There were two bags of Coco's preferred bacon bones, one of the peanut butter bones that she would also accept, and the last bag…

Vanilla teased her nose as she opened the bag of smaller cookies dipped in yogurt that made Coco's eyes light up.

"Are they the right ones?" Matt asked. Doubt was replacing his excitement the longer she sat there. Brooke knew that was unfair so she forced herself to get it together. "Home run. Touchdown. Nothing but net." Brooke urged him closer, one hand under his chin, so that she could kiss him the way she'd been afraid to earlier that afternoon. Worries about their audience were crowded out by the thoughtfulness of his sweet gesture.

When Matt leaned back, he was pleased.

But he was also clearly confused.

"She means you won," Clay said dryly. "We are not a family for sports metaphors as a general rule."

Everyone chuckled as Brooke offered both dogs an artisanal organic yogurt-dipped fancy treat from her favorite pet store in New York.

That Matt had delivered to her in the mountains of Colorado.

Not because she asked. He didn't display a single ounce of amusement—or worse—at shipping treats across the country for a dog.

Because in his heart, Matt Armstrong was sweet. Thoughtful.

And nearly impossible not to love.

The understanding of the danger she was in tensed her muscles.

Divorcing Paul had brought her low—so low it had taken her sisters to save her.

If this relationship with Matt fell apart, not even her sisters might be enough to put her back together.

As Brooke returned the bags to the box, she could see that Matt wasn't sure what she was thinking. He raised an eyebrow at her, but put his hand in the middle of her back to rub soothing circles. "Long day?"

Grateful and feeling the threat of tears in the background, Brooke nodded. "Yeah, but you made it so much better."

His slow smile made it easy to melt into his arms.

"Does this count as the ghostly scent of vanilla that signals a visitation from Sadie?" Jordan asked slyly.

Brooke's first instinct was to argue that it wasn't. How could it be? They could point to the actual source of the cookie scent in the air?

But everyone gathered there on the deck knew the myth. Could anyone convince her this counted?

When no one else spoke, Matt said, "I'm not sure we can easily rule out ghostly interference." Her surprise that the notorious ladies' man, perpetrator of the Matt Armstrong Effect, was building a case for the matchmaking ghost had to be written on her face. He held out his hand and flicked out one finger for each of his points of evidence. "It's a cookie. It's vanilla. I didn't order or request that."

"But the ghost has always been connected to the lodge," Brooke said. She wasn't sure which side of the argument she wanted to be on, but the fact that he was pro-ghost was proof that Matt was all in for this relationship.

He waved his hand to indicate that they were sitting in the shadow of the lodge. "And Sadie also loved New York. Who's to say she doesn't enjoy a visit there, too? None of us are paranormal experts."

Brooke stared into his eyes as he smiled down at her. "I say we keep an open mind."

Why did she believe that he was talking about more than ghosts, whether they existed and how they managed to travel across the country?

When Clay cleared his throat, Brooke wondered if he was about to send everyone home. She wasn't ready to leave Matt's arms. Not yet.

"I should have gotten used to my brother stealing my thunder," Clay said as he tangled his fingers through Jordan's hand.

Almost as if he was anchoring her in place.

"But I never expected it to be a variety of dog treats, you know?" Clay shook his head. "At this point, I've got to keep going." He turned to face Jordan. Her expression was cycling through confused, alarmed and some third emotion that Brooke couldn't name. She hoped it was excited, because Clay suddenly had a tiny ring box in his hand. "I've been carrying this for a month. It belongs on your finger, Jordan. You have done everything you can to prepare for Western Days.

You have invested time, blood, sweat, tears and so many hours into rebuilding this lodge. The way you dig in has impressed me from the start." He yanked his hat off and ran his hand through his hair. "Even when we were kids, working down at the marina, I couldn't take my eyes off you, and the woman you are today is…" His voice cracked so he cleared his throat again. "I want you to be my wife. Whatever comes next for us, the next project you dream up for this place or Prospect, we'll do it together. Please, will you wear this ring? Will you marry me?"

Brooke knew she was squeezing Matt tightly but the thrill was too intense.

She'd missed Wes's proposal to Sarah, but this was one of those moments everyone present, Hearsts and Armstrongs, would remember together for the rest of their lives.

Jordan didn't open the ring box and Brooke had a sudden panicked thought that her sister might say no.

Instead, she launched herself into Clay's arms in a Jordan way. Apparently, he had gotten used to that sort of reaction because Clay caught her with a quiet *oof.* "Taking that as a yes."

Everyone was laughing when he managed to untangle Jordan's arms from his neck for a minute to slip the ring on her finger. She was crying. Sarah was crying. Brooke sniffed loudly because...

Well, it was nice to shed happy tears.

When everyone stood to congratulate the couple, Brooke joined Sarah at the edge of the crowd.

"I hope he knows what he's getting into," Brooke teased Sarah as she slipped her arm around her sister's waist.

"Oh, he may not know the full extent of Jordan or the Hearsts, for that matter," Sarah said with a smile, "but he's up to the challenge. They're going to be so happy."

Brooke wondered how Sarah could be so certain, but it was easy to imagine Jordan and Clay right here in fifty years. She would still be a mess, and he would still be an Armstrong, solid all the way to the core.

"Yeah," Brooke agreed. It was impossible to imagine a future where Jordan and Clay were not together. As she watched Matt shake his brother's hand, she tried to picture where he might be in fifty years.

Then she realized that his future mattered, but at this point, it wasn't the most important question.

Until she could answer the question of where *she* might be in fifty years, imagining any kind of future with Matt was impossible.

CHAPTER FIFTEEN

ON THE FIRST day of the Western Days weekend, Brooke learned that, even though she'd attended the festival when she was a girl and she'd been helping plan this year's events, she'd failed to dream big enough about the size of the crowd and the job.

She hadn't anticipated the hours involved during the actual festival days, how the people arrived in waves, or the number of decisions that had to be made in a heartbeat while someone anxiously awaited direction.

Veterans like Lucky Garcia at the Garage, and Amanda Gipson at the Prospect Picture Show provided steady influence that kept the whole thing on the rails.

Brooke's consolation was that she was only responsible for trailing behind Matt. Every once in a while, she'd hand him something like he was the surgeon and the phone number for Annie Mercado's manager was a scalpel.

Luckily, she had prepared for that part.

They met at sunrise in front of Bell House.

The street through town had already been closed, blocked off at either end, so that any drivers who needed to get from one side to the other had to use side streets running behind the festival on the north side of town. The side-by-sides, four-wheelers and two odd golf carts they were using to carry things from one end of the festival area to the other ran up and down the roads on the south side of town. That left pedestrians able to roam safely on the main street and spend their money wherever they liked.

Brooke was impressed with the efficiency of the small town's setup. It was clear that Prue Armstrong and her volunteers had gotten Western Days down to a science. It was a shame that this system was limited to one big event a year because it could work for so many occasions.

All the parking spots lining the wooden sidewalk from Bell House to Homestead Market had been blocked off for vendors, so now a mish-mash of colorful tents, stands, tables and temporary walls were slowly filling up with arts, crafts, T-shirts, garden decor and a dozen other fun curiosities that Brooke was definitely going to inspect closely and possibly purchase later. Why? Spending was in the air.

Above the street level, large banners welcomed visitors to "Western Days in Prospect,

Colorado. Home of Sadie Hearst, the Colorado Cookie Queen." The dark navy blue letters were bold, but everything was framed in Sadie's beloved red-and-white gingham. Brooke knew her great-aunt would have been proud and pleased by their accomplishments.

Large signs featured both Sadie and her Cookie Queen Corporation prominently, and the full list of all the weekend's different sponsors had gone up on both ends of town as well as near the stage and in the park behind the Mercantile.

When Brooke reflected on all the work Matt had managed without her help, she was impressed. Western Days was a full-time commitment, not an easy project to add to an already-crowded work schedule. Suddenly, dropping the ball on the parade and the talent show made more sense. She was glad they'd ironed out their agreement when they had.

She also regretted that she hadn't gotten to Prospect sooner.

No one person should be stuck with a project this size. When it came time to plan next year's event, she'd make certain to say that loudly and repeat it until everyone heard her. He was resigned to the responsibility of the binder, but she was determined that he wouldn't carry it alone again.

Mother Nature had gotten Prue Armstrong's

sternly worded warning, and the weather was warm without being hot.

There was not a single cloud in the sky to start the day. Prue and her team of volunteers had deployed the town's collection of previous Best in Show prize-winning quilts to hang along the street. The top floor of the Mercantile displayed the entries for this year's quilting competition.

Brooke knew Sadie would have loved every colorful inch of her hometown that morning.

Matt had called the committee heads toward the front of the group to run down any last-minute questions and problems that had cropped up since their last meeting after talent show rehearsals the day before.

Even from here, it was easy to see that the hours were catching up with Matt, but his smile was still quick and everyone around him nodded confidently. At this point, there wasn't a lot they could do except monitor and adjust, but he made it easy to trust that that would be simple enough.

Honestly, he was an excellent leader. Matt could do anything, be whatever was needed. Walt and Prue had raised five boys just like him.

Brooke stood near the back of the crowd, clutching the clipboard Sarah had tossed at her as she ran out the door that morning. Apparently it was her lucky clipboard. Brooke wasn't sure what sort of luck she should expect, but she was hoping that Matt would seize this opportunity to write notes on actual sheets of paper instead of stray gum wrappers.

She also had two fully charged two-way radios, even though she didn't expect to be far from Matt's shoulder for the length of the festival. The security firm they'd hired had insisted all leaders be easy to reach via radio in case of an emergency.

Brooke carefully hooked the radio onto the waistband of the shorts Jordan had insisted were the correct wardrobe choice and tried to be optimistic about how long the radio would stay there.

When the crowd broke up in front, the volunteers for each committee followed behind, leaving Matt, Brooke, Mary Beth and Carla Romero, Mia's mother, behind.

"Mary Beth, this is Carla. Have the two of you met?" Matt asked as he put a hand to Carla's shoulder. "She's going to be your assistant today. If you need access to someone, Mary Beth can help you track them down."

Brooke stifled a grin at the way the older woman blinked rapidly to free herself from the Matt Armstrong Effect. With exposure, it was possible to build an immunity, but Carla had just rolled into town on Wednesday. She and Mia were ramping up their plans to build an online magazine dedicated to life in the West, launching with a behind-the-scenes look at Prospect and their annual festival.

Brooke watched the two women walk away before she turned back to Matt. "Good pep talk. Are we as ready as you promised everyone we are?"

He tapped the clipboard. "You bet. You wouldn't have it any other way." Then he motioned at her waist. "Have you been converted to denim? The shorts are very Prospect. That fanny pack, though…" He grimaced.

The bag had been Jordan's contribution. Instead of a lucky office supply like the clipboard, she'd scuttled Brooke's wardrobe choice the night before, insisting on the practicality of shorts and tennis shoes, and then offered her secret weapon: the fanny pack. Apparently, when a woman is renovating a lodge, she runs out of places to put all the things required from one place to the next and gets into a bad habit of leaving her cell phone where she can't hear it ringing, much less answer it.

That annoys her sisters, her friends and the man who thinks he's responsible for keeping her in one piece.

Clay had gifted Jordan the fanny pack, so Brooke had strict orders not to lose it. It was nice, all leather, and she'd seen more than one on the streets of New York, but they were slung across the chest.

That seemed cooler, so she'd gone with the diagonal as well.

Brooke sniffed. "I am nothing if not practical. This radio would not have worked with the sundress I picked out." She swung her hips to show off the two-way radio, a symbol of her importance. "And the first time you ask me for another pen, sunscreen, aspirin or a safety pin, you will apologize for ridiculing my belt bag. It's useful in the city, Matt. You'll catch on eventually."

He nodded. "Why would I need a safety pin?" He brushed hair from her cheek, and Brooke wished they could stand there in that shady spot forever.

But the clatter of setup and happy chatter of volunteers and early visitors was impossible to ignore.

Brooke's lips were twitching as she said, "Hard to say when anyone will need a safety pin, but ask me again on Sunday."

Before he could answer, a loud squawk came through the radio. "Matt, this is your mother. Do you copy?"

The way he braced himself was funny, but Brooke knew he expected his mother to do something over-the-top where everyone with a radio could hear.

He reluctantly took the radio she offered and said, "Go for Matt."

"Is it okay with you if I set up a table and chairs over in the festival storage area for the quilt show judges I've asked to come in from Denver? The secure doors are locked, so we don't have to worry about losing any of the quilts still in storage. I forgot to run that by you when we talked."

Matt tilted his head to the side as if he was waiting.

"I'm supposed to say over," Prue said, "so now I'm saying over. Over." Her irritation was obvious.

"As long as they don't mind if we're in and out to grab supplies we've got stored there, that's fine. I can go and unlock the door. Let me know when we need to lock up. Brooke and I both have a set of keys, too." Then he grinned at Brooke. "Over."

"—he understands what I'm saying without all your code words, Walt Armstrong," Prue was muttering as the radio beeped. "Thank you, baby. Your father may need you to rescue him from the quilt storage area if he keeps pestering me."

Matt cleared his throat and said, "Copy that." His lips were twitching as his eyes met hers. "Odds that they're still talking to each other by the end of today?" He waved at Reg McCall, who was motioning a car through the barricades at the end of the historical section of town.

Brooke fell into step beside Matt and had to hustle to keep up.

She supposed the question was rhetorical because Matt never slowed down long enough to resume their conversation. Until the sun set on Friday night, she and Matt walked up and down the festival layout, troubleshooting and problem-solving.

All eyes were on him, so it was easy enough to watch the Matt Armstrong Effect sweep over small throngs of people here and there. Early on Friday, he got to charm all the volunteers, the retirees who were making an early day of it and the visitors who had chosen the lighter day of the festival. When school was out, the crowd changed a bit, growing younger, but it was still like watching the sun rise whenever Matt stopped to talk. Women and girls of every age brightened under his focus, and it was impossible to hold that against him.

Removed from the intensity of his concentration, she easily saw that all Matt did was take a genuine interest in whoever stood in front of him. His flirting was light and fun and teasing. His concern was authentic.

"Is this how Matt is using your skills?" Sarah

asked as she tugged Brooke's shirt to pull her closer to the Sadie Hearst Museum. The small crowd and murmur of conversation inside that Brooke could hear from the sidewalk was gratifying. Both Sadie and Sarah should be proud of all the work that had gone into it. "Because I can use them better. Jordan says she can't leave the lodge. Two of the temporary staff we hired to help out have called in sick. Is there any way you can escort Michael around town? Jordan does not want him staying in the lodge, and I've got…" Sarah motioned toward the door before clapping excitedly. "There are actual, real live people in this museum I've been daydreaming about for months!" she finished in a loud whisper.

Before Brooke could answer, Matt leaned forward. "Is this Cousin Michael we're talking about? CEO of the Cookie Queen Corporation, our beloved sponsor and guest judge for the talent show?"

"That very VIP. Can you spare Brooke? Grant is bringing him into town before he heads out to the barn where they're setting up all the cowboy games for tomorrow. Michael may already be at the Mercantile even as we speak." Sarah bit her lip as she glanced over her shoulder at the Sadie fans watching the museum's video greeting.

Matt immediately nodded and took the clipboard and radio Brooke had been carrying for him. "You bet. I'll be checking on Betty and Coco in the office when I pass by. I'll call you on the radio if I need you." Someone called Matt's name from near the Prospect Picture Show and he immediately started walking, but he turned back. Brooke nodded in a hurry and he winked before rushing away.

"I wasn't sure he'd be able to pull this off," Sarah said, "but I gotta say, he seems to be on top of things."

Brooke touched the radio at her waist as she tried to shake the feeling of being…unnecessary. The sensation was a little like watching Paul sweep into whatever event she'd been meticulously planning to take all the praise.

The annoyance that immediately settled in her stomach surprised her, but she forced herself to try logic before that feeling escalated.

The situation was not the same at all. Matt was busy. The man had been outworking everyone, including her, so this wasn't a matter of him taking credit for work he hadn't done. He had needed her help because this task was huge, but showing Michael what they'd done with the corporation's investment was an important request.

If she repeated that enough times to herself, she'd get over being loaned out so easily. Probably.

It prodded the sore spot that reminded her that

she didn't have her own project in Prospect, but that was a problem to solve some other time.

"Guess I'm a tour guide now." She squeezed her sister's arm and pointed. "Michael at the Mercantile. Got it."

Sarah waved before returning to her museum visitors, and Brooke dodged a couple of slowly moving crowds before she saw her cousin's blond hair in the distance.

He called out to her. "Brooke! A friendly face. I was afraid I was going to be stuck with Jordan all day." Their cousin Michael shivered at the scary thought. Since he was the oldest of all the Hearst cousins—Sadie's great-nephews and great-nieces—Michael had always wanted to be in charge. Having been named CEO by Sadie had reinforced his belief, but Jordan had never met an authority she didn't want to challenge. Michael had been one of her favorite opponents for decades, so Brooke couldn't blame him for celebrating his escape.

"There's too much happening down here to be stuck with Jordan, I agree," Brooke said as she wrapped her arm through his. "Since we're here, let's start with the Mercantile."

He turned to open the door for her.

"It's changed a bit since we came to visit Sadie in the summers, hasn't it?" he asked as they stopped in the hallway.

"It's changed since I was here a couple of weeks ago," Brooke murmured as she moved closer to the end where a new bulletin board had gone up. Everything on it was rough; there were no slick posters, but someone had hand-lettered a list of upcoming events for the year, classes being offered through Handmade, summer weekends, food truck nights, that sort of thing. There were also nice photos of the lodge, after the landscaping was completed, and Bell House; both had phone numbers and websites at the bottom.

Had Prue taken her advice about using the hallway better? With enough time to polish and expand, this could be such an effective way to draw repeat visitors back to town.

When they stepped inside Handmade, Brooke was pleased to find large clumps of shoppers gathered near the bins of precut fabrics Prue had been working to build up for the weekend. The conversation ebbed and flowed with happy chatter as the women compared their choices. When she and Michael moved closer to the checkout, Brooke introduced Michael to Prue, who was vibrating with excitement.

"Can you believe it? The turnout is great," she said as she squeezed Michael's hand and pumped it up and down. "And I am thrilled to have the chance to thank you, Michael, for the sponsorships. I'm hoping you will not be a stranger to

Prospect. We've got a lot of exciting events coming up, plenty of opportunity to partner with the Cookie Queen Corporation from here on out."

Brooke watched Michael do his best to absorb the enthusiasm. There was no way he met that much goodwill in the course of every day. Eventually, he said, "I will definitely be back. Can't wait to tour the rest of the town, Prue."

The line to check out had grown, so he motioned Brooke back out to the hallway. "Want to skip the hardware store for now?" He bent his head to peer into the window. It seemed busy, too.

Brooke nodded. "Let's go find something to eat. I hear the food trucks are amazing. We can start down here in front of Homestead Market for a snack and have dinner on the other end. In the middle, you can tell me how impressed you are with what we've pulled together."

Michael whistled as he pushed the door open so they could step out. "We, is it? I should have known they'd put you to work as soon as you arrived. What I'm not quite clear on is what you're doing here instead of New York."

"Oh, it's a sad, clichéd story. My husband changed his mind about our marriage, and he wanted a divorce. He kidnapped my dog. Jordan, Sarah and I stole her back and made a quick getaway to the mountains like the outlaws we are." Brooke pointed at the banners stretched across the street in front of the Homestead Market. "Sadie would love those, wouldn't she?"

He squinted up at them before turning back to her. "And that's all of the divorce story you want to share?"

Brooke nodded firmly.

"That has all the elements of one of Sadie's stories, especially the outlaw piece, but you need to improve your dramatic delivery," he drawled before squeezing her shoulder. "I'm sorry to hear that about your marriage, but I'm starting to wonder if Prospect is going to call us all back here. Sadie must be enjoying every minute of this return, wherever she is."

He was right about the delivery. Sadie would have had him howling with the same material, but in that moment, it was easy enough to decide she was tired of telling the story of her divorce. She was ready to look forward, not back.

They started walking again as Michael said, "I have noticed that almost everywhere I turn, there's a reference to Sadie Hearst, the Colorado Cookie Queen and the Cookie Queen Corporation. When Sarah got to town, Prospect wasn't too high on any of those things."

Brooke smiled. "You know how the Hearsts are. We don't take *I don't like you* for an answer." They both laughed. "And it definitely doesn't hurt that you and the board of directors have invested in Prospect in a major way. If things keep going the way they are, you're going to need a vacation home on Key Lake to keep tabs on Sadie's town."

Jordan was going to kill her for even suggesting that Michael spend more time in Prospect.

That made her even more determined to bring it back up later. Besides, she could definitely mention that Prue had said it first. Jordan wouldn't argue with Prue.

"Gotta say, in some ways, this place hasn't changed a bit," Michael said, "but in others, I don't even recognize it." He motioned at where a crowd had formed a semicircle around a small band that Reg had lined up at the last minute to make use of the stage in between events.

"This is the biggest weekend of the year," Brooke said. "Prospect may be too sleepy for you the other fifty-one weeks."

They stopped in front of a BBQ food truck.

"I'm not sure what else I'll be having to eat," Michael drawled, "but I am definitely starting right here."

The smell was incredible, so Brooke immediately tugged him into the line forming in front of the window. When he was right, he was right, and at that moment Brooke was thrilled to have put her vegetarian days behind her.

"What Prospect needs is another event," Michael said as they inched forward one step. "Summer's probably busy enough, with a steady crowd headed for the lake. Maybe something after the leaves change but before the heavy snows…" He waved a hand to dismiss the suggestion. "Southern California boy here. It might be too cold and snowy for anything as big as this."

Brooke crossed her arms over her chest as she surveyed the town. "Cold and snowy reminds me of this Christmas village Paul and I visited one year in upstate New York. It was adorable. Lots of handmade crafts and gift booths. Right now, there's enough empty storefronts in the historical section that we might be able to set up vendor booths inside."

The day she'd gathered up all the sponsorship checks, she'd tried to visualize what kinds of stores she'd like to move in, but while they were empty, why couldn't the town offer them for a weekend show of some kind? She tipped her head back, the ideas exploding in her brain. "Christmas decorations in the park behind the Mercantile. Lights everywhere." When she realized Michael was guiding her to step up to the window to order, Brooke wondered how long she'd been daydreaming about adding a festival to Prospect's calendar. "Pulled pork sandwich, please."

She waited for Michael to order the same and two lemonades before stepping away. When they had their food, she led him back to the park she'd just been imagining strung up in twinkling lights for Christmas.

She reminded herself to stay in the here and now. Today, there was a special attraction for the kids visiting Western Days. Someone was teaching them to toss a lasso to rope an adorable wooden cutout of a calf. There was a photo opportunity with a small stagecoach, and some of the kids from the high school art club were painting faces.

They were all events that with a few tweaks could work in winter, too.

"I've eaten my sandwich while I watched your wheels turning." Michael sighed. "As nice as it is to sit here resting quietly in the shade, would you like to use any words now?"

"Do you know anything about chambers of commerce?" Brooke blurted out.

Michael frowned. "Anything in particular or…?"

"How to get one started. What the requirements are. How they're structured." Brooke crumpled her napkin as she finished the last bite of her sandwich. Was she getting serious about this idea?

Michael shrugged. "I think all you need is a group of business owners who want one. Maybe a lawyer to help with bylaws. I guess it would depend on what you want the chamber to accomplish, because there are probably fees to join. Is it all volunteer or are you going to hire staff? There might be some questions to iron out, but it doesn't seem all that complicated."

Brooke stood as he was speaking and took both their plates to the trash. Then she ran her arm through his again. "Let's go see what we need to buy on the way down to the other set of food trucks."

"Oh, okay, we're done talking chambers of commerce. I expected a pitch for the Cookie Queen Corporation to sponsor something else on behalf of one of the Hearst sisters."

"Not quite yet, but stick a pin in that idea. We may be coming back to it." Brooke patted his arm as Michael's weary chuckle floated behind them.

One of the biggest questions Brooke still needed an answer for was what she wanted to do next.

Jordan had the lodge.

Sarah had the museum.

They had plans to add on to each with wedding packages and the test kitchen studio where they hoped to make content for the Cookie Queen Corporation's website.

There wasn't any room for Brooke in those.

What if her piece of Sadie's legacy was Prospect itself?

Even Matt had Western Days, and he was so good at it that it made no sense to picture anyone else leading it.

Everyone had something to call their own.

If what the town needed was another festival, it made perfect sense for her to organize it.

Would anyone else in Prospect agree with her? And if they did, could she convince them that her "volunteer opportunities" had taught her everything she needed to know to lead it?

CHAPTER SIXTEEN

ON SATURDAY MORNING, Matt stepped inside his office, relieved to turn the lock and step into the shadows of his apartment where it was quiet except for two happy dogs. He and Brooke hadn't connected yet on the second day of the festival, and he was out of sorts and ready for a break. Managing the touch-base meeting before the festival opened for day two without her had felt strange. Brooke had delayed her arrival to bring Michael, Carla Romero, Annie Mercado and her manager into town.

While he hadn't seen her, he'd heard her answering questions on the two-way radio. His workload had immediately lightened as she addressed some of the requests coming in. That was nice, but more than anything, he wanted to see her.

Hold her.

Tell her good morning and ask about Michael and get her opinion on how the festival was going. She had the kind of eye for detail that he missed. As he sat down in the floor with Coco and Betty, who immediately leaned against him, he fought the urge to call her to the veterinary office for some important task he would make up off the top of his head.

She was busy.

He was, too.

There would be time enough later to catch up.

Coming to terms with this need to see her might take some time. He wasn't sure he'd ever experienced it before for anyone else.

All he wanted at that moment was to be stretched out on the lounger behind the office with Betty, Coco and Brooke in his arms.

There in the blessed silence he came to terms with the fact that everything had changed.

Like Billy Dawson had promised, he had met the one he didn't want to live without. Trouble would come, but that wouldn't change this feeling.

Doing hard things for Brooke made perfect sense. Like Whit Dawson and her talent show, if Brooke asked, he'd find a way to answer, no matter how big the challenge.

"What do you think, Coco? Is this love?" he asked and smiled as the pretty corgi licked the tip of his nose in a delicate yes.

"Brooke for Matt." The radio crackled as she waited for his answer.

"Go for Matt." He was tempted to do something gooey, silly, over the top, but he wasn't certain Brooke was ready for that public display of affection.

But it would definitely make his mother's day. Possibly month.

"Parade starts in twenty. We need you and all the other riders in the high school parking lot. Over." Her tone was all business, and he suddenly wanted some gooey for himself.

He rubbed both tired eyes. "Copy. I'm headed that way."

Then he pulled out his phone to send Brooke a text. Mama Coco is doing fine in the office. I'm on my way to the high school. I missed you this morning. Let's meet up at the Majestic's orange hammock ASAP.

He stared at his phone for a minute, hoping she'd see the text and respond immediately, but then forced himself to stand. After he gave both dogs treats, he bent to press a kiss on their heads. "Coco, you be good. No puppies until tomorrow, you understand?" He wasn't sure she agreed, but he locked up and hopped in the side-by-side that would cut through the back roads to get him up to the high school where they'd gathered the horses for the parade.

When he saw that everyone was already mounted, the horses restless, he hurried to join his brothers. His father shook his hand as he moved over to his horse. "Been a long time since we've all been together in this parade. Sure am proud of what you've accomplished, son."

Matt stopped and met his father's stare. The urge to explain that it was a machine his mother had created and it would keep working for years after they were all gone... Well, it was wiped away by the pride he could read in his father's eyes.

"It was a lot of work, Matt," Wes said from his spot atop Arrow. "You've done a great job."

Grant nodded behind him, and he realized that the whole family was watching him. It felt good to be the center of this kind of attention, and it was easy to accept. This felt right. Then he climbed up into the saddle. "Best day of my life, honestly."

His mother patted his hand. "Let's get this parade started."

A loud squawk of the radio distracted him for a minute. He heard Lucky ask for assistance with finding more trash bags. Had they run out already? Then he heard Brooke answer, and he knew she'd get it straightened out.

Matt urged his horse forward, and his family fell in behind him. He turned once to survey the lineup curving out of the high school parking lot. He'd cut it close, but this parade was a good show.

As they came closer to the end of town, the marching band started the high school fight song, so that when they made the turn into the heart of Prospect, the crowds had stopped and gathered along the parade route.

The emotion that hit him was a surprise, but the immense pride he felt at what they'd managed to accomplish made all of the aches and pains and lost sleep dim in his memory. His neighbors and friends were shouting and clapping. Western Days was a success.

When they got closer to the museum, he spotted Sarah and Jordan up on the sidewalk. They were jumping up and down. Where was Brooke?

The disappointment that she wasn't there shaded some of his excitement, but he tried not to dwell on her absence.

When the parade was over, they moved directly into the craziness of the Cowboy Games where Grant and Mia placed third, edged out of second place by his parents. Prospect's dentist and his wife took first by smoking the entire field of competition in the three-legged race.

After the games were finished, he hustled over to the stage to announce the quilt chosen Best in Show. By the time he made it through all of that, the talent show was looming large.

"Have you eaten anything?" his mother asked as she shoved a frosty lemonade and a hamburger into his hands while they stood next to the stage. The sun was setting, casting a beautiful glow along Prospect's historical old town and the crowd settling down in lawn chairs and on blankets for the final event of the long, fun day. "As I recall, food never made it to the top of my to-do list when Western Days was in full swing."

Matt sank down onto the metal steps leading up to the stage and gratefully drank half of the lemonade in one gulp. After he cleared half the burger, he sighed. "Thank you. I don't know how you did this, Mom." The *why* she had done it had gotten much clearer at the parade. Everyone in town was going to benefit from this weekend, and his mother would never let Prospect down, no matter how hard the work was. How she had carried this burden for so long without anyone making sure she had food to keep running was a mystery.

She patted his shoulder. "It gets a smidge easier with practice, I promise."

Matt raised his eyebrows at her to demonstrate his doubt, but he didn't stop chewing to argue. It wasn't important now; they had the talent show to finish up, and then the crowds on Sunday would shrink until all that remained was cleanup. He had survived the most grueling part.

And the sugar in the lemonade was restoring his will to live into next week.

"Have you seen Brooke today?" he asked. The last bite of the hamburger was the best bite, so he savored it as he watched his mother's slow grin spread.

He knew what that expression meant.

His mother was renewing her plans to claim the third Hearst sister as an Armstrong.

The nagging sensation that he was missing something important because Brooke wasn't next to him convinced him his mother might as well start jumping to all the right conclusions.

"Oh, yes, she's been keeping everything in town running like a dream while you've been hosting all these events. I was absolutely correct to suggest she help with this festival." She patted herself on the back instead of waiting for him to do it. Since he was too tired to stand, that suited them both. "Sure am happy you both came to your senses. I had to have faith you could both recognize a good thing when you found it." She wrinkled her nose. "I'm only referring to her help with Western Days, of course." She widened her eyes to show him she couldn't possibly be imagining anything of a romantic nature.

He was too tired to confirm all of her correct conclusions at that point. Her answer fit his question, but it wasn't the information he wanted. It was clear she was behind the scenes working.

What he wanted was to *see* Brooke. In person. Preferably near enough for him to put his hand on hers.

"No, I mean here. In the crowd. Do you see her?" Matt didn't care what his mother thought about him repeating the question. If she added up the two questions and his desire for one certain person to be nearby and came up with the correct answer, that was fine. She was the best person to help him win Brooke over to a real relationship once Western Days was finished.

Suddenly impatient, he pulled the radio off his belt. "Matt for Brooke. What's your location?" He adjusted the volume as he waited for her answer, but it didn't come.

His mother stood on her tiptoes and waved his father over. "Hon, is Brooke around? Do you know where she is?"

"Naw, want me to go for a look-see? She can't be far," Walt answered.

Matt watched the way his father wrapped his arm around his mother's waist. They were a combo of loving and cute that had always amused him.

Tonight? He was a little jealous and more determined to track down Brooke.

As Matt stood and ignored the pains that

sparked from the muscles in his legs, Reg Mc-Call marched up. Dr. Singh's office manager had put on his best black hat and jeans for his performance. Based on his rehearsal, the crowd was going to love every minute. "Is it showtime?" he asked. Energy seemed to pulse from him even though he was standing still.

Matt inhaled slowly and met his mother's stare. She blew him a kiss. "One more event, baby. You got this."

Reg handed him a microphone and Matt wondered if he had the energy left to do the show right, but it was too late to change the plan. He stretched his arms, wished he had one more gallon of lemonade to chug and trotted up the steps to the stage.

"Good evening, Prospect! What a good-looking crowd we have here tonight," Matt said in his best emcee voice. He'd said some version of that same thing for years and it always drew a loud round of applause. "I need to hear from you…" He paced to the center of the stage. "Is this the best Western Days yet?" Then he cupped a hand to his ear and waited for the cheering to stop. It was pretty gratifying to hear the level of noise in response to his inaugural stint running the festival. The crowd was happy, so he was ecstatic. "Tonight, we're going to sing. Some of us will dance. We have juggling, and at the end of this, you will all be making plans to be right back here for next year's Western Days. I promise."

The audience clapped wildly, but he was distracted because he spotted Sarah and Jordan near the sidewalk. Sarah was on the phone, while Jordan listened intently.

Where was Brooke?

When Sarah glanced up at the stage, he couldn't read her expression, but watching them both spin away from the crowd and trot toward his office convinced him that he was in the wrong place at the wrong time.

The way his mother raised her eyebrows at his silence caught his attention.

"Who is ready for some music?" Matt asked and nodded when the crowd responded. "Then, without further ado, let's have last year's champion, Mr. Reg McCall, up here to get this party started."

Matt trotted down the steps but grabbed Reg before he could hop up on stage. "Reg, one minute." He knew what he was about to do was a gamble, but he needed to find Brooke. Even if it meant walking away in the middle of the talent show.

His mother moved closer. "What's going on?"

"I'm not sure anything is wrong, but I need to check." He offered Reg the microphone. "And I might not be back."

Reg bent his head. "Come again?"

Matt was aware that the crowd was waiting. He had to make the decision. "Reg, have you ever considered moving from performer to host of the talent show?" The guy loved being on stage. He would be perfect to step up and run the whole thing. Why hadn't this occurred to him sooner?

Reg twirled the microphone in his hand. "I still get to perform tonight?" He pointed. "Both songs, not one."

Matt nodded. "There's no way I'd deprive our visitors from your performances, Reg." That was an easy yes.

Reg pursed his lips. "Okay, but I'm going to finish off the night with a third song." He held up both hands to stall Matt's answer. "You haven't given me any time to prepare jokes or intros or anything. I gotta leave 'em with a showstopper, Matt."

"Three songs?" Matt's mother mouthed in concern.

Matt knew they'd be excellent performances so he held out his hand for Reg to shake. "Fine. We have a deal for this year. Next year, we can negotiate our terms in advance, but I expect you're going to be the best host we've ever had." Then he held his hand back. "Of course, this will remove you from the running to win the talent show itself. That's only fair. Are you okay with that?" If Reg dropped out of the judging, Whit Dawson was going to be one happy wife. Billy would owe him big time.

Reg gripped his hand hard and shook. "I've been needing a new challenge. This is it. I won't let you down." Then he straightened his shoulders and leaped up the stairs to the crowd's applause.

His mother patted his back. "I hope we don't regret giving Reg all the power, but you go find your girl. Let me know if you need our help."

Relieved that his mother wasn't panicking about these last-minute changes to her show, he said, "Can you stay close in case there's a need for any kind of official representative on stage? I'll be back as soon as I can."

After she nodded, he trotted over to the judging table and squatted to tell Michael Hearst and Annie Mercado to scratch Reg McCall from the score sheet that Brooke had prepared. Then he started winding his way through the large crowd. The last place he'd seen Sarah was near his office. That had to be where he'd find Brooke.

CHAPTER SEVENTEEN

BROOKE REALIZED SHE was still clutching her cell phone so tightly that her fingers were aching about the same time she heard the front door to the veterinary office open. Betty turned her head to see who was coming but neither of them left their spots on the floor of Matt's apartment. Brooke knew it was going to be Sarah, but a wild hope that Matt had somehow decided to skip hosting the talent show and return to his office had her heart racing.

When her older sister hurried into the room, she was disappointed but so grateful not to be the only human present at her dog's delivery that tears came to her eyes. If she had stayed in New York, she would be doing this all alone.

For half a second, she'd told herself she could handle it all alone.

Then she'd remembered promising Matt that she was going to let her sisters in.

So she'd made the call and Sarah had answered. The relief was sweet.

When Jordan followed, Brooke said, "I am so sorry. I didn't mean to drag you both away from the show. Matt has said over and over that Coco will do everything that needs to be done, but I'm afraid something will go wrong, and I'd really rather not be by myself then. You could take turns waiting with me? I don't know." She hated how vulnerable she was feeling.

They both immediately stretched out next to her, one on either side, to peer under the table where Coco and puppy number one were resting.

"So, Coco wasn't a fan of the newspaper-and-cardboard birthing box you made," Jordan said. "Make sense, but what did she make her bed out of?"

Brooke inhaled slowly to get control of her emotions. "That's at least one pair of Matt's scrubs, possibly two. It looks pretty fluffy under the..." She didn't need to fill in the blanks. Birth was messy. Instead of trashing the convenient birthing box, they were going to be trashing Matt's scrubs.

"Does Matt know the babies are coming?" Sarah asked. "He was up on the stage when you called."

Brooke sighed. "No. I had my phone out to call him, but I heard him through the speakers. He..." She had argued with herself about sending him a text, but if she could do this and let him finish the big final event, she would. He deserved that. He'd worked hard.

She knew how it felt to put in so much effort and lose the chance to enjoy the rewards.

"I don't want him to miss any of this night," Brooke said finally.

Sarah wasn't convinced but she didn't argue. "How long has the first puppy been here? I read that it can take some time before the next one, but it shouldn't take more than an hour."

"And the placenta… It should come out after each puppy. If it doesn't, we need to get Matt no matter how busy he is." Jordan pulled her phone out of her pocket to check the time. "How long has it been?"

The realization that her sisters had been doing their own homework about Coco's delivery slowed her answer, but she said, "I came in right before showtime to check on Coco. I didn't want to miss any of the acts, but the puppy was on its way, so… What? Twenty minutes?"

"At most," Jordan agreed and put a timer on her phone.

They were silent as they stared at Coco. Betty had joined them.

"Does Coco appreciate her audience or no?" Jordan asked and the three of them smiled.

Just then, Coco stirred restlessly and they held their breath as puppy number two made its appearance. When there were two shivering puppies, Jordan said, "What a miracle." Her tone was more "I would like to barf right now" but she was doing her best to be supportive, so Brooke appreciated it. "I'll reset the timer for one hour. We only have to do this once more, right?"

"Yes, if we read the ultrasound right."

The front door of the office opened again. All three of them plus Betty were staring at the door when Matt marched in.

She didn't hesitate or even make the decision before she was standing and throwing her arms around his neck. Relief settled her queasy stomach when his arms wrapped tightly around her. "Thank goodness you're here."

Matt's dark frown as he stared into her eyes surprised her. "I would have been here sooner if you'd called me instead of your sisters. Or even if you'd called me after your sisters, Brooke." Then he closed his eyes and inhaled slowly. "How is Coco?"

His annoyance was clear. Brooke gulped before saying, "She seems to be doing well. We have two puppies so far. She didn't use the birthing box. Sorry about your scrubs."

His confusion wiped away the scowl. Then he reached for a stethoscope and squatted to stare under his kitchen table where mother and children were resting. "Jordan, Sarah, could you go warm up the towels I have sitting on the dryer? It's by the back door." He motioned vaguely. "And clear out the newspaper from the box. Warm towels will make the box cozier for Coco." He didn't wait for them to follow his orders.

"Hey, Mama, you've had an exciting day, haven't you?" he said in his gentlest voice as he stretched out under the table. The tone brought tears to Brooke's eyes, which was silly. She sniffed hard to get herself under control. "These scrubs have had a good life. Good choice, Coco." Brooke smiled at the way he rolled with the situation and made a mental note to ask Mary Beth to order him a full thirty days of new scrubs in every color under the rainbow. "Healthy mama. Healthy puppies, too, although they're cold, aren't they? We'll fix that. Let's see about Tripp? You ever meet anybody named Tripp, Coco? Because they're the third? I only know one, and he's the kind of guy who makes you wish they'd stopped at two, but your baby will be something special."

Brooke sat down next to him and let his calming chatter soothe her nerves.

By the time Tripp arrived and Matt had pronounced every dog and puppy in the room to be the best, the prettiest, and one hundred percent healthy and the whole event complete, Sarah and Jordan had set up a warm nest for Coco. Matt lured her inside before placing the puppies next to her to nurse. Eventually, the warmth soothed them all and they fell asleep.

When Brooke managed to tear her eyes away from Coco long enough to stare around the room, she found her sisters perched on the edge of the futon, Matt and Betty resting their heads close to Coco and the puppies, while she was sitting against the wall next to the kitchen table.

Muffled music was still coming through the walls from the stage outside, so she said, "Thank you for answering my call for help. You can catch the rest of the show if you like." When Matt turned his head slowly to narrow his eyes at her, she said, "Not you. Them. You have to stay here."

He sighed and Brooke raised her eyebrows at her sisters before motioning them to follow her. "There's a shortcut out the back. It should take you right next to the stage to catch the end of the show."

Sarah and Jordan immediately stood and tiptoed around Matt to follow her out the back door. "Go left at the alley and you'll be back on the street by the stage." Brooke squeezed her sisters closer. "Thank you. I'm so glad you came."

"Anytime," Jordan said when they stepped

back, "but you need to make a dramatic apology to your cowboy. You hurt his feelings by calling us instead of him."

"But it's the talent show," Brooke said. She'd figured if anyone was going to be on her side, it would be her sisters.

"Yeah, you were trying to do the right thing, but they don't always see it the way we do. Go ahead and apologize, promise to always call him first from now on and get on with your life," Sarah said with a jaded voice of wisdom. "It works."

Brooke watched them rejoin the crowd before turning back to find that Matt had taken his spot on the lounger. His arms were crossed against his chest. That was not a great sign.

She shuffled closer. "How mad are you?"

His lips were a tight line but eventually he answered, "You should give your sister's advice a try."

Brooke's panic eased a bit as he inched over to make room for her next to him. "I'm sorry. I promise to always call you first from now on." She crossed her legs and stared up at the sky. "Is that 'Friends in Low Places' Reg is singing?"

Matt nodded before shifting her closer to rest against his chest. "Yep, show tunes and Garth. Reg is a big fan of both. This year, since I thrust the hosting duties on him at the literal last second, he will be dropping out of the contest and performing a third song as a consolation prize. I'm anxious to see which way he goes."

"I'm sorry I put you in that position. You deserve to be soaking up every bit of the crowd's excitement." Brooke clutched his shirt, determined to make him understand her decisions. "I wanted you here more than anything, but I was trying to do the right thing." She stared into his eyes, willing him to believe every word. "I am also sorry about the truly egregious amount of biological matter that got on your scrubs tonight. I will replace them."

His chuckle tickled her ear as it pressed against his chest but he shook his head. "Nope, still mad."

Brooke studied his face as she tried to find the right words. "You have to understand that you aren't..."

He raised his eyebrows. "Dependable? Responsible? The right guy for hard times?" His expression was closed, as if he was braced for the answer.

"No! No!" The immediate ache in her chest surprised Brooke. There was the shadow of how he'd described his brothers and fitting in at the Rocking A in his words. "You aren't normal, Matt! You're so sweet. Caring. Helpful. In my world? That's not normal. I have to be strong and take care of things on my own. That's who

I am, who I've been for so long. And my ex…
My previous relationships have all required that
of me, so calling you away from something so
important to you… I couldn't make myself do
it, even though I wanted you. Calling my sisters
was growth!" She was desperate to make him
understand.

He blinked. "You might be the first person to
tell me I'm not normal, Brooke. It's a good thing
you followed it up with some explanation."

She closed her eyes. "Yeah. Could be I'm not
normal, either?"

"Or we're both absolutely, perfectly normal
and figuring out this relationship stuff is hard
work. I want you to call me first. No matter
what else is happening. You come first. Your
trust, your faith in me matters. I love my family that way, as a priority. I don't know how to
love you any differently. I need you to want me
right there, in the middle of whatever it is. It has
scared me my whole life to open up that group
because I don't know how else to live, and losing someone so important is devastating. But
you… You're already in the center of the most
important people in my world." He sighed. "And
I would put this moment right here above any
amount of applause on the stage. All day long,
I've been out of step because I missed you."

Brooke scooted closer so she could see his

face better. Those were not the words of a man who had friendly exes and future exes around every corner. Matt sounded like a man...in love?

"Yeah, I know," he said dryly. "Grant warned me about how quietly love sneaks up on a man, but it still caught me."

There was no doubt in his expression, either. Matt was certain of every word.

He made it so much easier to take the last big step.

"So, if you're in love with me, and I'm obviously in love with you because I decided to try to brave puppy delivery with only amateur backup instead of calling on my concierge vet—which was clearly within the scope of our agreement no matter what else was going on tonight..." She brushed her hand over his chest. "What are we supposed to do now?"

"Unchartered territory for me," Matt said, "but we could go see who wins the talent show?"

"You're sure Coco and the puppies are okay?" Brooke asked as she stood.

"Yep, we may need to wake them up to eat," he said as he checked his phone, "in half an hour or so. They've all had a big day." He took her hand and they walked slowly out to where they could view the stage.

Reg McCall and Prue were announcing the winner of the quilt raffle. After they called the winning ticket number, there was a shout and then everyone started clapping wildly for the winner, Carla Romero. Mia's mother had been saying all weekend that she was determined to win it. Brooke wondered how many raffle tickets she'd bought to make her claim come true.

Whit Dawson was named the winner of the talent show. Neither Brooke nor Matt were shocked by that, either. Whit Dawson? She was stunned and thrilled as she hoisted the silver trophy over her head and thanked Reg for dropping out of the competition.

"That's going to make negotiating Reg's performance next year more difficult," Matt muttered under his breath. "They've been vying for the top spot for years. She won because he wasn't competing, but I don't know if either one of them will be satisfied with that outcome."

Brooke slid her arm around his waist. "Maybe you could ask them to cohost next year."

He considered that. "They would either end up best friends or mortal enemies. I'll need all my strategy advisors to weigh in before I make a move."

"Smart." She squeezed him closer, determined to be there when it was time to set up next year's talent show.

Prue Armstrong stepped up to the front of the stage. "I must say, this year has been one for the books, hasn't it?" Prue waited for the crowd's applause to die down. "I have loved this weekend for decades, but this year, I admit that watching it change has been bittersweet. Not too long ago, I wondered if the crowds would keep coming back, but tonight we have new life. New people. New events. Still, at its heart, this weekend remains about community. From the bottom of my heart, thank you all for attending. We've got more big changes coming, but the focus of Western Days is and will always be Prospect."

Whatever she would have said next was cut off as Walt stepped up next to her.

Brooke glanced up at Matt. "What's going on?"

He frowned. "I'm not certain but this has the feeling of a…"

Walt bent smoothly down on one knee and held out his hand. Since he wasn't speaking into the microphone, they couldn't hear what he said, but Prue's response was "Oh, you silly cowboy, I thought you were never gonna ask. Yes!"

Reg grabbed the microphone and took it from Prue's flailing hands as Walt scooped her up and spun her around.

"Congratulations! Your parents are getting married," Brooke said with a laugh as he shook his head slowly.

"The whole family has wedding fever," he muttered but he pulled her closer.

"Well, it's not every year we're going to end this show with a proposal, but it's right for an anniversary like this. One hundred years!" Reg held his hands up to clap and the crowd joined in. "Come back and see what we put together for one hundred and one. Tonight, I have one last song, and I'm pleased as can be about how it fits this night. As you're packing up to go home, please enjoy 'You're Still The One' by the Queen of Canadian Country, Miss Shania Twain."

Brooke turned to face Matt. "Did you put him up to that? That's what you said we were dancing to. In your dream!"

He gave her a wicked grin. "You remembered that? I wasn't sure you caught it." Then he slipped his arms around her waist. "We were dancing like this."

Brooke smiled up at him as they shuffled in a circle. "Is this a two-step?" She was almost certain that would involve actual steps, while this was more hugging and swaying.

But she liked it so she wasn't going to argue.

CHAPTER EIGHTEEN

BY THE TIME the Western Days after-party was winding down on Sunday night, Brooke had watched everyone in the room treat Matt Armstrong like he was a celebrity. Congratulations and effusive thanks flowed as freely as the celebratory champagne. Her concerns about being expected to do work that others would take the credit for must have been top of mind because he made sure to correct every single person that it had been teamwork, wonderful volunteers, the eye for detail of people like Brooke that had gotten them all across the finish line together.

His cheeks had taken on the adorable blush he'd worn that first meeting when his mother had made everyone clap for him. When he finally sat back down next to her, he said, "I'm sorry. I'm doing my best not to take credit for your work." He waved a hand. "For anyone else's work, including yours."

Brooke caught his hand. "I see that. I appreciate it."

"And we're okay," he added.

"We are. I'm proud of you." Brooke nodded. "But here's what I need you to do."

He leaned forward.

"I'm about to stand up and make a suggestion." Brooke had studied it from every angle, and the idea wouldn't leave her. She knew what she wanted to do next.

"And you want me to support it," he said. "Of course I will."

Brooke smiled slowly at him. "You have no inkling what I'm going to say."

He shrugged. "You're smart. You've gotten to know us, this town. I'm in favor of it." Then he held up one finger. "Unless it involves you leaving for any reason."

Brooke shook her head. "Nope. Prospect is stuck with me for now. I never realized how much I missed my sisters when I was caught up in New York. They're here. I like it here."

He frowned. "And that's all?"

"I figured it would be hard to convince you to move to New York or LA." She sipped her champagne and waited for him to catch her meaning. She could live somewhere other than Prospect, but she didn't want to do it without Matt. Not yet. Maybe not ever.

His grin made her happy. "I like that answer."

Before Brooke could tell him the basics of

her plan, Prue stood up and clinked her spoon against her glass to get everyone's attention. "I know you're all exhausted and giddy from the champagne and the success of this weekend, but I have to offer my sincere thanks. I know my methods for…" She cleared her throat. "My methods for encouraging volunteerism have their critics, most of them related to me, but we have done so much this weekend to set up our town for success. You all are a part of that, and I hope you reap the benefits for years to come."

The rowdy applause took a minute to die down. "On that note, I'd like to take one minute to imagine where we go from here."

Matt thumped his head on the table in front of him. "It's too soon to start planning for next year."

Brooke ran her hand over his back as his mother narrowed her eyes at him. "In this, we agree. However—" Prue rolled her eyes when all of her sons groaned aloud "—however, we *can* build on this."

Then she motioned gracefully at Michael Hearst. "We have a corporate expert in our midst, and Michael and I shared a lovely lunch today behind the Mercantile. The empanadas from the Garcia food truck? Seriously, you can't find better anywhere, and Chef Caruso will back me up on that."

The man in question nodded dutifully while Faye Parker patted his chest.

Brooke shook her head at the suspicious way Jordan watched Michael as he stood. "We did, Prue, and I loved your suggestion about a nice holiday home on Key Lake because the Cookie Queen Corporation is going to be partnering with Prospect closely for the content we need now that Sadie is gone."

Jordan shrugged as if she couldn't argue with that.

Brooke watched Sarah turn away to hide her amusement at Jordan's reluctant acceptance.

"How does that impact our future?" Wes asked from his spot next to Sarah. "The town, not our family. For the family, it means we're going to need an event hall for Sunday night dinners because the crowd will not fit in the Rocking A's kitchen anymore."

Clay shook his head. "Why do I think Mom's dance floor for the big my-son-ran-away-to-Vegas-and-got-married-and-all-I-got-was-this-party party is about to turn into something much, much more complicated?"

Prue crossed her arms over her chest. "You know, we could roll the Majestic's wedding gazebo and our need for party space and an enormous dinner table together to come up with…"

She shook her head. "Never mind about that. Prospect... We're talking about Prospect."

"You need another festival and Brooke Hearst has a proposal," Michael said quickly, obviously aware that he would be interrupted again soon. "And you need someone whose job it is to head up these events. I have heard that starting a chamber of commerce for the town is pretty simple, especially if you have the right person in mind with a whole collection of skills already. Like planning meetings, rounding up volunteers, working with business leaders, that sort of thing."

When Michael turned back to her, Brooke realized that her mouth was hanging open.

Matt slipped his arm around her shoulders. "Brooke is perfect to set up another festival for..." He peeked at her out of the corner of his eye, waiting for direction as he tried to keep his promise to support her.

Even as Michael had stood up in front of the crowd and done the hard work.

He'd tossed her a pitch. All she had to do was hit it out of the park.

"December." She sighed. "Or possibly mid-November."

Brooke stood. "We could do a twist on a Christmas market. Set up stalls outside or in the empty storefronts in the historical part of town. With a frontier theme? Have classes taught by artists like Prue. Faye could do cookie exchange classes which would tie in with Sadie's brand and the museum." She rubbed her forehead. She'd rehearsed in her mind how to sell this, but Michael's intro had her rattled.

"If we decided to hold a meeting of businesses interested in a Prospect Chamber of Commerce," Matt said, "we could discuss the timing and nail down the events for a winter festival and what kind of benefits the businesses in Prospect could expect from organizing it together." He slipped his arm over Brooke's shoulder. "Brooke can set up a time and place for the first meeting and we can go from there."

"Only if you want to," Prue said slyly. "I wouldn't want to volunteer you for this big project." She smiled innocently, even though they both were aware of the way this meeting echoed their first face-off in the Mercantile.

"I want to. I want this." Brooke wended her way through the tables in the dining room to hug Prue before Sarah and Jordan gathered around her. "This is exactly what I was looking for. I don't know if Sadie had any idea what would happen when she left the three of us her lodge, but every day, it's clearer to me how much Prospect meant to her." She met Matt's stare over the crowd. "She was able to dream big here. The lodge, the museum, these festivals, and whatever inspiration comes next... Everything we need to make these wishes come true is right here in this room."

Then the crowd was cheering for her, and when she and Matt walked back down to his office to check on Coco and the puppies, Brooke realized she'd never experienced such a sense of satisfaction.

Not in any of the other jobs she'd taken on.

And not holding hands with any man other than Matt Armstrong.

"You would have backed up any wild suggestion I spouted, wouldn't you?" Brooke asked. Her lips twitched at the memory of his immediate support.

"You bet. I'm going to be your number one hype man," he said, "although Michael seems to be challenging me."

Brooke sighed. "Your mother was putting him up to that. Like maybe she expected me to be a problem if she made the suggestion, but Michael? Well, he's family, head of the business and all that."

Matt tipped his head back. "Yep. I can see the connections now. You may be able to give my mother a run for her money when it comes to strategy."

"That is a true compliment, Matt Armstrong," Brooke said. "I'm beginning to think you like me."

"Number one fan." He wrapped his arms around her waist. "And it's a pretty large fan club, so we're going to need to set up a VIP section just for me."

EPILOGUE

BROOKE HEARST RAN her fingers down the silky skirt of the champagne-colored wedding dress as she listened to her sisters discuss what still needed to be done before the wedding ceremony. They had gathered the bouquets, the deep crimson dresses and shoes for all the bridesmaids, and Jordan was handing out glasses of champagne while they waited for the ceremony to start.

"The only piece we're missing is the bride," Sarah said as she spun away from the window.

"Has she changed her mind?" Jordan didn't look overly concerned as she moved over to the window. Keena and Mia were seated in front of the lighted vanity they'd installed in the bride's dressing room in the wedding pavilion a week before.

It had taken some time to find the right location for the event center, one that would allow visitors to make use of the Majestic's parking lot but would not disrupt the view from the lodge, its restaurant or the two new houses the Armstrongs were building up on the ridge overlooking the lake.

Every person in the family had pitched in on construction and decor.

And they were about to have the first wedding.

Outside, under the open-air pavilion, chairs were set into aisles facing the lake.

The small indoor reception area held a beautiful cake, plates, silverware and more champagne.

But the decorations were minimal.

The beauty of the Rocking A on one side and the Majestic Prospect Lodge on the other were all the bride wanted.

That and every single member of her family in attendance.

For Prue Armstrong, that meant all of Prospect.

"Has anyone seen Prue?" Keena asked. "I don't personally know about cold feet, since I took the Vegas way out of this, but I expect even a woman who is marrying the same man a second time can get them."

"I'm here. No cold feet for me!" Prue said as she hurried inside. "Walt couldn't find his best hat because I had put it in the top of the closet to keep it his best hat. It's white. You ever seen what happens to a white cowboy hat in a barn? It's ugly. He didn't tell me what had him in such a snit until I was getting ready to leave, so by the time I climbed up to get it down…" She held her hands out as if to show her late arrival. "I need hair and face but not too much." She plopped herself in the chair in front of the vanity and motioned Keena and Mia closer. "Let's go, girls."

Brooke joined Sarah and Jordan in front of the window that overlooked the lake. They had created a family wall next to the windows with a casual photo of Sadie Hearst in the center. She was wearing jeans and a Majestic Prospect Lodge T-shirt with bare feet as she stood on the edge of Key Lake, young Brooke standing beside her. Brooke guessed she was about six in the photo, but she was happy to see all of her front teeth were present in her smile as she clung to Sadie's leg. Young Jordan and Sarah were splashing in the water behind them.

She couldn't remember the occasion of the photo, but it almost had to have been her mother who took it.

Other photos were circled out around them. Her parents were there. So were Walt and Prue. All of the Armstrong sons had a spot, with Keena and Mia. And Damon and Micah were there, and the large open spot at the bottom would be filled by the family photo they took after Prue and Walt got remarried.

Since it had been her suggestion, Brooke was proud of the way it had turned out.

When she saw the Armstrong men gathered in a semicircle outside the doors to the reception hall, she understood what had captured her sisters' attention. All six of them were wearing dark suits. The effect was devastating.

"Is there a ring in your future, little sister?" Jordan asked before she polished off her glass of champagne. Sunlight caught the diamond on her finger. "Double weddings are kind of boring. A triple wedding? Those are rare."

Brooke hugged Jordan and Sarah. The faint scent of vanilla filled the air, but no one remarked on it. Was she the only one who could smell it?

"Single, double or triple, you all better get a move on if we're going to have all the weddings finished by the time Western Days rolls around again," Prue said while Mia curled her hair and Keena worked on her manicure. "It's going to take all of us to make it bigger than we did this year."

Brooke patted Jordan's shoulder as Sarah whispered it would all get done in time.

It wouldn't surprise Brooke at all if there was a ring in her future.

And it didn't worry her in the least.

She already knew the right answer was yes.

* * * * *

HARLEQUIN
Reader Service

Enjoyed your book?

Try the perfect subscription for Romance readers and get more great books like this delivered right to your door.

See why over 10+ million readers have tried Harlequin Reader Service.

Start with a Free Welcome Collection with free books and a gift—valued over $20.

Choose any series in print or ebook. See website for details and order today:

TryReaderService.com/subscriptions